'You!'

He doffed his tall hat and executed a mannerly leg as steadily as if they had been in a London drawing room and not on a heaving deck. He was smiling. 'As you see! Jack Chiltern at your service, ma'am.'

'What are you doing here?' she demanded, unaccountably pleased to see him. 'Have you been following me?'

He smiled lazily. 'Why should I do that?'

'To take me back.'

Born in Singapore, **Mary Nichols** came to England when she was three, and has spent most of her life in different parts of East Anglia. She has been a radiographer, school secretary, information officer and industrial editor, as well as a writer. She has three grown-up children, and four grandchildren.

Recent titles by the same author:

MISTRESS OF MADDERLEA

JACK CHILTERN'S WIFE

Mary Nichols

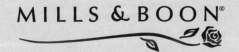

MILLS & BOON®

First published in Great Britain 1999
Harlequin Mills & Boon Limited,
Eton House, 18-24 Paradise Road, Richmond, Surrey TW9 1SR

© Mary Nichols 1999

ISBN 0 263 81839 X

Set in Times Roman 10½ on 12 pt.
04-9911-80828

Printed and bound in Spain
by Litografia Rosés S.A., Barcelona

Chapter One

1793

The atmosphere in the rectory library was charged with tension. It crackled like lightning in a leaden sky, presaging a storm which threatened to engulf the three people who stood grouped around the hearth. The Reverend William Harston, still in the black evening coat and breeches he had worn to Viscount Beresford's Hunt Ball, stood with his back to the dying fire, facing his niece, Catherine, known to family and friends as Kitty. His dark features were sad and disappointed rather than angry, a fact which filled Kitty with remorse. But that remorse was tinged with defiance.

She, too, was still dressed for the ball in a high-waisted white silk gown with a square neck and three-quarter-length sleeves which ended in lace ruffles, as befitted a young lady of nineteen still in the single state.

Beside them, almost between them, stood Kitty's stepmother, Alice. Her plump frame spilled out of a voluminous gown of pink satin. She wore an old-fashioned white wig and patches on her heavily powdered face. The powder was wearing off and did little to hide the red spots of anger on her cheeks.

'Sorry! Sorry! Is that all you can say?' Alice's green eyes gleamed with malice. 'You behaved like a harlot…'

'Madam, you go too far,' William interposed. 'Pray, moderate your language.'

Alice ignored him and continued her tirade against Kitty. 'You think "sorry" will see an end of it? We will never live it down. Never. It makes me quite ill to think of what we have just witnessed. The most flagrant impropriety imaginable…'

Kitty had made up her mind not to rise to her stepmother's taunts, to be calm and dutiful and accept whatever punishment her uncle meted out to her. He was her father's brother and her guardian and she respected him. But that was too much of an injustice. She looked up, violet eyes sparkling, and turned to the overbearing woman who had married her late father.

'That's not fair!' she said. 'It was only a kiss and meant nothing. Don't tell me you never allowed a gentleman to kiss you before you were wed, because I will not believe it.'

'That's enough, Catherine!' her uncle snapped. 'Apologise for that at once.. You should go down on your knees in thankfulness to have a mother who cares for your reputation and the good of your soul.'

It was more than Kitty could bring herself to do and she hung her head and said nothing. After all, she had done nothing so very terrible, except allow Edward Lampeter to dance her straight out of the ballroom on to the terrace, where he had proceeded to kiss her soundly.

The trouble was that he had not taken her far enough

and some of the guests at the ball had seen them, had seen, too, that she was enjoying the experience. Her stepmother had been one of them and lost no time in drawing her uncle's attention to the spectacle, and in such a noisy way that even those who had hitherto been oblivious had seen them and either smirked behind fans or chuckled aloud.

Uncle William had forced them apart, pushed Kitty behind him and stood facing Edward in icy control of his temper, before muttering a warning that he would call on him the next day and hustling Kitty from the room and out to his carriage. Alice had been furious at their abrupt departure from so prestigious an event but, in Kitty's eyes, she had made matters far worse by her display of outrage. There was no need to make such a fuss, unless she wanted Kitty to be publicly disgraced.

The carriage ride home from Beresford House, across the park to the rectory, had been made in silence, except for the clop of horses' hooves and the jingle of harness. Only when they were behind closed doors did her uncle speak. 'Do not think you are going to be allowed to go to bed, young lady. Into the library with you.'

Kitty had thrown off her cloak and given it to the waiting Judith, who looked from one to the other and, noticing the black looks of her employer and heightened colour of Mrs Harston, wondered what scrape Miss Kitty had got herself into now.

'Go to bed, Judith,' the Reverend commanded, before ushering his niece and her stepmother into the library.

It was the only room in the house Alice had not been allowed to transform. It was the only room he could go to when he needed solitude, a room for quiet relaxation, a room for doing business and discussing family matters. Here he could put on his stern face and exert his authority as leader of his flock of parishioners and head of the household, something he seemed unable to do anywhere else in the house since he had taken his brother's widow into his home.

Kitty suspected he had not wanted to, but had done so for the sake of the children. Kitty still missed her mother, even after eight years. Her mother had been so gentle, so loving, so understanding of her high-spirited daughter, even though she was often ill and, in the last few months of her life, bedridden.

Her death had changed Kitty's cheerful, easy-going father. He became almost morose, and involved himself more and more with looking after the poor. He had been a country doctor and a good one, just as he had been a good father; too good, she sometimes thought, because it was thinking of his motherless children which had prompted him to marry Alice a little over a year later. And anyone less like her darling mother could not be imagined.

If old Judith was to be believed, Alice had set her cap at Papa before he met and married Anne, the youngest daughter of Lord Beresford, and she had been furious at being spurned.

When the first Mrs Harston died, Alice had, in almost indecent haste, rushed to comfort the widower. And he, needing a mother for his children, James and Catherine, had succumbed. Whether he had regretted making her the second Mrs Harston, Kitty did not know, for he had never given any sign of it.

But he had given way to Alice's demands in every particular, allowing her to redecorate and refurnish the house to her own somewhat flowery taste, connived in the spoiling of their son who arrived a year after their marriage, and pandered to her imaginary ills, so that Kitty became exasperated at his weakness.

But it wasn't Alice's nagging or his weakness that carried him off in the end but typhoid, which he, as a physician, was treating at the infirmary. She had been fourteen at the time and James seventeen, almost a man, while little Johnny was only eighteen months old. On his deathbed Papa had asked Uncle William to look after his children and he, being the good man he was, had undertaken to do so.

Uncle William, unmarried and unworldly, had allowed himself to be persuaded by Alice that he needed a housekeeper as much as she and her fatherless children needed a home. She had taken over the rectory in the same way she had taken over the doctor's home.

But though she tried, she had not been able to subdue Kitty's bright spirit, her love of life, her quest for adventure, for new experiences, almost impossible in the rarefied atmosphere of the rectory of a quiet Berkshire village. Hence, the kiss.

'Just when Lord Beresford was beginning to accept me and her ladyship was showing some friendly feeling towards me, you must perforce disgrace us.' Alice's diatribe went on. 'What must they think? I'll tell you, shall I? They will think I do not know how to go on, that I do not know enough of genteel behaviour to pass it on to my daughter…'

'Stepdaughter,' Kitty murmured.

'Catherine!' warned her uncle in a low voice. 'That is unkind in you. Your stepmama has shown you nothing but kindness and treats you as if you were her own.'

'For which I get no thanks,' Alice put in, addressing Kitty. 'Why, if we had played our cards aright, Lord Beresford might very well have given you a Season;

you are his granddaughter, after all, and he has financed
your brother's Grand Tour. He would have treated you
both even-handedly. We could all have had an enjoya-
ble time going out and about with all the top people.
We might have been presented at court.

'You could have found a suitable husband and set up
your own household,' she went on, hardly pausing for
breath. 'It is too late now—his lordship will not invite
us over his doorstep again and I shall be snubbed by
everyone and not asked anywhere.'

It was obvious to Kitty that her stepmother's concern
was all about her own aspirations to be accepted by the
upper echelons of society. Alice's father had made his
own way up in the world, building up a manufacturing
business and becoming comfortably off. Kitty admired
him for it, but his own daughter had despised him. She
had never written to him and never visited him.

To hear Alice gossiping with her cronies, you would
think she was a duchess at the very least. And she loved
to boast that she had connections with Viscount Beresford, which were tenuous to say the least. Tonight at
the ball, for instance, she had almost hurled herself at
the poor man, gushing and primping and telling him
how she loved dear Kitty like her own, even though she
was often wilful and disobedient.

She had sighed heavily, fluttering her eyelashes at
him over her opened fan. 'Girls need a strong hand, do
you not think so? Not that your dear Anne would not
have been strong if she had been able. She was ill for
so long and dear Henry so engrossed with looking after
her, which was only proper of course. But it is no wonder the children were allowed to run riot.'

It had given Kitty a perverse pleasure when her
grandfather, tall and upright, had pursed his lips and

said, 'Yes, indeed?' in a tone of voice which would have cowed anyone with a thinner skin than her step-mother.

'Oh, yes, my lord. I could see that dear Henry was devastated when she passed away. Being a woman of sensibility, I longed to comfort and succour him and his motherless children after his untimely bereavement; God made it possible.' She had sighed again. 'It was not easy. And after the poor dear man passed away himself, I was left to manage alone and, being a slave to poor health myself…'

There was nothing wrong with Alice's health; it was just an excuse for idleness, to give Kitty more and more to do. She did it willingly for her uncle's sake, and for Johnny, her six-year-old half-brother whom she adored. When the occasion demanded, such as an invitation to Beresford Hall, Alice could be as energetic as anyone there. And certainly her tongue never rested.

'There! You can see how right I have been all along, William,' she went on, when Kitty remained silent. 'She has been thoroughly spoiled. If I were you, I would wash my hands of her, send her to your Aunt Henrietta in Scotland. She will be suitably strict with her and the climate might cool her ardour.'

'No!' Kitty cried, afraid her uncle would do as she suggested. Her great-aunt lived in splendid isolation in the far north west of Scotland. She was almost a recluse, refused to go out and was very rude to any visitors who called. It would be tantamount to a prison sentence. 'Uncle William, am I a criminal to be sent away from you? What have I done that is so very bad, except to be young and want to enjoy my life?'

'Kitty, please don't make matters worse,' he said.

'Apologise to your stepmother and let us discuss what is to be done in a calm and sensible manner.'

For the love and respect she bore him, Kitty turned and gave the apology with as good a grace as she could muster.

'That's better,' he said, giving a sigh of relief, but he did not smile. Indeed, his countenance was even more sombre than usual. 'Now, I will tell you what I have decided.'

Kitty turned towards him, trying to convey a plea in her large, expressive eyes which would soften his heart. Could he not see that Alice wanted to be rid of her and had seized this opportunity to have her sent away? Her stepmother hated her for being too much like her dead mother, whom her father had adored.

Surely Uncle William had noticed the little acts of cruelty Alice had meted out when they first came to the rectory: the stinging rebuke; the quick cuff round the ears; sending her to bed without her supper for the slightest misdemeanour. Even now, when she was grown up, she was subjected to constant reminders of her failure as a daughter.

She was too outspoken, her deportment was a disgrace and her social graces sadly lacking. By social graces Kitty understood she meant the artificial manners in company which went by the name of politeness. Alice was the master of cutting innuendo. Why did her uncle not see it? Or perhaps he saw it and chose to ignore it for the sake of peace and quiet.

Even now he was taking Alice's side and refusing to hear her explanation of what had happened. If they sent her away, Alice could act the injured party. She could almost hear her plaintive voice. 'Why, I did my best with the girl, but she would not have it. We did not want to send her away, but what else could we do?'

Kitty was forced out of her reverie when she realised the Rector had spoken. 'I beg your pardon, Uncle, what did you say?'

'I said you will marry him.'

'Marry? Whom should I marry?'

'Edward Lampeter, of course.'

Kitty's mouth fell open. 'Uncle, I can't do that. He has not offered for me and we do not have that affection which is necessary for a happy marriage.'

'What is that to the point? He is single and of good family, not as well-heeled as I would have liked, but that can't be helped. The money your mother left you will be your dowry and that should suffice…'

'You call that punishment!' Alice broke in, just as surprised as Kitty by her brother-in-law's pronouncement. 'It is more like a reward. What she needs is a little discipline and your Aunt Henrietta is just the person to give it to her.'

'Not while there is a chance to salvage the situation,' he said. 'At least this way we can pass it off as a little premature exuberance on the part of the young couple, that we had intended to announce the betrothal at a gathering of our own later in the year but, in view of the couple's impatience, we have decided to bring it forward…'

'I won't agree to that,' Kitty said. 'And Edward won't agree either. We should not suit. Uncle, please do not put either of us to the humiliation of being refused.'

'Neither of you will refuse,' he said, setting his lips in a thin hard line. 'The young man is honour-bound to make an honest woman of you.'

'I won't. I can't. Oh, Uncle, please don't make me.'

His voice softened as he looked at her. 'Kitty, it won't be so terrible. Edward is not old or ugly, or drunken—at least, no more than any young man of his age—and he will soon settle down.'

'Perhaps he doesn't want to settle down. Have you asked him?'

'No, but before we left Beresford House, I spoke to his father. We are to meet again tomorrow afternoon at his London home to discuss the matter.'

'I won't go.' Now she really was frightened and appalled, but defiant too. 'I won't be party to ruining Edward Lampeter's life or mine, just for one stolen kiss, which meant nothing.'

'You are not expected to go,' he said flatly. 'You will remain here until I return to tell you what arrangements have been made. Now, I suggest you go to your room and reflect on your conduct tonight and what it has brought you to. Then say your prayers and ask forgiveness from Someone who is more able to absolve you than I.'

Kitty knew there was no arguing with him while he was in his present mood, nor while her stepmother stood by to make sure he did not weaken. She curtsied to them both and turned to leave the room. Shutting the door behind her, she gathered her skirts in her hands and ran along the hall and up the oak staircase to her room where she flung herself on her bed.

She would not weep. She would not! Neither, she told herself, would she marry Edward Lampeter. She liked him, was even fond of him, but he was certainly not her idea of a husband. They had known each other ever since they were children; he had been James's playmate and she had often tagged along behind them when they went riding and fishing and getting into the sort of mischief young boys always get into.

He could be fun, but that was half the trouble, he never took anything seriously, and he was only two years older than she was, hardly more than a boy. When she married, it would be someone she could look up to, a man with strength of character, a man who could make her feel like a woman, not a playmate, a man she could love, who loved her.

She smiled suddenly, remembering that kiss. It had been a new experience for her and, she had to admit, a delightful one. She was not the first girl he had kissed, that had been obvious, and it had gone on rather a long time, which suggested he had enjoyed it too. But she was quite sure he had never thought it would lead to marriage.

Was he, even now, being given the same ultimatum as she had been given? She could imagine his reaction and, while it was not very flattering to her, she could hardly expect him meekly to obey. Or would he? Did his light-hearted view of life include an indifference to whom he married? He would not agree, would he? Oh, he must not!

If only James were here, he would know what to do. He would talk to Uncle William and Edward and make everything right again. But James, being a boy and older than Kitty by three years, had escaped to university and after that had taken himself off to Europe to do the Grand Tour, and she missed him dreadfully.

She scrambled off the bed and crossed the room to a small walnut escritoire, where she rifled through the drawers for James's last letter. She found it and took it to the candle to read it. The light was almost unnecessary for she had it almost by heart. Written from Florence, it was full of enthusiasm for his travels. He wrote well, filling his prose with light and colour, peopling the pages with the strange characters he had met.

'I think I shall visit Paris on my way home,' he wrote. 'I am curious to see if it has changed much since the Revolution.' The letter had been written several months before and since then there had been news of riots and beheadings and, worst of all, the imprisonment and coming trial of King Louis.

James, who could be more than a little rash at times, would not be so foolish as to embroil himself in other people's troubles and would surely return by sea. On the other hand, perhaps it was only Paris that was dangerous and the rest of the country was peaceful, in which case, travelling overland would be the safest. Safest of all would be to stay where he was until the troubles came to an end.

He seemed to be enjoying Florence and wrote at length about its antiquities and the hospitality of the people and the social occasions he had attended. That, she knew, was a reference to the young ladies he had met. Had he kissed any of them as Edward had kissed her, for the fun of it?

That was what was so unfair about being a woman; you could not have even the tiniest flirtation, however innocent, without you were branded a wanton. What was it Alice had called her? A harlot. She had only a vague idea of what a harlot was, but she knew it could not be anything but bad, especially as the remark had drawn an exclamation of remonstrance from her uncle.

She wished she were a man; life would be so much more fun. A man could travel the world, without the worry of abigails and chaperons; he could get involved in all sorts of adventures and everyone labelled him a jolly good fellow. Why couldn't a woman do that?

Why not? Why not leave home—it would be better than marrying against her will, wouldn't it? Other women did it, why couldn't she? Alice wanted to be rid of her. She would be rid of her, but not to Scotland.

The prospect began to excite her and she paced the room, trying to think of a way in which it could be accomplished. Her uncle would never agree to let her go and to travel you needed money, a great deal of it.

She had the money her mother had left her, but she could not draw on that until she married and then it would be given to her husband. That was something else that wasn't fair. Her uncle gave her a monthly allowance from the trust her father had set up, but that was only pin money and he could stop it at any time. Could she borrow and, if so, from whom? The idea, when it came to her, was so outrageous, she knew she had to try it.

Judith had long since retired to her own bed and would certainly try to dissuade her from going if she was roused. No one must know where she had gone, no one at all, because she would be fetched back and Alice would have her way about sending her to Scotland. That would be worse than marrying Edward.

She would be sorry to leave the rectory, but lately it had become more a place of confinement than a home, and she would be sorry to leave Judith and little Johnny, whom she loved, but staying would be intolerable whether she agreed to marry Edward or not.

She had to get out of her ballgown and its petticoats, something her uncle had obviously not thought about when he dismissed the maid. It had tiny buttons down the back which she could not reach and after struggling for a few minutes, she took a pair of scissors from her needlework drawer and cut herself out of it. Poor Judith, she had spent hours stitching the lace round the sleeves and neckline and pressing the yards of silk in the skirt; goodness knows what she would say when she saw it had been ruined.

But there was no time to think of that. A coach, on its way from Bath to London, called at the King's Head in Beresford village every morning at five-thirty and she meant to be on it.

It was still dark when she let herself out of the house, wearing a simple blue wool dress and caraco jacket, topped by a blue cloak with a fur-lined hood, for it was bitterly cold. Her feet were encased in half-boots. She carried a small handbag in one gloved hand and a carpet bag containing a change of clothes in the other.

Stealthily she made her way down the steps and along the drive to the London road, hoping no one would go to her room and discover the note she had left on her pillow until she was well on her way.

She had never been about at that time of day before, and never alone, so that the experience was both exhilarating and frightening, except, of course, that the step she was taking was irrevocable and she had no idea what the future held in store for her.

She arrived at the King's Head just as the coach rattled into the yard, its mud-begrimed wheels and sweating horses proclaiming that it had been driven hard through the night in order to reach the metropolis by daybreak. Kitty, having paid her fare, climbed aboard and settled into her seat, while the horses were changed, then they were off, galloping through the countryside as dawn lightened the sky and the domes and spires of London appeared in the distance.

Beresford village was only an hour's ride from the capital, and it was still barely light when she left the coach at the Golden Cross and set out to look for a hackney. It was still very early but already, as she walked up Haymarket, which supplied the nearby stables of the Royal Mews with hay and straw, towards Piccadilly, the streets were becoming busy.

Two milkmaids, their yokes slung across their shoulders, hurried to Green Park where their charges waited patiently to be relieved of their overnight burden. A chimney sweep, with his brushes over his shoulder and his little climbing boy trotting reluctantly at his side, made his way to his first call. Errand boys, clerks, washerwomen passed her, giving her a glance of curiosity, but no more than that.

She crossed the road to avoid a drunk rolling homewards and turned the corner into Piccadilly just as a hire carriage approached. Without thinking, she held up her hand and stepped into the road. The driver, half asleep, pulled on the reins so sharply the horse nearly fell back on its haunches.

'Lunatic!' he yelled. 'D'yer want to be killed?'

'I wish to hire your cab.'

He looked down at what he had taken to be a servant girl on an errand for her mistress and found himself gazing at a raven-haired beauty who, though young and very petite, was obviously not a servant. Her complexion was pale and her oval features perfectly proportioned, framed by the hood of her cloak, which was too expensive a garment for a servant to be wearing. Her agitated manner and the bag in her hand gave away the fact that she was running away. He was not sure he wanted to be any part of that.

'Ain't for hire,' he said, preparing to move on. ''Bin up all night, just going home to me bed.'

'I'll pay you double.'

He hesitated.

'For goodness sake, man,' said a male voice at her elbow. 'Don't dilly-dally, can you not see the lady is in great haste?'

Kitty spun round to see who had spoken and found herself looking into a broad chest which sported the most vivid waistcoat she had ever seen. It was of bright blue velvet, embroidered all over with gold and silver thread and trimmed with scarlet braid. And she was prepared to wager the little buttons cascading down its front like teardrops were diamonds.

Slowly she raised her head to look up over a flamboyantly tied cravat, which spilled over the waistcoat, to the face of its owner. He was handsome…my, he was handsome, dark as a gypsy with a firm chin, almost black eyes which held a hint of amusement, and black hair tied back with a blue velvet ribbon to match the waistcoat. A many-caped overcoat was slung carelessly across his shoulders, as if keeping out the cold was the least of its uses.

Smiling, he reached across her to open the door of the cab. 'Be my guest, ma'am.'

She hesitated, not at all sure how she ought to behave, but then, remembering that the reason she was on the streets of London at this ungodly hour was because she had not behaved as she ought, she decided she might as well continue in the same vein. Her life with her uncle and stepmother had ended the minute she had stepped out of the house; whatever lay before her was of her own making. She smiled, thanked him coolly and stepped up into the vehicle, leaving him to hand in her bag.

The driver, sitting with his hands on the reins, looked on in undisguised amusement as the man stood in the road, still holding the door open, so they could not proceed.

'Where do you wish to go, Miss—?' the stranger queried.

'To Brook Street,' she said, settling herself in her seat and ignoring the hint that she should provide her name.

'What a coincidence, that's just my destination,' he said, jumping in beside her, flinging his coat on the opposite seat and revealing a cutaway jacket. 'We can travel together.' He rapped on the roof with his cane and they were away.

Kitty inched herself as far away from him as she could—which wasn't far, considering the narrowness of the vehicle—her body tense with nerves. What had she done? Supposing he abducted her, or took her for the harlot her stepmother had called her—what could she do? Would it do any good to shout for help?

The few people who were about on the street had seen her climb willingly into the vehicle and were continuing on their way, minding their own business; they would not interfere. It was less than two hours since she left home and already she was in a quandary. She did not look at him, but gazed out of the window as if there was something of great interest to be seen in the road.

'You are nervous,' he said. 'Are you afraid of me?'

'Certainly not!'

'Then perhaps you ought to be.'

She gasped and turned to look at him. 'Why?'

He smiled. She was an innocent. 'No, you are right.

You have nothing to fear from me. I am not in the habit of abduction and I would be a fool to molest a schoolgirl, however pretty and desirable.'

'Sir, you are impertinent. And I am nothing of the sort.'

'Not a schoolgirl, or not pretty and desirable? The first I can only guess at, the other I can certainly vouch for.'

She did not answer, knowing that she should never have entered into conversation with him in the first place. Was he flirting with her?

'Am I to assume you are running away from home?'

She remained silent and was disconcerted when he laughed. 'Your silence is more eloquent than any reply. Why are you running away?'

'I am not running away. I am going to visit Sir George Lampeter in Brook Street,' she said, deciding that mentioning Edward's father might add more respectability to her errand.

'Sir George, eh? He with the handsome son? You are surely not eloping? I must say, it is less than gallant of the gentleman to expect you to call for him. I had always thought it usual for lovesick swains to climb ladders to bedroom windows to rescue those they love from wicked stepmothers.'

She turned to him in surprise. 'What do you know of it?'

So, that was the way of it. He assumed a serious expression; it would not do to laugh at her. 'Nothing, nothing at all, my dear, I was just teasing.'

'Then I beg of you to desist. I am not eloping. It is my uncle's wish that I should marry Edward Lampeter.'

'Your uncle's wish?'

'My guardian.'

'And you and you uncle have crossed swords over it?'

'You could say that. On the other hand, it is none of your business.'

'My, we are sharp, are we not? And so early in the morning too. Have you no liking for Mr Lampeter? I am not acquainted with the gentleman but I know of him, he is personable enough. And eligible.'

'I did not say I did not like him. I like him well enough.'

He sighed melodramatically, enjoying the encounter. 'Ah, then he has done something to annoy you. Stolen a kiss, perhaps?'

She felt the colour flare in her cheeks. How could he possibly know that? 'Sir, you are presumptuous.'

He chuckled. 'When a beautiful young lady is in distress, then I do presume, it would be unchivalrous not to. Tell me, if he has not upset you, why have you no wish to marry him? I assume that is what this is all about.'

'I do not love him.'

'Ah, love!' He leaned back in his seat and surveyed her, from her dark curls, tied back with a velvet ribbon because she had had no one to help her arrange them, to flushed cheeks which gave her a sort of gamine charm, from a sturdy little chin to a slim figure which was far from childish. 'He's a lucky fellow.'

'Edward?'

'No, the man who has your heart.'

'There is no one.' With cheeks flaming, she turned to look out of the window again, wishing she had never allowed herself to be drawn into conversation with him, wishing she had refused to enter the coach.

'Impossible!' He laughed. 'Young ladies are always

falling in and out of love, that is why their elders and betters have to help them make up their minds.'

'You do not understand,' she cried, before she could stop herself. 'It is not like that at all. I do not want to marry anyone.'

'Never?' he teased.

'Not until I meet the right man.'

'Then you are going to Lampeter to give him his *congé*. You know, I could almost feel sorry for him, except that it might be a blessing. In my experience, young ladies are not renowned for their steadfastness. The smallest difficulty and they fly into the boughs and stamp their pretty little feet…'

She gurgled with laughter. 'Quite a difficult accomplishment, stamping one's feet while sitting in a tree. I am sure I could never do it.'

He smiled lopsidedly. So the minx had a sense of humour, even when she was in trouble. Unless he missed his guess, she would need it if she really had run away.

'Is Lampeter expecting you at such an early hour? The house will hardly be astir.'

'No.'

'You propose to go alone and ring the front-door bell?'

'Why not?'

'Why not? My dear Miss…' He paused, still smiling. 'You did not tell me your name, but no matter, I can understand your reluctance. You will set the household on its head if you do anything so outrageous. Do you know what you are about?' He paused and turned in his seat so that he was almost facing her and his knees, clad in slim-fitting breeches and white silk stockings, brushed her skirts, sending a little frisson of alarm through her. 'But perhaps that is your intention. Perhaps you want a scandal?'

'No, of course not.'

'Then, if you would allow me, I might be able to help.'

'How?'

'I could go to the door and fetch Lampeter out of the house on some pretext or other and bring him to you. It would be better than going to him, don't you think?' He was looking at her with his head on one side and broad grin on his face.

'It is not funny!'

He assumed an expression of severity which was even more comical and Kitty, in spite of her annoyance with him, found herself smiling in response.

'That's better,' he said. 'You have a beautiful smile. I cannot think how Lampeter could fail to be moved by it. Now, will you allow me to come to your aid?'

'No.' But it was not a very firm negative.

The carriage turned into Brook Street and slowed to a halt. 'Where to exac'ly?' the driver called, leaning over so that his head was hanging upside down above the window.

'Wait,' his male passenger commanded, then, to Kitty, said, 'Well? Do you want me to fetch the lucky fellow out to you?'

'No... Yes... I don't know.' To Kitty, who had not made up her mind how she was going to make the opportunity of speaking to Edward alone, the stranger seemed the answer to her problem. But did she really wish to be indebted to him? She did not even know his name. He might be the devil himself. Come to think of it, he did look rather devilish with his dark looks, dark hair and equally dark eyes. But the eyes had a glint of

gold…and would the devil wear an embroidered blue
waistcoat and a mulberry suit?

'What kind of an answer is that?'

'Very well. I shall be much obliged if you would
fetch Mr Lampeter here, to me. The house is the one
on the far corner.'

Having told the cab driver to wait, he disappeared,
leaving Kitty to contemplate her folly, a course which
left her feeling more lonely and vulnerable than ever.
She sighed heavily. The die had been cast and the only
thing she could do was carry through her plan with all
the resolve she could muster.

The wait seemed interminable, but just when she
thought Edward must have refused to come, or he had
perhaps not returned to London after the ball, although
he had told her that was his intention, she heard the
sound of footsteps and he climbed into the carriage beside her and shut the door.

'Where is…?' She did not know the dark stranger's
name and surprised herself by even mentioning him,
when there were more important things to be discussed.

'Gone on his way. I must say, Kitty, you do have the
most extraordinary calling cards.'

'He seemed a perfectly ordinary gentleman to me.'
She was conscious of the irony, even as she spoke. The
man was far from ordinary.

'That waistcoat! Did you ever see such a garment?
Not one to hide his light under a bushel, is he?'

'You know him?' She was sorry he had not returned;
she had not thanked him properly for his trouble. But
this was no time to be worrying about a stranger; she
had some persuading to do.

'I've seen him at the gaming tables on occasion,' he
said. 'Devilish lucky fellow, too, and known for a hard

man. The ladies seem to like him, though I can't say why they should. Ain't sure he's even a gentleman. How did you come to meet him?' He looked at her, as a suspicion crossed his mind. 'He's not… Oh, Kitty, I never took you for a…' He paused, unwilling to utter the word.

'Edward! I hope you know me better than that.'

He smiled with relief. 'To be sure I do. But what are you doing here? And so early in the day? Have you been to bed?'

'No.' She turned to look at him and noticed he was still wearing the gold satin evening suit and white stockings he had worn at the ball; his fair hair was tousled and there was a distinct stubble on his chin. 'Then, no more have you.'

'And you chastise me for that! Kitty, I wonder you have the effrontery, considering where you are. Last night was bad enough—do you wish to ruin your reputation entirely?'

'Last night was your fault,' she snapped. 'And it is because of what happened last night that I had to see you today.'

'Can't it wait? I went on to White's for a few hands after the ball and have only just returned home. I'm deucedly tired.'

'You can go to bed when you've heard me out. You know my uncle is most displeased? In fact, he is furious.'

'That much I deduced at the time, but an apology to him and to your good self when he calls on me today will surely set everything to rights. He must know I meant no harm.'

'Whether you meant it or not, it has certainly been the result. He is determined to see us married.'

'Married!' He sat up with a jerk. 'That's going too far!' He leaned forward to search her face. A very pretty face, to be sure, and one he was very fond of, but... 'It's a hoax, that's what it is.'

'It is no hoax, I promise you.'

'But why? You ain't a bad-looking girl. I'd go so far as to say you were one of the handsomest, and your grandpapa is a Viscount and wealthy too, so why pick on me? You can have any of the young bloods in town this year.'

'I don't want any of them.'

'Just me?'

'Not you, either.'

'You don't?'

She laughed at the comical mixture of relief and indignation on his face. 'No, I don't. It is Uncle William's idea and he will brook no argument, possibly because if he does my stepmama will insist on him sending me to my great-aunt in Scotland.'

'No, don't believe that. You're bamming me.'

'No, I'm not. Did you know he is meeting your father this afternoon to discuss arrangements for a wedding?'

'No, by Jupiter, I did not. My father will skin me alive.'

'But he will agree with what my uncle proposes?'

'Very likely,' he said morosely. 'He has been rattling on at me to marry and settle down this past year, but I'm only twenty-one, for heaven's sake, and I want to see something of the world before I do.'

'Why didn't you do as James did? You could have gone with him.'

'James is older than me by more than a year, as you know, and he was sponsored by Viscount Beresford. I have no means to finance a protracted tour. I planned to enter the navy as the next best thing. But to be leg-shackled…' He paused, contemplating the prospect. 'I would make a terrible husband, what with drinking and gambling and staying out all night.'

'I am well aware of that, Edward. If I loved you, I might overlook it, but as I do not love you and never will, not in the way of a wife for a husband, I do not propose to saddle myself with you.'

'You are going to refuse me? Oh, you darling girl, I could kiss you all over again. In fact, I think I will.' And he reached out towards her.

She pushed him away. 'No, Edward, I do not think you should.'

'What would you have me do?'

'You need do nothing, except to act the jilted lover, if you want to. I shall not mind.'

'I say, that's coming it a bit brown, ain't it?'

'You are a nice man, Edward, and we have been friends since we were children and I used to trail after you and James. I would like to think you are still my friend.'

'Always, dear girl, always.'

'Then give me money, as much as you can manage. I want you to buy me off…' She sounded perfectly calm though, inside her blue wool gown, her heart was beating furiously.

'Buy you off?' He was visibly shaken that such a suggestion should come from a young lady who had been carefully nurtured. 'Has your uncle put you up to this?' Noticing the look of consternation on her face, he checked himself. 'No, he would not do such a thing, being a man of the cloth and an honourable one. Your stepmama, perhaps? Now, *she* might.'

She ignored this slur on Alice. 'No one put me up to

it. It was my own idea. They do not know I have left the house, though when Judith goes to my room to wake me she will see the letter I left and take it straight to my uncle. I have no doubt he will look for me, but I do not want him to find me.'

'You surely do not expect me to hide you? God in heaven, the Reverend will scalp me.'

'There is no need for you to hide me or even for my uncle to know I've been to see you. I shall be gone long enough for any scandal to die down, but I must have funds. You do understand, don't you, Edward?'

'And if I can't lay my hands on any?'

She shrugged. 'We will be condemned to a loveless marriage.'

He sighed heavily. 'Very well, I will do my best. Go home and wait for me.'

'No, I am never going home again. And I dare not go to any of my known friends because Uncle William is bound to go looking for me. I want you to take me to an hotel and book a room for me.'

'Out of the question,' he said firmly. 'Do you take me for a mountebank? You are a gentlewoman, you cannot stay in a hotel alone. Nor yet with me. We should never live it down—'

'My stepmama has already said we should never live down what happened last night either. It seems I am to live the rest of my days with my folly. I am past such considerations. Surely you know a discreet little rooming house tucked away somewhere?'

He laughed suddenly. 'You know, Kitty, you really are the most extraordinary girl. I could almost fall in love with you.'

'Well, don't,' she said crisply. 'Just do as I ask.'

'It's unthinkable you should go anywhere unaccompanied,' he said. 'Take a companion or a maid. Ask Judith. Ten to one, your stepmama will turn her off without a character.'

Kitty sighed. He was right and she had been thoughtless to leave without making provision for the servant, who had been nurse and companion to her and her mother before her. Alice would be glad of an excuse to be rid of her. 'I couldn't ask her. It would mean taking her far from home and goodness knows how many adventures we shall have.'

'Far from home,' he repeated in alarm. 'Kitty, where are you going?'

'Better you do not know.'

'Then let me fetch Judith to you.' If anyone could dissuade Kitty from her folly, it would be Judith and, to be honest, he was out of his depth and needed to hand her over to someone more competent to deal with her.

Kitty's bravado was all on the surface and the idea of having a companion on her travels grew on her. Would Judith come? 'Can you ask her without letting anyone else in the house know?'

'I will do my best.'

It was not until she was alone in a bedroom of a small, unfashionable hotel that the enormity of what she had done came to her, and she began to shake uncontrollably. And the thought of what she had yet to do almost made her turn from her resolve and rush straight back home.

But the memory of the scene with her uncle and stepmother in the small hours of the morning, and the countless pinpricks of unkindness meted out to her by Alice over the years, stiffened her spine.

She would not stay where she was not wanted and she would not marry a man she did not love, however many young ladies had done so before her and would do so in the future; if it meant loneliness and hardship, then so be it. She would endure it stoically. Quite how much hardship she was not yet to know.

Chapter Two

If he stopped to think, Edward might guess what was in her mind, Kitty thought, as she climbed into bed that night, having first taken the precaution of hooking a chair back under the door knob, but it might not come to him until it was too late. And he might remain silent, not wanting to implicate himself.

He returned the following morning just as she was finishing a frugal breakfast in her room after a sleepless night. He was accompanied by her maid. Judith Sadler was a woman of middle years, almost as round as she was tall, with reddened cheeks and small blue eyes which easily sprang tears, as they were doing now, as they embraced.

'Oh, Kitty, my love, what have you done?' she cried. 'Your uncle is silent and white-faced and your step-mama is screaming at him what an ungrateful wretch you are. They would have it that I knew aforehand what you were going to do and the mistress bade the Rev-erend beat it out of me. They could not believe I did not know where you were, nor couldn't I believe it my-self. How could you break my poor heart so?'

'I am truly sorry, Judith, but you might have stopped me—'

'For sure, I would.'

'But you came when I sent for you?'

'And why would I not? If ever you needed a body's help it is now, and who else but me could you trust?'

'No one, dear Judith,' Kitty said, looking over the grey head at Edward. 'Was it very difficult?'

He smiled, turning his hat in his hand, anxious to be gone. 'I paid a young girl to call on the rectory and say Judith was needed urgently by her sister who was ill and needed someone to look after her children until she recovered.'

'But Uncle William knows Judith has no sister.'

'Mistress didn't know it and the Rector was out,' the maid said. 'She was glad enough to let me go.'

'Thank you, Edward,' Kitty said.

'My pleasure,' he said, though he looked far from pleased.

'What about that other matter?' she asked, hoping that, in fetching Judith to her, he had not forgotten about the money.

He put a small purse of gold coins and some paper money on the table beside her empty coffee cup. 'I managed to call in a few debts and borrow some more, but I wish I knew what you were going to do. The Reverend is sure to think of me before long and then what shall I say?'

'Nothing. I have written to him again, trying to explain why I have done what I have done. I pray he will understand and forgive me. Will you see that it is delivered to him tomorrow, after mid-day?'

'Why not today?'

'Because I don't want him to stop me.'

'He will say that I should have stopped you. And he would be right. I don't like it, Kitty, not above half I don't.'

'You can have the letter delivered anonymously; he need not know you were involved at all. I told you, you can act the jilted suitor.'

'I shall look a fool.'

'No, everyone will say what a lucky escape you had.' She took his hands in both her own. 'I am truly grateful, Edward. I could not have managed without you.'

He laughed. 'Blackmail is a very strong weapon, my dear. I had no choice.'

'You had, but I am glad you did not take it.'

'Goodbye, my dear, and good luck.' He kissed her lightly on the cheek and left.

Kitty turned to Judith, who stood in the middle of the room with a small travelling bag and a basket at her feet. The poor woman looked pale and worried to death, but she was, above all else, loyal to Kitty and would follow her and look after her through thick and thin, fire and water.

'Fact is, Miss Kitty, I ain't exac'ly sorry to be leaving the rectory. Not that I would have left while you needed me—your poor dead mother asked me to look after you and look after you I will. I suppose that's why your stepmama never did take to me. She would have turned me off the minute you were married.'

'You goose, Judith, I would have taken you with me. Which is what I am doing now. You will come, won't you?'

'I couldn't have borne it if you had asked someone else to look after you.'

'You aren't going to try and tempt me to go back then?'

'Would it serve?'

'No, it would not.'

'Then I shan't waste my breath.'

'Thank you, Judith. You know I was very desolate and frightened, but now you are here, I feel so much better.'

'I took the liberty of bringing some more of your things,' Judith said. 'I thought you might be going somewhere a mite warmer.'

She heaved the basket onto the bed and opened it to reveal two lightweight gowns, one in green silk, the other blue muslin, a thin lawn petticoat, shoes and a pelisse, as well as a carriage dress in brown taffeta for travelling and a flannel petticoat to wear in the January weather then prevailing and which they would not leave behind for some days.

'What made you think that?'

'You left Master James's letter lying on your bed.'

'Did anyone else see it?'

'No, Miss Kitty, I put it in the basket and brought it with me.'

'Oh, now you are here I feel quite cheerful again, so you may take that sorrowful look off your face and smile. We are going to have some high old adventures, you and I, and we are going to enjoy them. Can you imagine James's face when he sees us?'

Judith could not. That meeting was so far in the future that even thinking about what might happen in the mean time filled her with foreboding. But she smiled and began repacking the basket and Kitty's valise.

It was four o'clock the following morning when the two women arrived in Dover after travelling in a public coach since seven the previous evening. They were cold, tired and hungry, not to mention filthy.

'We must bespeak a private room here,' Judith said, as they climbed stiffly from the carriage. 'For I declare I can't go a step further until I have washed, eaten and slept.'

Kitty, who had quite regained her spirits, laughed. 'It is less than twenty-four hours since you left home and already you are complaining.'

'I am not complaining,' Judith denied the accusation sharply. It would never do for her mistress to think she was not up to the rigours of the journey or she might be left behind. Already she had had her own way about crossing the channel by the shortest route, having a great terror of the sea.

She would rather face revolution in France than be drowned trying to sail round it, she had told Kitty. Adding that, if she were sick, how could she look after her darling? And that, she declared, was the one purpose of her life, to look after her charge and protect her from all the dangers that faced them, from lascivious sailors and Frenchmen who would chop off her head, to bad food and bed bugs.

'Very well, we will stop here for a few hours, but then we must go to the harbour and find out when the next packet is due to leave, for I mean to be on it.'

'And what story do we put about for a lady and her maid to be travelling alone without so much as a link-boy for an escort?' Judith demanded, as she picked up Kitty's luggage and followed her into the inn. 'Everyone will know at once that you are running away.'

'I am not running away. I have just lost my parents and am going to Italy to join my brother, he being the only relative I have left in the world. It is as near the truth as makes no difference.'

'Your poor uncle would not think it so.'

'No, but when we reach Calais, I shall entrust the captain of the packetboat with another letter to him, so that his mind is set at rest.'

It was Judith's opinion that a letter from the other side of the Channel was more likely to inflame the Rector's mind than set it at rest, but she did not voice it.

Picking up their luggage, Judith followed her mistress into the inn and demanded a room in a way which brooked no argument. They were soon ensconced in an upper chamber, enjoying a meal of chicken, ham, meat pie, fish and vegetables. What they could not eat they wrapped up and put in their baggage against a future need, not knowing how well provisioned the ship would be, or how difficult it might be to buy food in France. And then they lay down to sleep.

Kitty was woken three hours later by the clatter in the yard outside their window which told her another day had begun.

She padded across the floor to look out of the casement and saw, in the growing light of dawn, that a coach had just arrived from London and its passengers were alighting. There were two portly men in frieze greatcoats and buff breeches and a tall man with dark hair tied back with a black ribbon who was, at that moment, doffing his hat in goodbye to a clerical-looking gentleman and his plump lady.

At first Kitty thought it was her uncle and stepmama come to fetch her back. However, on looking closer realised this was not so, but it served to remind her of the need for haste and she quickly roused Judith; fifteen minutes later they were out on the street and making their way down to the harbour.

They had the hoods of their cloaks up over their heads against the bitter, sleet-laden wind which blew from the north-east, numbing their fingers and toes. But it was a good wind for sailing and they hurried to the quay where they saw a schooner preparing for sea. People were coming and going from it and the sailors were busy on the deck. Kitty left Judith minding their baggage while she went to the ticket office and paid for their passage, then urged the reluctant Judith up the gangplank of the *Faery Queen*.

They were directed below decks to a small dingy cabin which, so they were told by the crewman who conducted them there, was usually occupied by several ladies. 'But you have it all to yourselves,' he said, depositing their baggage on the floor. 'This not bein' the season for travelling, so cold and wet as it is, and what with the Frenchies as like to chop your head off as not. If I was you I should turn right round and go ashore ag'in.'

They could not have taken his advice even if they had wanted to because, at that moment, there was a great crack above their heads as the wind filled the sails and the deck beneath their feet began to tremble.

'Oh, God be merciful, we're sinking!' Judith exclaimed, clutching at Kitty.

The sailor smiled. 'Bless you, we ain't sinking, we're under way, as smooth as you please.' And with that he left them to go about his duties.

'Shall we go on deck and say goodbye to England?' Kitty suggested. 'I am sure you will feel better if you can see what is happening.'

They returned to the deck, holding on to superstructure, posts and rigging, anything to help them keep their balance, until they were standing side by side at the rail, watching as the ship slowly made its way out of the shelter of the harbour.

'Well, well, if it isn't my little runaway.'

Kitty whirled round to face the man who had spoken, the man with whom she had shared a cab little more than forty-eight hours previously, the man she had seen getting out of a coach at the inn. She had been so intent on the clerical gentleman, she had not recognised him then.

'*You!*'

He doffed his tall hat with its narrow curly brim and executed a mannerly leg as steadily as if they had been in a London drawing room and not on a heaving deck. He was smiling. 'As you see! Jack Chiltern at your service, ma'am.'

'What are you doing here?' she demanded, unaccountably pleased to see him. He was solidly real in a shifting world; someone from England. How did he know she would be on the packet? Had she let her intentions slip when talking to him in the coach? 'Have you been following me?'

He smiled lazily. 'Why should I do that?'

'To take me back.'

'If that were so, I would surely have made a move before we set sail. I can hardly swim ashore with you. My presence on this ship is pure coincidence, I promise you.'

'Oh.' She turned from him to look at the receding coastline as the ship met the open sea and began to pitch and roll. The unexpected movement flung her towards him. He caught her and steadied her, holding her just a fraction longer than was proper before releasing her.

'But I am curious,' he went on, deliberately setting aside the pleasure her small body next to his had given him. 'Tell me, Kitty, what is so objectionable about Edward Lampeter that you cannot abide being in the same kingdom with him and must flee the country?'

She gasped. 'How do you know my name?'

'Lampeter murmured it when he required me to give a description of the person who commanded his presence so early in the morning. He said he would not stir for any little bit of muslin who might opportune him; his words, not mine, I add. It was not until he had been convinced of your identity that he agreed to go to you.' He sighed melodramatically. 'I am only sorry that it was to so little purpose.'

'What do you mean?'

'Why, that you did not come to an understanding. I should have thought a life with him would be infinitely preferable to the course you have chosen. Or perhaps he did not offer?'

'Sir, you know nothing of it but what I was so foolish as to confide in you. Pray forget it.'

'With pleasure, ma'am. I have more important things to occupy me than a madcap girl who does not seem to realise she is jumping from the frying pan into the fire.'

'Nonsense!' she said with some asperity. She did not know why she continued to converse with him, he was so arrogant and not at all civil, but he had the kind of presence you could not ignore and, if she were honest, she felt a little safer with him beside her. 'I know there is some unrest in Paris, but we mean to bypass the city—'

'You call the bloodiest deed ever to disgrace the name of France *some unrest*!' he interrupted. 'Less than a week ago, they sent their King to the guillotine. Pray, tell me where have you been hiding yourself that something which has cast a cloud over the whole of Europe should be of so little import to you? Do they not have newspapers in your part of the country?'

She was shocked by the news but quickly recovered herself. 'Naturally they do, but I rarely see them. Uncle William thinks they are not fit reading for genteel young ladies. When he spoke of it, he said it would come to nothing; a people could not depose a king and right would prevail.'

'And so you remain in blissful ignorance, which is no bad thing, except that you have taken it into your silly head to hurl yourself into the fray.'

'You overstate the case, sir. We are not hurling ourselves into anything, we intend to stay only at respectable inns and avoid trouble.'

'Easier said than done, Kitty, believe me. But tell me, where are you bound? Purely as a matter of satisfying my curiosity, you understand. Or is this simply a whim to travel without a destination?'

His condescending attitude infuriated her. 'Sir, I did not give you permission to use my given name. But, since you ask, I am going to join my brother in Italy.'

He whistled. 'Right through France? Child, you are mad. Did you not know France is also at war with Austria and half of Europe and will undoubtedly soon be in conflict with England? Do you have papers stating your business? And passports? You will need them to pass through the barriers and cross the borders.'

Before she could tell him that she lacked these requirements, Judith, who had been standing beside her growing paler and paler, was violently sick, and she turned from him to look after her maid. Taking her down to the cabin, she helped her to bed and sat beside her, bathing her brow, until she was calmer and fell asleep.

Later, longing to escape from the malodorous cabin, she returned on deck. The short day had turned to night and she stood by the rail again, breathing deeply, thankful that she appeared to be a good sailor. The sea was calmer now and, above the billowing sails, the stars made a dark pincushion of the sky. They made her think of home, of her uncle and little Johnny.

He would be missing her as she missed him: missed his giggle when she tickled him, his rapt attention when she told him a story. She prayed his mother would have patience with him and perhaps find him a loving nursemaid. She wondered fleetingly what her grandfather, the Viscount, had made of her disappearance; undoubtedly Alice would have put it in the worst possible light.

'Beautiful, aren't they?' said a voice at her elbow.

She did not need to turn round to know who stood beside her; she recognised the voice, knew the large capable hand that grasped the rail only inches from her own, felt his tall presence overshadowing her. 'Yes, they are.'

'It is strange to think that those same stars are twinkling over the whole northern hemisphere, over France and England, rich and poor, good and evil, faithful and faithless. You would think they would be more discriminating, wouldn't you?'

'We are all God's creation,' she said, wondering at the tinge of irony she detected in his voice.

'Indeed, yes.' He stood looking down at her, seeing the glitter of tears on her lashes in the moonlight and feeling a sudden surge of compassion which he quickly stifled. 'But I believe you are already regretting your precipitous flight.'

'Not at all,' she said, as coolly as she could, though his nearness was making it almost impossible. 'I have always wanted to travel, I'm looking forward to the experience.'

'It is an experience you may learn to regret,' he said. She had courage, he would give her that, and it was courage she would need in the weeks ahead of her. If he was not so pressed for time, he might be tempted to offer to escort her, but then smiled at his own stupidity. Hadn't he learned his lesson yet? 'In those clothes, you will stand out like a beacon. The *sans-culottes* will strip you naked and worse before taking all your money and denouncing you for an aristo.'

Kitty, who considered herself very plainly dressed, looked down at the fur-lined cloak and sturdy half-boots she wore and then back up at him. In the darkness it was difficult to see his expression, but his eyes were watchful. 'What does *sans-culottes* mean?'

He grinned. 'Is your French not up to translating it? It means ''without breeches''. In other words, those who wear *pantalons* and not knee-breeches.'

She found herself blushing. Alice would never use either word and always referred to gentleman's nether garments as Inexpressibles. 'I still don't understand.'

'It is a term applied to the working classes, labourers, shopkeepers, craftsmen. Since they wield a great deal of power these days, it is advisable not to upset them. And being better dressed than they are upsets them.'

'Your puerile attempts to frighten me are wasted,' she said, determined not to let him see how nervous he had made her. 'I am an Englishwoman, not a French aristocrat, so what have I to fear? I have done no wrong and shall do none.'

He laughed suddenly. 'Oh, my eye, a genuine innocent! And you think your haughty manner will be enough to keep you safe? Rest assured, nothing could be further from the truth. Will you, for instance, know how to deal with this?' And before her startled senses could warn her what was coming, he had taken her into his arms and was kissing her.

It was nothing like the gentle kiss Edward had given her which had roused nothing in her but innocent delight at her daring. This man's mouth was hard and demanding, forcing her lips to part, engulfing her, shutting out everything else around her, the wind in the sails, the creak of the rigging, the low voices of the crew, everything except the surge of something growing and expanding deep inside her, something wild and ungovernable which took her breath away.

With one arm still about her waist, he put his other hand up to her neck, caressing it with his thumb from ear to throat, making her shudder. When his fingers found the ribbon that tied her cloak, she suddenly realised what was happening and pulled herself away.

She stood, eyes glittering, breast heaving, unable to speak, unable to think of anything except the effect that kiss had had upon her. She raised both clenched fists to him, but he simply grabbed them and held them fast.

'That was only a small taste of what you might find yourself having to endure,' he said as calmly as he could, though his own heart was pounding. He knew he ought to ask pardon, but apologising would put him in the wrong and render the lesson ineffective. 'Others would not be so careful of you.'

'Careful!' she hissed, unwilling to scream and alert

the crew to her plight. She doubted if they would come to her aid, if she did. 'I cannot think of anything more lacking in care. Do you take me for a…a…?' She could not say the word.

He released her hands. 'No, I meant only to demonstrate to you the dangers which might beset you. Talking seemed to have little effect.'

'All you have demonstrated, sir, is that you are a cur.'

She turned, intending to go down to the cabin, but suddenly realised that the coast of France, which had been a distant line on the dark horizon when she came on deck, now loomed large and she could dimly see buildings and lights and people. Even as she hesitated, the sails were furled and a rope was thrown out and they were being hauled alongside the jetty by a tugboat.

'If you had any sense,' he said, addressing her stiffened back. 'You would not disembark, but stay aboard and return to England. Better the devil you know…'

Kitty might have been tempted to take his advice, if Judith had not been so anxious to have *terra firma* under her feet again that she declared she would rather face a thousand bloodthirsty Frenchmen than spend another minute at sea. Kitty told her nothing of her latest conversation with the tall stranger—she realised she still had no idea who Jack Chiltern was—and, picking up their baggage, helped her maid up on to the deck and down the gangplank on to French soil.

The other passengers had disembarked before them and were each going their separate ways. The two women stood undecided on the quay with their bags at their feet, looking about them for a cab to convey them to a hotel for the remainder of the night. They could see no such vehicle. What they did see was the stranger, who had been striding purposefully ahead of them, stop and turn. He stood for a few seconds, watching them, then strode back.

'Damn you, woman!' he said. 'I cannot abandon you.' Kitty was so thankful to hear his voice, she forgot to reprimand him for his language, although Judith bristled with indignation and would have said something if Kitty had not laid a hand on her arm to restrain her.

'Come with me,' he went on, picking up the valise and basket. 'I'll see you safely settled in a hotel, if you can call it by that name, but more than that I will not undertake to do. I have other more pressing errands.'

'Thank you.' It went against all her inclinations to be civil to him, let alone grateful, but she had to admit she needed help and, as he was the only one to offer any, she should not be too proud to accept.

He conducted them along the street and round a corner, where he stopped in front of a building which looked more like a tavern than a hotel. Above the door the sign of a cockerel creaked in the wind. He ushered them over the threshold into a dimly lit parlour, where several people were drinking. All of them were meanly dressed, the men in pantaloons, rough collarless shirts and a garment that was somewhere between a sleeveless jacket and a waistcoat. Some also wore long overcoats.

The women were in skirts and blouses with red, white and blue shawls tied about their shoulders or waists. All wore the crimson caps of the Revolution, with their tricolour cockades pinned on the side.

'Citizen Chiltern!' The innkeeper came forward and, clasping both their escort's arms, embraced him. 'It is good to see you again, *mon vieux*. Come into the back room and you can tell me all your news.'

'I'll tell you later, Pierre, my friend,' their escort said

in fluent French, stepping aside to allow Kitty and Judith to precede him into the next room where a bright fire burned. He put down their bags. 'First, I must dispose of certain encumbrances. Can you find a room for these two?'

The man looked doubtfully at Kitty and Judith who stood uncertainly just inside the door, looking longingly at the fire. 'Jack, I'll do anything for you, you know that, but…'

'One night, then put them on a south-bound diligence in the morning and forget you ever saw them.' He pulled a purse from the capacious pocket of his great-coat and extracted some coins which he laid on the table.

'They have passes?'

'No, they travel light.'

'Too light, *citoyen*, too light.' He looked Kitty up and down, noting the warm clothing. 'And in other ways too heavy.'

'I know, but what can I do? They have thrown themselves on my mercy…'

'And you cannot resist a pretty face, I know it. Where do you go in the morning?'

'To Paris.'

'Without them?' He nodded at the two women.

'Without them. But I would not have them molested. They need passports and papers to travel through France. An escort part of the way, if you can provide one.'

'*Mon Dieu!* You do not ask much, do you?'

Jack laughed. 'Put Gerard on to it.' And again gold coins were extracted from the purse and laid beside the others on the table.

'I shall need their names and their destination and a valid reason for travelling.'

Kitty, who had learned a little French in the schoolroom, had managed to follow the gist of what had been said. 'I am going to Italy to live with my brother, my parents both being dead,' she said, moving to stretch her cold hands towards the blaze. 'Is that reason enough?'

'And this one?' The man pointed a blackened finger at Judith.

'She is my maid, Judith Sadler.'

'Maid, eh?' He smiled at Judith and chucked her under the chin which made her recoil. 'No, not a maid. Citizeness, you are a free woman, free to come and go as you please.'

'Of course she is,' Kitty said, grasping the situation. 'I meant she is my friend. Yes, very definitely my friend.'

'And you, *citoyenne*, who are you?'

'Kitty Harston, plain Kitty Harston. My brother is James Harston, should you need to know that.'

'What!' The exclamation came from Jack.

She turned to look at him. The astonishment on his face was comical. 'Harston,' she repeated. 'Did Mr Lampeter not tell you that when he told you my given name?'

'No, he did not.' He sat down heavily in the nearest chair. '*Mon Dieu*! This alters everything.'

'How so?'

He ignored her and turned to the innkeeper. 'Pierre, we shall have to think again.'

'What do you mean?' Kitty demanded. 'Do you know something of my brother?'

'Shut up, woman, and let me think,' he said in English.

'Did you ever hear such ungentlemanly language?' Judith protested. 'Kitty, I cannot think what we are doing here, allowing ourselves to be bullied in this fashion. I begin to think it was a bad day when you met up with the scoundrel. I am quite sure he is doing all this on purpose to frighten us.'

'Do you know something of my brother?' Kitty asked again, thoroughly alarmed by the thunderous look on Jack Chiltern's face. 'If you do, I beg of you to tell me. He is not…not dead, is he?'

'Not that I know of, but he is certainly not in Italy.' He stood up suddenly and spoke to the innkeeper in French. 'Pierre, give the citizenesses your best room and something to eat. I will go and see when the *Faery Queen* is due to return to England. These two must be on it.'

Kitty, who had followed most of what he had said, was thoroughly alarmed. 'Mr Chiltern, I beg of you to tell me, where is my brother?'

'In Paris, ma'am. At least, he was there two weeks ago.'

'Then we go to Paris tomorrow.'

'Oh, no, we don't. If you think I am going to saddle myself with a couple of *ingénue* tourists, you are mistaken.'

'Then don't. We did not ask for your help and will continue without it.'

Pierre demanded a translation, which Jack furnished him with and which resulted in ribald laughter.

'It is not amusing, my friend,' Jack told him. 'You know how important my business is and how much in haste I am to see it done. I must either return them to

England or take them with me. Either way...' He shrugged.

'Leave it to the morning,' Pierre suggested. 'No one goes anywhere after curfew and the tocsin has long since sounded. And besides, Gerard will need time to forge the papers. Yours, too, because Jack Chiltern is no longer safe in France.'

All of which served to heighten Kitty's anxiety. She realised she knew nothing whatever about Jack Chiltern; he could be anyone, a French nobleman, an English spy, a French spy, a pirate—with his dark complexion he certainly looked piratical enough—a murderer, an adventurer who preyed on helpless women, or simply a gentleman of leisure, making the Grand Tour, just as her brother was doing.

Was that how they had met? Why had he brought her to this inn and how was it that he knew so much about forging papers? And the innkeeper and his patrons were undoubtedly revolutionaries.

Pierre went to the door and shouted for his wife and that good lady, dressed as everyone else was in rough peasant clothes, laid down her knitting and brought in a watery potato soup and some thick black bread and, after Kitty and Judith had tried to swallow some of it, conducted them upstairs to one of the rooms. There was only one bed and no fire, but Kitty was past worrying about such inconveniences. She was beginning to think Jack Chiltern had been right; she had jumped out of the frying pan into the fire.

'Perhaps we ought to go back,' she said, hurriedly taking off her gown and boots and getting beneath the blankets in her underclothes. 'But I am loathe to give him best. And if we went back, where would we go? Not home, for my stepmama would crow like a cock over our downfall and I should be sent to Scotland on the next coach going north. Or Bedlam. She is bound to say I have taken leave of my senses...'

'And who's to say she wouldn't be right?' Judith said, following Kitty's example and joining her in the bed. 'The whole escapade has been madness.'

'You did not have to come with me.'

'I know that, but where else would I go? Mrs Harston would not give me houseroom and, besides, someone must look after you, though I seem to have had little success, so far.'

'Oh, Judith, you have been a tower of strength to me. Now, tell me what you think. Honestly, mind.'

'I am sure, Miss Kitty, that I have always been honest, as you well know.' Her voice, muffled by the bedclothes, was huffily indignant.

'Go on, then.'

'Your brother would undoubtedly give you welcome and, if the gentleman is right, and he is in Paris, why, that's not so very far to travel and we'd be on good solid ground all the way, would we not?'

Kitty laughed and hugged her. 'Very well. We will not allow ourselves to be bundled back on to that packet like so much cargo. We go to Paris.'

Jack sat before the backroom fire, his long legs thrust out before him, a mug of ale in his hand, listening to Pierre telling him the latest news of Paris. The execution of the King had resulted in popular rejoicing, as if that one act would see an end to all their problems. 'Louis Capet was more fool than traitor, I think,' Pierre said, referring to the King by his popular name. 'Who but a fool would leave incriminating documents in his apart-

ment for all to see? And trying to flee the country, that
was the height of folly.'

'He may have been a fool, my friend, but he was also
a king,' Jack said. 'The people may come to regret their
treatment of him. France will jump from the frying pan
into the fire, just as the innocent Miss Kitty Harston has
done.'

'How did you come upon her? It is not like you to
dally with females when you are working.'

'It was none of my doing,' he said. 'Women are an
abomination, always making demands, always interfering...'

Pierre laughed. 'A sweeping statement, *mon vieux*,
and one I cannot agree with. I have no fault to find with
madame, my wife. She has suited me well these twenty
years.'

'You have been lucky.'

'So you may yet be. What of the citizeness upstairs?'

'James Harston's sister, God save me, and where is
James? Right in the thick of it. They are two of a kind,
that pair, impulsive, entirely without sense, but courageous. But there are times when courage is foolhardy.'

'You will send them back?'

'I certainly ought to and I ought to go with them, if
only to protect them and try to mitigate the trouble they
will surely find themselves in on arriving home.'

'You can't go back now, there is too much at stake.'

'That I know. I must leave as soon as the curfew is
lifted.' He paused to drain his glass. 'Is Gerard here
yet?'

'Yes, he is in the kitchen, eating—he is always hungry, that one—but he will join us directly. But you must
decide on a new identity before he gets to work.'

'What do you suggest?'

Pierre looked thoughtful. 'The time is not far off, I think, when England and France will be at war and *les Anglais* will be even more distrusted than they are now. It is time you took your mother's nationality.' He grinned suddenly. 'But not her noble birth.'

'That poses no difficulty.'

'A farmer, perhaps. You still have that safe house just outside the city?' Jack nodded and he went on. 'If you are seen coming and going daily from the market with your cart, the men on the barriers will become used to you.'

'And my name?'

'Jacques will do, easy to remember. Follow it with… let me see…' He grinned. 'Faucon, how's that?'

'The Hawk. Yes, it will do very well.'

As he spoke a very tall man, thin as a pole, whose rags hung on him like fluttering pennants, came into the room carrying a satchel which he placed upon the table. They turned to watch as he drew out parchment, pens and inks. 'So?' he queried.

'Citizen Jacques Faucon, smallholder,' Jack said, watching him write slowly and laboriously. 'Thirty-one years old.'

'Married?'

'No.'

'Pity. A farmer needs a wife, too much to do alone and no one willing to work any more…'

Pierre looked at Jack and then nodded his head to the room over their heads. 'He has a point. A ready-made wife…'

'No,' Jack said, bluntly. 'They go home.'

'The young one seems determined to go on. You cannot make her go back.'

'I cannot make her come with me either. Nor do I want to be saddled with her.'

'It will help your disguise. Jack Chiltern always works alone. Jacques Faucon is a family man.'

'She would never agree. And what would her brother say?'

'If she is as determined to go as she says she is, it would be safer for her, too. He would understand that.'

'She is not French and, though she can make herself understood, I doubt she speaks the language well enough to pass as a native.'

'Then you once went to England and took an English wife, a foolish lapse and one you have lived to regret many times over, for she is a veritable shrew.'

Jack laughed aloud. 'I think she might enjoy playing that part, for she has no great liking for me. But what of the other one?'

'Her mother, even more of a scold.'

'It is all very well for you to jest, citizens,' Jack said, amid their laughter. 'But I am in the devil of a quandary.'

Pierre stopped laughing. 'Your work is important too, *mon ami*, and personal feelings can have no place in your life. If Providence provides you with a way to make it easier, then you should take it.'

'I wish to God I had never met her.' Even as he spoke he was aware that it was not true. Miss Kitty Harston had attracted him from the first. He admired her beauty, the way she spoke, the artless things she said, her lack of fear, even when he had kissed her. He had done it to frighten her, but instead found himself being roused to a passion he had stifled for too long. And she had not been frightened; in truth, her response had been a delight and he had felt a surge of joy, followed quickly by remorse.

She was an innocent, fragile as porcelain, almost as transparent as glass; he had spoiled something which was beautiful and should have been cherished, had crushed it with his brutality. It was for her future husband to awaken her, not the embittered man he had become.

'Too late, my friend, too late.' Pierre turned to the forger. 'Papers for the women, too.' Then, filling Jack's glass again, he added. 'I'll wager five *livres* that when it comes to it, the women will have the last word.'

'They usually do,' Jack murmured morosely.

Kitty was up at dawn, dressing in the brown taffeta travelling dress and scraping her hair into a bun before repacking their belongings and discarding fripperies. One night in France had shown her that Jack Chiltern was right, they must not stand out in the crowd. She did not fancy being mauled by any of the rough-looking patrons of the Cockerel, and it was her guess they were typical of the population as a whole. When she had finished, she woke Judith and they ate the food they had brought with them.

'Well, do we throw ourselves on Mr Chiltern's mercy this morning, or shall we manage without him?' Kitty asked.

Judith considered the question for some time, looking at Kitty speculatively. 'On the one hand, we know nothing of him. We do not even know if he is trustworthy but, on the other, he helped you without reward when you left the rectory and he seems to know where your brother is. Which weighs the heavier? It is for you to decide but, if we go with him, you must hold yourself aloof and not indulge in battles of words, for you will surely lose.'

Kitty ignored the implication that she was argumentative; she knew that only too well. 'Supposing he has already left without us?'

Judith stood up and helped Kitty on with her cloak. 'Then, child, you will be saved the decision.' She picked up the baggage and made for the door. 'Come, my love, by tomorrow or the next day, you will be with James and he will look after you.'

Kitty followed her out and they went down to the parlour, where *madame* was busy sweeping. She looked up as they approached and nodded her head towards the back room without speaking. Kitty turned and made her way there.

An unshaven Jack was sitting at the table, devouring a hunk of bread. A bottle of red wine and a full glass stood on the table in front of him. The innkeeper was sitting opposite him, watching him eat. Jack rose as soon as the women entered, but it was a Jack much changed. Now he was dressed in grubby black trousers tied about the middle with a length of rope. His shirt was of coarse linen and was topped by a ragged black coat which was so old it was turning green. He wore no hose, but half-boots worn down at the heel.

'Good morning, Miss Harston,' he greeted her. 'Did you sleep well?'

'Tolerably,' she said, unable to take her eyes off him. 'But we were so fatigued we took no note of our miserable accommodation.'

'Breakfast?' he queried, indicating the unappetising loaf and the bottle of wine.

'No, thank you, we have had our breakfast. We took the precaution of bringing food with us.'

He smiled. She was capable of thinking ahead, after all. 'A sensible precaution,' he said. 'And does your good sense extend to returning to England where you will certainly be able to eat more heartily than in this afflicted country?'

'Food is the least of my considerations, sir. I am concerned for my brother. I will not go home without him.' She paused, remembering Judith's admonishment not to have a verbal battle with him. 'I am sorry that we should be such a burden to you, Mr Chiltern, but I entreat you to allow us to accompany you to Paris. We should not be the least trouble, I promise you. And I have a little money…'

'Then hide it well,' he said, wondering if he did not like her better when she was being quarrelsome. 'And address me as Citizen Faucon, if you please.'

Kitty's eyes lit up. 'Then you will take us?'

'Damn you, woman, if you will not turn back, you give me no choice.'

'Sir, you will not swear at my darling,' Judith put in.

'I shall swear when I damn well please,' he snapped. 'And you and your mistress had better become used to it. It is not a picnic we are embarking upon.'

Kitty turned to Judith, who was about to answer back. 'Shush, Judith, remember what you said to me.'

Judith lapsed into silence, though the effort made her feel like bursting.

'You will do exactly as you are told, however uncomfortable and inconvenient, do you hear?' he went on. 'Your lives may depend upon it.'

'Of course.' Kitty thought he would make a great actor; his sense of high drama bordered on the ridiculous, but she managed to stop herself airing her opinion. Perhaps he *was* an actor; she had not thought of that, an actor who seemed not to be able to tell the difference between reality and the stage. And she and Judith were expected to play a part too. She was even more convinced of it when he turned and, picking up what looked like a bundle of rags, handed them to her. 'Put these on.'

'These rags?' Judith demanded, taking them from Kitty and shaking them out. 'Why, they are not fit for beggars.'

'And beggars cannot be choosers,' he said. 'Put them on.'

Kitty took the indignant Judith by the arm and led her upstairs again. 'It is naught but a masquerade, Judith, and we must indulge him,' she said, taking off her dress and donning the peasant costume of skirt, blouse and shawl. 'And, though they look dreadful, they are not verminous.'

'He means to humiliate us.'

'No,' she said. 'He is gruff and ill-tempered to be sure, but I do not think he would do that. I am sure it is necessary not to appear too refined.' She laughed suddenly. 'I promised you high old adventures, did I not?'

'So you did, but I doubt you ever dreamed we should go about looking like riff-raff.' She had been putting on her own costume as she spoke. 'Oh, if your poor mama could see us now.'

'If Mama had been alive, we should not be in this pinch, should we? Now, put on this cap. There is one for each of us.' She handed Judith the red Phrygian cap of the Revolution which seemed to be universal wear for both men and women in France at that time. Thus attired, they bundled up their own clothes and carried them to the lower room where Jack Chiltern was waiting for them.

Chapter Three

Jack walked round them, inspecting them carefully. 'Too clean,' he said and, reaching down to the cold hearth and rubbing his finger along the soot-laden bars, he spread a little on their faces and on the backs of their hands, ignoring Kitty's expression of distaste and Judith's protests. 'Now, let us be off. You may wear your cloaks in the carriage, but take them off and hide them under the seat if we are stopped.'

He shook hands with Pierre and, picking up a small leather valise from the floor and one of the ladies' bags into which they had crammed the clothes they had just removed, he strode from the room. Kitty followed him, head held high, while Judith picked up the basket and went after her mistress to the accompaniment of laughter from Pierre. 'Sooner you than me, my friend!' he shouted.

With the women behind him, Jack made for a battered old carriage which had certainly seen better days. It had once had a coat of arms on the door, but this had been obliterated with red paint. The paintwork on the rest of the vehicle, which had once been a glossy black, was faded and peeling. The upholstery had disappeared and all they had to sit on were slats of rough wood.

The roof had a hole in it and the windows had been replaced by only half-cured hide curtains. Kitty wasn't sure which would be worse, the smell of the skins or the cold she would have to endure if she insisted on having them removed. As for the single horse, it looked ready to drop from starvation. 'Is that the best you can manage?' she asked.

He laughed. 'Why, it is a magnificent carriage, my lady, none better in the whole country. It once belonged to a *comte*, but alas, he no longer has a need for it.' His laughter died. 'Now, get in, I have no time to waste.'

He handed them in, folded the step and shut the door, then climbed up on the seat. A moment later the poor old horse was urged into motion and the wheels began to roll.

'Merciful heaven, I shall eat this filthy cap if we arrive in Paris safely,' Judith said, as they jolted along at little more than walking pace.

'At least we have been spared Mr…Citizen Faucon's company, and we shall see something of the country-side.' She lifted the malodorous curtains so they could look out.

What they saw was devastation. The fields grew lank with weeds, the cattle looked half-starved, the buildings were crumbling and, what was worse for them, the roads were full of potholes so that they were continually being flung about. Judith rummaged in their baggage, which had been put on the opposite seat, and made cushions of some of their clothes.

'I shall be able to press them when we arrive at our lodgings in Paris,' she said, convinced that, once reu-

nited with Master James, their nightmare would end and
all would be well.

They travelled all day, stopping at wayside inns
where they were thankful to stretch their legs and have
something to eat and drink, though it was only thin
soup, coarse bread and, at the place where they stopped
for the night, one scrawny chicken between them. Only
the chink of coins prevented them from having to share
a bed with several other women.

Where Jack slept they had no idea, he did not say,
but Kitty guessed he would probably prefer to sleep
with the horse than share a room with half a dozen other
men.

Jack considered the risk of showing they had money
against their discomfort and decided that, until they
were close to Paris, he could take it, but he made it
known he despised the women for their fastidiousness.
'The bitches forget times have changed,' he grumbled
to the assembled company. 'But they will know it when
we get to Paris. I am escorting them to the Palais de
Justice.'

'Aristos?' someone queried.

'No, not so lofty, *citoyen*. But they have been hoarding flour. Can't have that, can we?'

'Where's the flour now?'

'Distributed to the needy in their village,' Jack said,
hoping no one would ask for more details.

His listeners lost interest. The women were not nobility and there was no food to be had from them. They
turned their backs and continued with the conversation
they had been having before the newcomers arrived.

Kitty and Judith, huddling together in a narrow bed,
trying to warm each other, had long since realised that

high old adventure was not what they had thought it would be. High old adventure was cold and hunger and fear, and not understanding the language, or the people, or their escort who treated them with contempt and called them bitches and refused to allow them to speak. He was a tyrant, every bit as bad as the mob who had chopped off the head of King Louis. Perhaps he was one of them.

But though Kitty told herself with increasing vehemence that she disliked him and wished heartily that they could be rid of him, she knew that they would be lost without him. Within the constrictions imposed by the situation he did try to ensure their comfort and, somehow or other, he found food for them. And, whenever the people they met became too curious, he protected them, shouldering the questioners away and ensuring they were not molested.

At dusk on the fourth evening when they could see the outlines on the city of Paris on the road ahead of them, Kitty's hopes began to rise. They immediately fell again when Jack turned off the road on to a rough track, rank with weeds and overshadowed by uncut hedges. It was so dark they had no idea where they were being taken. Terrified, they clung to each other as the carriage jolted over the ruts.

'Where is he taking us?' Judith asked. 'Does he mean to do away with us here and rob us of all our belongings? Oh, I wish we had never come. I had thought we should be in Paris tonight and instead he takes us heaven knows where.' She began to wail. 'Oh, what is to become of us? It is not the guillotine we should fear, but him. He has frightened us into believing he would help us, when all the time…'

'Oh, Judith, do be quiet,' Kitty said, wondering if her maid might be right after all. But what had the man to gain? They had nothing worth stealing and, whatever he was, she did not think he was a thief. There was more to it than that. Perhaps he was planning some devilment. Did he see her as a threat to those plans? But that was foolish; she had no reason to threaten him. And what could she do anyway?

She had put herself in his power, had begged him to help her, had willingly entered this ramshackle vehicle which was bad enough on what passed for good roads, but which now threatened to fall apart with every bump. She had truly been the architect of her own downfall but, what was worse, she had involved poor Judith.

She thought of trying to jump out and run, but Judith could not do that and Kitty would not leave her. Besides, however fast they ran, he would soon catch up with them. She sat back in her seat, trying to devise a scheme to outwit him, but none came to mind.

Fifteen minutes later, they stopped before the door of a small farmhouse, which appeared deserted. No light shone in the windows and no dogs barked. They heard their escort jump to the ground and then his footsteps as he came to the coach door and opened it. 'This is as far as we go tonight.'

'But this is not an inn,' Kitty protested, making no move to alight. 'Why did you bring us here?'

'We cannot travel after curfew, you must know that by now, and this is a safe house. No one comes here but those I know I can trust. You do understand me, I hope?'

Both women nodded.

'Good. Then get down, if you please, and follow me.'

There was nothing to do but obey.

He opened the farmhouse door and ushered them inside. A minute later he had struck a flint and lit an oil lamp which cast its soft glow over what must once have been a comfortable home. There were chairs and tables, even a bookcase and a glass-fronted cupboard containing crockery. A worn carpet covered the middle of the wooden floor and there were curtains at the window. Kindling and logs had been placed in the hearth ready to make a fire and he bent down and put a light to them.

'You will soon be warm.' He moved over to the window and closed the shutters, then returned and lit another lamp from the first. 'I'll show you to your rooms.' He paused on his way to the door to look at Kitty, who stood with her eyes wide and her mouth slightly open in surprise.

She presented a strange but delightful picture. The rags she wore did nothing to diminish her beauty, or the fine lines of her figure, nor did they make her into the coarse peasant she purported to be. She was simply a gentlewoman playing at dressing up and his heart missed a beat. How could he keep her safe? How could he protect her, except by degrading her, bringing her down to the level of those with whom he was obliged to associate?

He must harden his heart, keep his mission in the forefront of his mind, and he could only do that by constantly reminding himself of Gabrielle and the vow he had made to her father to find her and bring her back. Gabrielle…

He shook himself and led the way up the carpeted stairs to the next floor where he flung open one of the doors and ushered them into a bedroom. Putting the lamp on a table by the window, he pulled the curtains closed. 'You may dress in your own clothes tonight,' he said. 'We will dine in a civilised fashion.'

Just this once, he told himself, just this once, he would relax a little, enjoy her company, encourage her to talk, even argue a little; he guessed she had an alert and intelligent mind. Tomorrow…tomorrow was another day.

When Kitty returned downstairs, clad in a rather crumpled green silk gown decorated with rosebuds and with a fine lace shawl to keep her shoulders warm, she was taken aback to see a young woman coming from the room where Jack had lit the fire.

She was dressed in a plain wool gown of a light brown colour with a starched white collar. Her hair, pushed up under a lace cap, was fair and, though she was thin, she was by no means starved. What was so pleasing was that she was spotlessly clean; cleanliness seemed to have been generally abandoned since the Revolution.

She stopped when she saw Kitty and indicated the room she had just left. 'He waits for you,' she said, speaking slowly in French in order that Kitty might understand.

'*Merci.*'

Kitty entered the room and found Jack opening a bottle of wine. He was dressed in black breeches and white silk stockings with black clocks. His shirt ruffles were pristine and he was once again wearing the blue velvet waistcoat. A dark blue coat hung over the back of a chair.

The table in the middle of the room was covered with a white cloth on which were set cutlery and glasses and a covered tureen, which she did not doubt contained the ubiquitous potato soup which might, if they were lucky, contain a few pieces of stringy meat. She guessed it had been cooked by the young woman she had seen, which indicated he had been expected.

Who was she? A servant? But as far as Kitty could tell there were no servants in France any more which, if true, must mean that a great many otherwise deserving people must be out of work. How could the Revolutionary notion of *liberté*, *egalité*, *fraternité* justify that? She would ask him over dinner; it might make for a lively debate. But was the woman his sister or his wife?

The thought that he might be married unaccountably depressed her and she pushed it from her mind and turned her attention to her host, as he lifted the lid of the tureen and a delicious aroma of chicken and leeks assailed her nostrils. 'That smells good, Mr... *monsieur*...' She floundered.

He smiled. '*Monsieur* is as bad as Mister, my dear. If you cannot put your tongue round *citoyen*—and who can blame you?—then call me Jacques.'

'I cannot call you that, we are not so well acquainted.'

'Oh, come, Kitty, we are very well acquainted and will become even more so before long...'

She drew in her breath sharply. 'If you think what I think you do, then, sir, you will be sorely disappointed. Just because you had the audacity to take me by surprise and steal a kiss, does not mean I will allow you to...to...' She stopped, unable to put her fear into words.

'You will not allow!' He threw back his head and laughed because she had misunderstood him, but decided against telling her so. It was more entertaining to leave her thinking the worst. 'How, pray, would you prevent me? Scream for help? I assure you, no one will come.'

'There is Judith.'

'Ah, the inestimable Judith. I have no doubt she would be a formidable opponent.'

'Where is she? She was not in her room. I had thought to find her here.'

'What! And have her spoil our little tête-à-tête!' He paused to look at her. Her face was a picture of bewilderment and dismay, her expressive violet eyes open wide, her lovely lips slightly parted, unknowingly inviting more ungentlemanly behaviour, like that kiss. He could not forget it.

What he had intended as a lesson to her, to demonstrate the dreadful fate which could befall her if she continued with her escapade, had been a salutary lesson to him instead. He had meant to be harsh with her, to take some of his own frustration and anger out on her, but instead he had found himself enjoying the taste of her lips, the feel of her softly curved body against his, the warmth of her. She had managed to rouse feelings in him of tenderness and compassion and a desire which had nothing to do with lustful gratification, however hard he tried to convince himself of the contrary.

'Your maid is dining in the kitchen with Lucie,' he went on, because she seemed to be struck dumb. 'They will be company for each other even if they cannot converse.' He smiled, wishing she would relax. She stood there, facing him, every muscle tense, as if waiting for a blow to fall. 'Two silent women, a rare phenomenon, to be sure.'

'It is nothing to jest about. You arranged that so that you might be alone with me.'

'Naturally, I did. Her presence would certainly put a damper on proceedings.'

'What proceedings?'

Was she really as innocent as she seemed, or was it all a ploy to disarm him? 'That depends on you.'

'Sir, I asked you to escort me to Paris because you know my brother and could take me to him, and for no other reason. If you had any notion of anything else, I must disappoint you. If you cannot behave like a gentleman, I will retire to my room.'

'Without your dinner? Are you not hungry?'

'Not so hungry that I will stay and allow you to take liberties.'

He laughed. 'Do you have the least idea what that means?'

'I know I should dislike it intensely.'

'You would not, I guarantee it.' He did not know why he was taunting her so. Was he testing her, seeing how far he could go before she was reduced to tears? He hated seeing a woman in tears; it always made him angry. He could deal with her better if he was angry. Anger was better than compassion. Compassion made you weak. Surprisingly she did not falter, neither did she attempt to leave the room.

'You are insufferably arrogant and conceited,' she said.

'Audacious, arrogant, conceited,' he said softly, changing his tactics. 'Can you find no merit in me at all?'

Unable to lie, she said nothing; she would not let him turn the tables on her and put her in the wrong. She looked from him to the door, and from the door to the table and its steaming tureen. She was very hungry.

'So be it,' he said, cheerfully abandoning his teasing.

'Let us call a truce. It will not serve for us to be forever at odds, we still have some way to go. Now, sit down and eat, it might be the last nourishing meal you have for some time.'

Reluctantly Kitty sat down, knowing she could not fight him physically. Her only recourse was to appeal to his sense of chivalry. He must surely have one, or he would not have brought them thus far without harming them, or allowing them to be harmed by others. But he made a very strange knight.

'Now,' he said, filling a plate from the tureen and putting it in front of her, 'we will stop this cat-and-mouse game and talk sensibly.'

She began picking at her food, but hunger overcame good manners and she tucked into the delicious food with every appearance of enjoyment. But she was still wary. And curious.

'Who is she?' she asked, realising he was not eating himself but was watching her with a delighted smile on his face and eyes twinkling.

'Who?'

'Lucie. I thought at first she might be your wife, but then I thought no, because she would not leave us to dine alone. A servant, perhaps. Are you allowed servants in France these days? Your friend, Pierre, did not seem to think so. Perhaps she is a relative…' She prattled on, not giving him time to answer. 'She is very pretty.'

Not nearly as beautiful as you, my dear, he thought, watching the animated face of his guest and wishing there was some way he could stop time, freeze it so that she need never change, but stay always bright and cheerful, never to know cold and hunger and brutality.

'Yes, Lucie is pretty. And good, which is more important.'

'She is your lover, then?'

He laughed and poured wine in her glass. 'She was what English people might call a serf in the old days, tied to her *seigneur*, but since the Revolution she is free to work for whom she likes, which is good in theory but does not always work in practice.'

'Are you her *seigneur*?'

'No. She chooses to work for me. I pay her wages to keep this house clean and cook for me when I am here. Does that satisfy you?'

'She doesn't wear that hateful red cap.'

'If she went into Paris, she would. As you must.'

'Do you have a wife?'

'Yes.'

'Oh.' She digested this piece of information and wondered what difference it made. None, she told herself sternly, none at all. He was going to take her into Paris and reunite her with James and then she need see him no more. She gave him a brittle smile. 'Where is she? In England?'

Her face was so expressive, the violet eyes seemed to mirror her soul and he understood her thoughts almost as if she had spoken them aloud. It gave him a *frisson* of pleasure which vanished when he thought of Gabrielle, leaving him bitter and morose. 'She is in France.'

'In Paris?'

He shrugged. 'Who knows?'

'Oh, I am so sorry,' she said. 'I have been very selfish, haven't I, burdening you with my troubles and accusing you, when all you must be thinking of is going to your wife? I have delayed you and crossed you at every turn, it is no wonder you are so down in spirits.'

'I am not down in spirits, far from it,' he said, deciding not to correct her misconception. He had never found it easy to talk of Gabrielle and the last thing he wanted was Kitty's sympathy. 'I have no reason to believe she is not safe.' He raised his glass to her. 'We will talk of other things.'

'Very well. This food is delicious, which just goes to show that France is not in such bad straits as you would have us believe.'

'It does nothing of the sort, it shows only that money can still buy a few luxuries if you know where to find them.'

'How much money?' she asked, thinking of her dwindling resources.

'A great deal, I am afraid.'

'Oh. Then how does James go on?'

'He earns his bread and wine, just as we all do.'

'You, too?'

'Yes.'

'How?'

'Better you do not ask.'

'Could I?'

'Could you what?'

'Earn my bread and wine. Edward gave me as much as he could, but it will not last very long with the prices so high here. I must find a way of earning my keep.'

'What can you do?'

'I could teach English. Or sew.'

'Hardly skills in great demand in France at the moment,' he said, smiling at her. 'Have you ever done any play-acting?'

'Of course not. Uncle William would never have allowed it.'

'Not even charades?'

'We did sometimes play charades at Christmas when Mama and Papa were alive. My stepmama does not care for the pastime. Why do you ask?'

'Because, tomorrow, I want you to act my wife for all you are worth.

'Your wife! But how can I? You are already married.'

'Jack Chiltern is married, I give you. But I am not Jack Chiltern, I am Jacques Faucon and my papers state that I am married.'

'Oh, I see,' she said slowly. 'But surely, when you are stopped, you could simply say you had left your wife at home.'

'I could, but how would that help you, my dear? You want to get into Paris, don't you?'

'Yes, of course, but to be your wife…'

'In name only, of course. The last thing I want is an emotional entanglement, I promise you.'

'No more do I,' she retorted. 'Neither do I wish to become embroiled in anything illegal or disreputable. I know nothing about you. Who are you? What are you doing in France? Are you French? You certainly speak it very fluently.'

He smiled. 'You should have asked those questions long ago, before we ever left Calais. It is too late now, don't you think?'

'I thought I could trust you.'

'Trust is a two-way thing, my dear. It must work both ways or it does not work at all. So, think carefully. Do you still trust me?'

She looked at him with her head on one side and considered the question. He *had* been arrogant and conceited, he *had* taken advantage of her naivety to kiss her, he *had* taunted her, *had* been tyrannical and would no doubt be so again but, in spite of all that, she was grateful for his help. Without it, they would never have left Calais. 'I suppose I must.'

He laughed. 'Hardly wholehearted assurance, but no matter. We go on together, eh, *ma petite*?'

'I do not seem to have much choice.'

'Then listen carefully to what I tell you.'

She put her knife and fork down and listened as he outlined his plan, a plan which filled her with trepidation but also gave her a surge of excitement, as if new doors were being opened to her, doors to new experiences, new delights, perhaps new horrors, and it was up to her which she opened.

He emphasised that he would be on hand to support and protect her, but she must follow his lead and do exactly as he said. 'There must be no faltering,' he said. 'Nor must you behave haughtily, however provoked. You must remember you are not of genteel birth— nothing will inflame the Guard more than an aristo pretending to be a peasant. And Judith is your mother, not your servant, is that clear?'

'Yes, yes, but my French is not very good.'

'That could be a problem…we shall have to admit you are English. I married you on a visit to England several years ago. You never think of it now, but cleave to France and the new administration.'

'Do you? Cleave to the new regime, I mean.'

'Jacques Faucon certainly does. He is fanatical about it.'

'But Jack Chiltern?'

'Jack Chiltern does not exist. From now on, we will never mention that name.' He stood up and held his hand out to her. 'I suggest you retire for the night. We have to be away from here by first light. I am afraid you will have to leave your baggage behind, Lucie will take care of it for you until we all come back here, God willing.' He raised her hand to his lips. 'Goodnight and *au revoir*, Miss Harston. Tomorrow I shall greet citoyenne Faucon, *n'est-ce pas?*'

Kitty went up to her room in a daze, the feel of his lips still tingling on the back of her hand, his soft voice saying goodnight still echoing in her ears. How could he do this to her, make her feel as though she were melting away? She did not want to sleep, she wanted to savour it. But warmth, good food and wine, and the fatigue induced by five days of uncomfortable travelling overcame her and she slept soundly.

'What I want to know is what have we got ourselves into?' Judith demanded, the following morning. 'I never thought I should have to dress in rags and pretend to be your mother while you passed yourself off as that…that charlatan's wife. How could you agree? How could you think I would agree?'

'If you don't want to come, you could stay here with Lucie…'

'No, I could not!' Judith rounded on her. 'If you think I would be so unmindful of my duty, you are mistaken. I came on this jaunt to look after you, and look after you I will.'

She had been dressing in her ragged costume while she spoke, but she was doing it slowly, lacking enthusiasm for the adventure, unlike Kitty. She set the red cap on her grey curls and, looking in the mirror over Kitty's shoulder, grimaced with distaste. 'We know nothing of him. We have no idea what manner of man he is…'

Kitty looked up and faced the worried reflection in the glass. 'Then how do you know he is a charlatan?'

'He dined with you alone. If Lucie had not insisted you were perfectly safe and looked as though she might hit me over the head with a skillet if I insisted, I should have burst in to rescue you. I wish I had now. Your good reputation will be in shreds.'

Kitty laughed. 'Oh, Judith, I no longer have a good reputation, surely you must know that?'

'But to act his wife? What will you do when…' she gulped '…when the time comes to retire? You cannot possibly share a room with him.'

'Long before then we shall be with James. He will take care of us. It is only so that we may pass safely through the barriers.'

Kitty, who had finished dressing, was surveying the results in the mirror. It was not realistic enough. She lacked the haggard look of most of the women she had come across; her eyes were still bright with untroubled youth, and her hair shone with Judith's brushing. She picked up a pair of scissors from the dressing table and hacked at her long tresses.

Judith was horrified. 'Kitty! What are you doing?'

'Cutting my hair. Have you not noticed that nearly all the women here have short hair? I suppose it is easier to keep free from vermin.'

'Ugh! But I suppose you are right. Here, give me the scissors.'

Kitty handed them over and sat patiently while her long hair was cut short and watched in surprise as it sprang into tight little curls. 'Why, I do believe I like it,' she said, setting the red cap on top. 'Now for the eyes.'

A finger run along the chimney produced enough blacking to smudge her eyes with fatigue, and with the addition of a line or two across her brow, served to make her look older and more careworn. She stood up and slouched slowly across the room, her shoulders drooping. 'How's that?'

'It will serve, though I cannot say I approve.'

'You must do the same.'

Judith was too plump to look haggard, so Kitty contented herself with pulling her hair out of its neat coil and making it stand out round the cap, then blacking one or two of her teeth, which produced loud protests from her maid. 'You are making me look an old hag.'

'Exactly. We cannot afford pride, Judith, which is why I agreed to Mr Chil—' She stopped and corrected herself. 'Jacques' plan. Come on, he will be waiting.'

Outside the front door, they found the old horse harnessed to a farmcart loaded with cabbages, most of which were rotten and gave off a very unpleasant smell. Jacques, once more in ragged trousers and a well-worn greatcoat, thick with grease, was busy burrowing in the produce, hiding his leather bag.

When it was done, he stood and looked at them, surveying them from head to toe, then laughed. 'Very good, my dears, though I fancy you are too well shod. But no matter, a farmer can buy his wife a new pair of boots now and again. Rub them in the mud to make them look more worn and get on the seat. The sun will be up soon and we must join the line at the barrier.'

Lucie came from the house, carrying two small blankets which she handed to Judith. 'To keep out the cold,' she said. *'Au revoir, madame, ma'amselle.'* She turned to Jack. '*Bon chance, monsieur.*' Her grey eyes spoke more than her words; there was in them a look of un-alloyed adoration.

He pulled her to him and kissed her on each cheek. 'Go home to your *maman* until I send you word I need you, *ma chérie.*'

He jumped up beside Kitty and the cart rumbled off along the lane they had traversed the night before. Rain mixed with sleet whipped against their faces and, in spite of Lucie's blankets and the fact that both wore two or three petticoats beneath their rags, their fingers and toes were soon frozen, but they knew it would be useless to protest, nothing could be done about it.

Jack himself seemed impervious to the weather; he was becoming more and more morose, hunching his chin into his coat collar. He appeared to shrink, to grow older and craggier before their eyes, until he hardly seemed the same upright, muscular man who had brought them from Calais. He did not speak. His un-gloved hands, raw with cold, maintained their steady grip on the reins as the old horse plodded on with its burden.

A few minutes later they pulled out on the main road and jolted towards the distant huddle of buildings and spires which Kitty assumed was Paris. Gradually the roads became busier as other carts joined in a procession. There were walkers, too, women and children, carrying produce in baskets. They were poorly clad and looked down at the ground as they walked, as if they had nothing to look forward to. Was this what the great Revolution had done to the people of France? They were the ones who had jumped from the frying pan into the fire.

The line of carts came to a halt as the woods and

fields gave way to a few sparse buildings. 'The *barrière* of Saint-Denis,' Jack murmured, as they stopped. 'Now is the testing time.'

It took half an hour to reach the front of the queue; by then, Kitty was taut with nerves, as she watched some people being let through and others, whose papers, or perhaps only their looks, had been unsatisfactory and they were dragged off to be interrogated.

'Papers, citizen,' one of the guards demanded, holding a grubby hand up to Jack, who silently groped in his pocket and handed over the forged documents. While the guard perused them, his companion walked all round the cart, then stopped to stare up at Kitty.

Kitty looked dully back at him, trying not to let him see she was trembling. She pulled the blanket closer round her and stole a sideways glance at Jack. He seemed totally relaxed although the guard was taking an inordinate time to examine their papers.

'What have you got in the cart?' said the one who was staring at Kitty.

'Potatoes and cabbages,' Jack answered for her.

'Anything else?'

'No.'

The guard moved to the rear of the cart and began throwing the produce out. Kitty was afraid he would soon discover the case. Something must be done or they were lost. She pushed Jack's shoulder and began shouting at him in lamentable French, calling him a pig and a dog and beating her fists against his body, grunting with the effort.

For a second he did nothing, then he turned and cuffed her back, shouting even louder to drown her voice. It brought the guard back to their side.

'The citizeness is a handful, old fellow. Can't you shut her up?'

'Would that I could,' he said, trying to grapple with Kitty's flailing arms. 'Why, this is nothing to what she gives me at home. Grumble, grumble, all day long; I have not done this, I have neglected to do that. I don't know why I didn't leave her behind.'

The first guard had stopped looking at their papers and was standing watching them with a broad grin on his face as Kitty rained blows on Jack. He retaliated by slapping her face, an action which was as sudden as it was unexpected and silenced her.

'What is she complaining of?' the guard asked, while Kitty put her hand up to her cheek and pushed Judith away when she attempted to comfort her.

'Say nothing,' she hissed.

'She complains of the cold, as if I could do anything about the weather.'

The man looked at Judith. 'That one is quiet.'

Jack laughed. 'Being well-padded she does not feel the cold. And she knows better than to hold up the National Guard when they are only doing their duty.'

'Are you going to stand there talking all day?' someone shouted from the cart behind them. 'We've got work to do, even if you haven't.'

'On you go,' the guard said, returning their papers. 'And if you take my advice, citizen, you'll leave the shrew behind tomorrow.'

'I might do that,' Jack called, as the barrier was lifted and they rumbled slowly into the city down the rue Saint-Denis, once a wide street of fine houses, but now looking decidedly dilapidated.

It was several minutes before anyone spoke and then

it was Jack. 'What was all that about?' he demanded of Kitty.

'Charades, you said, act the part.'

'I didn't tell you to bring the whole National Guard down on our heads.'

She grinned. 'No, but I stopped them finding your case, didn't I?'

'What makes you think that it was important enough to take such a terrible risk?'

'You hid it, didn't you? And though it is a matter of indifference to me whether you are arrested or not, I did not want it discovered before we found James.'

He threw back his head and bellowed with laughter. 'Oh, my, you'll be the death of me,' he said, wiping his eyes.

'You ungrateful boor,' she protested. 'You pummel me black and blue and slap my face and then have the gall to laugh. That is the last time I shall try and help you.'

'Good,' he said. 'Your help could have us all guillotined. From now on, remain silent and do nothing.'

She was still smarting, both literally and figuratively, and she would not give him the satisfaction of cowing her. 'And if I don't agree?'

'Then you will be left to your own devices and sooner or later someone will start asking questions; if your answers are not entirely satisfactory, you will be arrested.'

'What would I be accused of?'

'Anything, it does not matter. It would soon be turned to an indictment as a traitor to the Republic.'

'How can I be a traitor to France when I am English?'

'A spy, then.'

'What about you?'

'Me?' He turned to look at her. Beneath the surface dirt her cheeks were pink and he regretted that slap with all his heart, but she had started the scuffle and he had been forced to make it realistic. And he had to make sure she did not repeat the experiment. 'I should deny all knowledge of you.'

'I don't believe you. The devil himself would not stoop to such an act of cowardice. You are bluffing.'

'You think so? I advise you not to call my bluff, my dear, or you might have a rude awakening.'

'Oh, Kitty,' Judith wailed. 'I never thought our position could be worse, but it is getting more dire with every minute. What are we to do?'

'Shut up, woman,' Jack said brusquely.

'Yes, Judith, do be quiet, please. We are in Mr Chiltern's hands and must trust him whether we like to or not.'

'I am not Mr Chiltern, I am Jacques Faucon, your husband. citizen of France. Please remember that.'

'All the same, you might at least acknowledge that I tried.'

'You tried,' he said laconically, staring straight ahead so that he did not have to look at her. She could melt the hardest heart and, though he pretended, he was not hard enough. She had been magnificent, beating him and screaming like any fishwife; if there really had been something of importance in that case, she would have saved the day. 'Do you think I am fool enough to conceal anything incriminating in a pile of cabbages? The case contains nothing but a bottle of brandy.'

'Is that all?'

'That is all.'

'But why hide it?'

'Something hidden is something someone wishes not

to be found. The men would have triumphed in uncovering it. A smuggled bottle of cognac confiscated is a small price to pay for being allowed to pass.'

'It was meant to be found?'

'Yes. Now we will speak of it no more.'

She obeyed, falling silent. In truth, she was already regretting her impulse to show off her acting abilities; it could easily have resulted in tragedy, if he had not been quick thinking enough to answer her blow for blow. She had deserved to have her face slapped.

The streets were busy in spite of the cold and wet. But nearly everyone was dressed poorly and wore the red cap of the Revolution. Many of the men wore black-and-grey striped trousers and coats, while the women were clad in kirtles and wool-shag blouses, with the tricolour scarf knotted round their waists. Some had blankets thrown about their shoulders. All were bare-legged and wore heavy wooden *sabots* on their feet.

'Why are there no gentlefolk?' she asked.

'Oh, there are. What you see is the fashion. Even the wealthy wear it to show they are one with the people.'

'But do they have to appear so dirty?'

'Soap is dear,' he said.

The wide road became narrower and dirtier as they made their way into the heart of the city, towards the river, but before they reached it, they turned off into an alley. It was dark and dismal, its overcrowded tenements leaning against each other, its cobbles wet and greasy, running with rotten vegetation and excrement. Judith flung her apron over her mouth and nose and Kitty did her best to quell the feeling of nausea which rose in her throat.

'Where in God's name are you taking us?'

'Be quiet.' This was a dangerous part of town and he was tense and on edge.

A few minutes later, having passed through with no more than an odd stare of curiosity, they came to the rue Saint-Antoine. 'This is where it all began,' he whispered. 'Up there is the Bastille, taken by the mob in its search for weapons and powder.'

'Surely you are not taking us there?'

'No, but this is the district of the artisan. It is here that some of the grand furniture English homes set so much store by used to be made. The demand has fallen off of late.'

'In these hovels?'

'Yes.' He pulled up outside one of them and jumped down, turning to help them alight. 'You will be safe here.'

He threw a small coin to a ragged urchin to keep an eye on the horse and cart and conducted them into a dingy hallway. An open door to their right revealed a workshop, full of lengths of wood and half-finished chair legs. The floor and benches were covered in sawdust. Two people were at work, but they hardly spared the newcomers a glance as they passed and made their way up to the next floor. Jack knocked on the first of a series of doors.

It was opened by a man of about Jack's age, wearing the universal trousers and rough wool shirt, over which was tied a large leather apron dusted with sawdust. He was a big man with tousled hair and shaggy eyebrows, also covered with sawdust. 'Jacques!' He held out his hand and Jack shook it. 'You are a day late.'

'Yes, Jean, my friend, I know, but it could not be helped. I am not alone.' He turned and beckoned the two women to come forward. 'This is Kitty and this is Judith. We need your help. May we come in?'

'Yes, of course.' The man seemed a little reluctant to Kitty, but she could hardly blame him; she was coming to understand the fear that everyone seemed to have, the need to be vigilant, to view every newcomer with suspicion until they had proved themselves. Without Jack they would not even have passed the barrier, let alone found anyone to help them.

'Kitty, this is citizen Jean Clavier and this…' He turned to a woman who had risen from a chair before the fire. She was warmly clad in a wool gown with a shawl collar and long sleeves. She wore no cap and her short curls were a rich, bright auburn. 'This is Thérèse, his wife. They are good friends of mine.'

Kitty and Judith both bent their knees and inclined their heads in greeting.

'Lord, don't do that!' Jack said. 'No one does that in France now, you will give yourselves away.' He turned to Jean. 'You see the problem I have?'

'Why are they here?' Jean growled, not liking what he saw. 'You're not smuggling aristos, are you?'

Jack laughed. 'Not out of Paris, my friend, they wanted to come in.'

'Then more fools they. And fool you are to help them. They will hinder you.'

'I know, but they have been able to be of some service to me. You see before you citizen Jacques Faucon, his wife Kitty, a shrew if ever there was one, and her mother Judith, who remains silent and eats us out of house and home, which is why she has more meat on her than either of us.'

It was as well this speech was made in French and Judith could not understand a word, except her own name. She smiled at Jean and Thérèse, while Kitty endeavoured to smother a giggle.

'You had better tell me all, *mon ami*,' Jean said, drawing Jack into an adjoining room. 'There have been developments while you have been away.'

What the two men said to each other, Kitty never knew, but it resulted in a grudgingly given agreement that she and Judith could stay there while Jack went out to try and locate James and conduct some business of his own. 'I have to go to the market and sell my produce,' he said. 'It is important to keep up appearances, and the market is a good place to hear the latest news.'

Kitty bade him *au revoir* with a grateful heart; rough-hewn he might be, bad-tempered at times and not apt to spare her maidenly blushes, nor her pride, but he was strong and fearless and, for some reason she could not fathom, his deeds belied his words when it came to caring what became of her. She really did trust him, which was why she was dismayed when he had not returned by nightfall.

Jack's non-appearance seemed to bother Jean Clavier too, for, after a frugal meal of salted herring which they all shared, he paced restlessly about the room, while his wife sat knitting by the fire, her needles clicking in the silence. A log dropped in the hearth, sending forth a shower of sparks, making Kitty jump. Jean pushed the log back with his clogged foot and stamped on the hearthrug which bore testimony to a great many sparks from previous fires; it was pitted with little black holes.

'Well, he'll not come tonight,' he said, as the tocsin sounded over the city. 'He'll not risk being out after curfew.'

His wife put down her knitting on the table at her

side and stood up. 'Come with me, *citoyennes*.' She lit
a candle with a spill from the fire, set it in a holder and
led the way out of the room and up a narrow staircase
to a room in the attic. 'You may sleep here tonight.'
She set the candle down on a chest. 'Snuff this out as
soon as you can, candles cost a fortune and we cannot
afford to waste them. Goodnight, *citoyennes*.' With that
she left, shutting the door behind her.

'She's not exactly welcoming, is she?' Judith said,
surveying the narrow bed, tucked under the sloping roof
and wondering about bugs.

'I expect she is afraid. She sees us as dangerous and
she expected Jack to come back for us long ago.'

'Where is he, do you think?' Judith asked, as the
hours ticked by and neither could sleep.

Kitty sighed. 'I wish I knew, Judith, I wish I knew.'

Chapter Four

Jack was sitting in the back room of a café in the Palais Royal, gambling with as evil-looking a bunch of cut-throats as anyone would wish to meet. They had all been drinking heavily on thin red wine, laced with cognac from the bottle Jack had brought with him. Kitty had saved it from the guard at the *barrière* and he was putting it to good use.

The Palais Royal belonged to the duc d'Orléans, who had converted the ground floor into a colonnade of shops, clubs and cafés. Even though it was near the noisy market of Les Halles, the once-quiet precincts had become popular with idle Parisians for gambling.

The upper classes dared no longer show their faces, but gambling still went on there, and that led to other things: plots, counter-plots, rumours of plots. Here agitators and journalists congregated, talking sedition, writing posters, printing pamphlets and exchanging gossip. It was said that the Revolution had started here in 1789.

Over three years had passed since then and though the Legislative Assembly had tried to govern the country on behalf of the people, nothing much had changed;

prices of bread, soap and candles were still exorbitant and taxes as crippling as they had been before. Now the government called itself the National Convention, but stability was as far away as ever and everyone was angry and afraid.

What could a government prepared to execute a king be capable of doing? Mere nobles had no chance at all unless, like the duc d'Orléans, they embraced the new regime. They were arraigned, found guilty and executed, all in the space of a day or two, but still more were crammed into the prisons. Jack, who could find no sign of young Harston, was beginning to wonder if he were one of their number.

He was acutely aware that Kitty and Judith were waiting for him, but what he would do if he did not find James he had no idea. Take them back to Lucie and hope they would be safe? He certainly could not go back to England with his mission unaccomplished. Drat the women!

He had spent some time in the market, selling cabbages and asking questions, but had learned nothing except that France had, while they had been on the road from Calais, declared war on Britain and Englishmen were certainly not safe in Paris. James, who loved to play dangerous games, would not have let that stop him. He had told Jack he meant to infiltrate the meetings of the *Enragés*, an extreme revolutionary party, and find out what they were up to.

'Our Government will pay handsomely for such information,' he had said. 'I will prove I can be of use to them and that will persuade them to give me other assignments. If you go to Horse Guards when you arrive in London, tell them that.'

Jack, who had been given instructions by the War

Department to stop James from acting the fool and pack him off home, had been sitting at the gaming table most of the night, steadily losing money, hoping to hear news of the young man. The men he played with were *Enragés*, but obtaining information from them was hard work and time consuming, especially as he could not ask them outright.

'Sugar and soap doubled in price,' one of them said, in an interval in the play. 'Coffee up to forty *sous* a pound, candles twenty. The people will not stand for it. It is all a plot to bring us to our knees and restore the aristos.'

'What are you going to do about it, then?' Jack growled, shuffling the cards before dealing.

'Put the food stores in the hands of the people, control the prices, punish hoarders and speculators.'

'Very commendable,' Jack commented drily, dealing expertly. 'But how will you keep law and order? More trials, more people imprisoned? Aren't the prisons overflowing already?'

'Who needs prisons when we have Madame Guillotine?' another said, running a thin finger across his throat.

'And you think that will satisfy the people?'

'No, how can it?' the first man said. 'The lust for blood is insatiable. There are traitors behind every door and even those who are hailed as patriots today will be traitors tomorrow, you mark my words.'

His words were chilling, but Jack recognised the truth of what he was saying. 'But what of the war? How can we hope to defeat *les Anglais* if we are continually watching our backs?'

'*Les Anglais* will defeat themselves. The Revolution

will spread to England and King George will soon know what it is like to bow to the will of the people.'

Jack had to tread carefully now. 'How do you know this?'

'From an Englishman.' He paused to lay a card, while Jack held his breath. 'Young puppy full of fire, hates all aristos, even English ones. He told us all it needs is the spark to ignite it.'

'Where is he now?'

The man shrugged 'Who knows? Gone to light the spark, perhaps. I haven't seen him this last week. We have enough to do looking after our own. Until we are rid of all the aristos, we shall not rest. The Austrian whore must follow her husband to eternity, along with the bastards she has spawned.'

'When will that be, do you suppose?'

'Soon.' He looked closely at Jack. 'What interest do you have in the widow Capet?'

'None at all.' He paused, knowing it was risky to go on, but remembering his promise to his father-in-law, he decided to risk it. 'My interest is in the *ci-devant* comte de Malincourt,' he went on, fingering the handle of a wicked-looking knife he had stuck in his belt. 'I have a score to settle with him.'

'Him!' Another of the four broke in, contempt in his voice. 'He fled with his family to England, in 'eighty-nine, cowards and traitors all of them. I spit on them.' And he spat on the floor at his side before taking another mouthful of wine from the glass at his elbow.

'His daughter married an Englishman, so I heard,' the fourth man put in, then laughed. 'Cuckolded him with a citizen from the French Embassy in London, who brought her back to Paris.'

'That so?' Jack asked lazily. 'Where are they now?'

'Why do you want to know?'

'If the father has escaped, then the daughter will do.'

'I hate to disappoint you, *mon vieux*, but Madame Guillotine got there before you.'

'She's dead?' For a split second he let his shock and horror show, but quickly took control of himself. '*Mon Dieu*, and I had been looking forward to doing the job myself. How did it happen?'

'The diplomat had ambition, he wanted to join the élite of the Jacobin Club. The price was the lady's head. He paid it gladly.' He looked down at the card Jack had just discarded. 'Fool! Why throw away your best trump? Anyone would think you felt sorry for the bitch.'

Jack pulled himself together to answer him. 'No, it's one less Malincourt in the world.' But he felt sick. Gabrielle, the beautiful, the enticing, the siren, his faithless wife, was dead. She had been taken from prison in a tumbril to the Place de la Révolution where, surrounded by a howling mob, her lovely head had been severed from her body. No woman deserved that fate, whatever she had done.

The game ended and the winner scooped up the pot, just as the tocsin sounded the lifting of the curfew. Jack pushed back his chair and stood up. 'I must go to my work.'

'What work is that, citizen?'

'Clerk to citizen Blanchard, the brewer.'

They laughed. 'A good job, citizen. You should hang on to it. Bring a few extra bottles with you tonight.'

He said he would, though he doubted he would see them again. He had to find James Harston and the sooner the better. Life for an Englishman—or an Englishwoman—in France was set to become very uncomfortable; the sooner James took his sister home to England, the better. He told himself that he would be well rid of the pair of them.

By the morning of the third day Kitty was beginning to despair and Madame Clavier was growing more and more tetchy. On one occasion Kitty heard her telling her husband they should turn the Englishwomen out before they themselves were denounced for harbouring them. To give him his due, Jean had turned on her angrily, saying Jack was his friend, a brave and honourable man who had important work to do, and he would not turn his back on him. But even he had sounded worried.

'I think we are a burden to them,' Kitty said, when Judith remarked once again that *madame* was lacking in hospitality. 'It is clear they are very poor.'

They were dressing in their garret room, which was so cold the inside of the windows was patterned with frost and there was a layer of ice on the jug of water which stood on the table beneath it. 'Offer them money, then, for I am heartily sick of fish and vegetable soup.'

'If Mr Chiltern is not back by mid-day today, I shall assume he is not coming and we will leave.'

'You think he has abandoned us?'

'*Madame* thinks so and he did threaten it.'

Judith stared at her. 'But do *you* think it?'

Kitty sighed. She had done nothing but find fault with the man ever since she had met him, but until he had left them, she had not appreciated how much he had done for them, much of it to his own inconvenience. Now, she wished she had showed herself more grateful. Without him to make decisions, to tell her what to do, she felt lost.

And deep down inside her, so deep she refused to acknowledge it, was the memory of that kiss. Had she really reacted so warmly? What must he have thought of her? No wonder he treated her with so much contempt; she deserved it. But she wanted him back. She wanted him back for all sorts of reasons she dare not analyse.

'I don't know what to think, but I cannot just sit here and do nothing,' she said. 'Perhaps he has been taken into custody for having forged papers, perhaps he has been waylaid by cut-throats and thrown in the river, perhaps something terrible has happened to James and…'

'And perhaps you have a lively imagination, miss.'

'What would you have us do?'

'Me? Why ask me?' the maid said huffily. 'You did not ask my opinion before you left home, or I might have given it. You chose to trust a complete stranger, who is most decidedly not a gentleman, so what can I say? You must do as you please.'

'Oh, Judith, please don't let us quarrel, we have troubles enough without that.'

Judith softened. 'I am sorry, my love. It is all this waiting about and idleness. I never could abide being idle. But if we leave, where could we go?'

'To the British Embassy. They must know the whereabouts of all English people in Paris.'

They sat in their room in the cold rather than get under Madame Clavier's feet, but they went down in the middle of the day and were given a bowl of soup made of fish bones and onions, which was so thin it had little nourishment.

Afterwards they offered Jean money and told him

they were leaving. He protested they should wait a little longer for Jack, but his wife contradicted him.

'He must have been discovered,' she said. 'He's in prison or dead. And we shall be next if we give shelter to France's enemies. Let them go.'

It looked as if there might be a serious falling out between husband and wife which Kitty solved by putting a gold sovereign on the table and leaving, followed by Judith. Once outside, Kitty hesitated, wondering which way to go, then decided to walk towards the centre of the city, where they would be able to ask directions.

The noisome alleys were busy and they walked close together to avoid being separated. Bands of women were flocking along the streets, shrieking obscenities and carrying bags of flour and sugar. Some were armed with pikes and knives; a few had muskets. Nervously Kitty and Judith pressed themselves against the wall to allow them to pass.

'I never saw such a bloodthirsty lot,' Judith said after the women had passed on. 'Where are they going with all that stuff? Do you suppose they've looted it?'

'Perhaps, but it need not concern us,' Kitty said, anxious to be away from what was obviously a very unsavoury area and to find somewhere more wholesome. 'Let's hurry.'

But there was no escaping the rioting women. They were everywhere, dashing into shops and coming out loaded with food, shouting, *'Vive la République!'* as if that justified what they were doing. Kitty and Judith, trying to make a way through the crowds, found themselves carried along with the tide.

'Please let me pass,' Kitty said, pushing against the shoulders of one woman who barred her way.

The woman's answer was to knock her to the ground, so that she was almost trampled underfoot.

'Have a care!' Judith shouted, wading in to push aside the women who surrounded her mistress. 'Let my lady up. You will trample her to death.'

'What do you say?' another shrieked, stopping in her tracks. 'What language is that?'

Judith did not understand, so she ignored the harridan and bent over Kitty to help her to her feet, revealing the hem of a warm flannel petticoat beneath her peasant kirtle.

'*Mon Dieu*, what have we here?' the woman cried, lifting Judith's skirt and flinging it over her head. 'Look at this! Petticoats and drawers!' And with that she kicked Judith's backside, toppling her face down into the mud, amid raucous laughter.

'And this!' another said, pulling Kitty to her feet and subjecting her to the same treatment. 'Two petticoats, one flannel and one fine cotton trimmed with lace. And look here, a corset! *Citoyennes*, I do believe we have found ourselves a couple of aristos.'

All this was spoken idiomatically and very quickly, so that Kitty's French was unequal to the task of translation, but she did recognise the word 'aristos'.

'No,' she said in halting French. 'We are not aristocrats, but ordinary British citizens.'

'*Anglais!*' One of the women spat at them. 'Enemies of the Republic. Enemies of France. *À la lanterne!*'

The women seemed to have forgotten their original purpose and abandoned the flour and sugar. They grabbed Kitty and Judith and forced them to march with them, shouting, '*À la lanterne!*'

Kitty struggled in vain and Judith's invective against the heathen scum, as she called them, along with other names Kitty was shocked to hear, only served to inflame the mob even more and Kitty was obliged to tell her to be quiet.

At regular intervals all along the banks of the Seine, facing the Palais de Justice, there were posts erected to hold street lamps, but it was clear they were used as instruments of execution, for many of them held dangling corpses. Kitty was sickened by them and terrified when she realised that the women meant to add her and Judith to their number.

'No! No!' she screamed, trying vainly to break free. 'We have done no wrong.'

Somehow Judith threw off her captors and hurled herself at those who held Kitty. 'You let her go! Let my darling go, you imbeciles!' The last word was easily translated which increased the women's fury; several of them flung themselves at Judith, holding her while others found a rope. In front of Kitty's horrified eyes, they fashioned a noose and put it over Judith's head, then flung the rope over the projecting arm of the lamp post and hauled the struggling woman to the top, screaming with triumphant laughter. *'Voyons l'aristos! Crache donc sur l'aristo.'* And, suiting action to words, they spat on the hem of Judith's skirt as it passed them at face level.

'Oh, God have mercy!' Kitty cried, as others grabbed her and marched her, stumbling, to the next lamp, leaving Judith's still-twitching body swinging in the breeze.

'No! No! No!' Kitty screamed as they slipped a second rope over her head.

'Wait, *citoyennes*,' one of them said. 'Let us not spoil those beautiful petticoats.'

In seconds Kitty's clothes had been stripped from her, leaving her in nothing but a shift. She felt the rope tighten about her neck as they began to haul on it. The breath was forced from her body and blessed darkness closed in on her.

The women who crowded the streets impeded Jack's progress. He encountered them everywhere he went: the Palais Royal, the Palais de Justice, the Tuileries, scene of so much destruction and bloodshed when the King was arrested, along the rue Saint-Antoine to the Arsenal and in every connecting road. It was clear that this was what his fellow card-players had predicted, probably incited.

It would be foolhardy to continue his search for James; it was more important to return to Kitty and Judith and ensure their safety. He was thankful that at the moment the rioting women were only interested in food shops, but it would not be long before they began systematically raiding other premises and the woodworkers might easily be next. If the ladies were found on Pierre's property, then his life would also be forfeit.

But when he arrived, he was shocked to learn the English women had left. Pierre told him he had tried to detain them, but they insisted.

'Where have they gone?'

Pierre shrugged. 'I heard the young one say something about the British Embassy.'

'Didn't you tell them we are at war? That makes them enemy aliens. You should have made them stay.'

'And lost our own heads for our pains?' Madame Clavier put in. 'No, citizen, and though we do not condone the killing of a king, it is done now, and we are loyal citizens of France.'

'Yes, I beg your pardon,' he said, realising his anger was unjustified. They had helped him only so long as they thought his first consideration was for France and the French people, but now France and Britain were at war, he could no longer rely on their support. He did not blame them, but it did mean the sooner Kitty and Judith left Paris, the better.

'Jean, I will go now, but make sure you have no evidence for anyone to find. You understand me?'

'Yes, rest easy, there is nothing to find except this.' He held out the sovereign. 'The young one left it as payment for their board. Gold it may be, but I dare not spend it. Take it, I do not want it.'

Jack delved in his overcoat pocket and extracted a small leather bag. From this he selected two *louis d'or* which he dropped into Jean's palm. 'Two for one, is that fair?'

'Thank you.' He took Jack's hand and held it in a firm grip. *'Bon chance, mon ami.'*

Jack clattered down the stairs and out into the street. Resisting the temptation to run, he strode purposefully down the street, passing knots of women on the way. *'Vive la République!'* they shouted at him.

Laughing, he answered them and passed on his way unmolested, but his thoughts were not on the women, but on Kitty. What had become of her? If she found the British Embassy closed because of the declaration of war, what would she do? Look for her brother? But James was not to be found and Jack feared he might have been arrested. The same fate might well fall to Kitty and her maid.

There were a dozen overcrowded and ill-documented prisons in Paris and anyone could easily be locked up and never heard of again. Or guillotined. The shock and revulsion he had felt on learning of Gabrielle's fate rolled over him once again and he realised he was not as hard-hearted as he liked people to believe, and if, through his negligence and uncaring attitude, Kitty also died, then he would be twice damned.

He had taught himself to smother his emotions, believing them to be a sign of weakness, especially since Gabrielle had taken all the love he had lavished on her and thrown it in his face. He had sworn never to allow another human being to rule his heart, but now he was forced to admit he did have a heart and one that could feel pain and tenderness. And, if that were so, what else could it feel?

He began to run, pounding the slippery street, unmindful of the strident yelling of a band of women, who congregated along the Quai de la Mégisserie opposite the Palais de Justice. He had almost passed them when a glimpse of white lace carried on the top of a pike caught his eye. White lace was not the usual material used for their banners and he paused to look. It was then he heard a voice screaming in English. 'No! No! No!'

He turned and dashed into their midst, just in time to see Kitty, almost naked, hoisted to the top of the lamp post. For one terrible second he stood still, staring up at her, feeling sick and hating himself for bringing her to this. Then the need for action forced him to his senses and pushed his way forward, grabbing the rope from the women who had not yet tied it off. 'What are you doing, citoyennes?' he demanded. 'What has this woman done?'

'She is an enemy of the Republic. *Une Anglaise* and an aristo.'

He knew he could not fight them off and must persuade them to let him have her body. And quickly. Already Kitty's face was blue and though he tried to let her down, the women were pulling against him. 'No, she is a poor misguided simpleton, whom I have the misfortune to have married.'

'Are you rich enough to clothe her in lace?'

'No, as you see, I am a humble farm labourer.'

'Then where did she get this?' One of the women waved a petticoat under his nose.

In the last two or three years he had learned to think fast and if there was any hesitation in his answer it did not show. 'She stole that from the home of our former *seigneur* after he and his wife were arrested. Don't all women like pretty things? They took her eye and what must she do but put them on.

'I told her it would lead to her downfall. I warned her but...' He paused and shrugged, not wanting to appear in a rush, though every second was critical. 'Please, *citoyennes*, you have done what you had to do, let me have her body for burial. Fool that she was, she was my wife and I cannot bear to see her left there to be pecked by hungry birds.'

They looked from one to the other. 'Oh, you might as well have her,' their leader said, suddenly letting go of the rope so that Jack found himself almost bowled over as Kitty dropped into his arms. 'We are more interested in food. Come, *citoyennes*, to the warehouses next.'

Jack put Kitty on the ground and knelt beside her to take the rope from her neck. The knot was tight and it was some seconds, which felt like hours, before she was free of it. He breathed a sigh of relief when he saw a light pulse fluttering in her throat. He grabbed her scattered clothes and scooped her up in his arms before looking about for Judith. 'Where is her mother?'

One of the women who remained pointed along the

street and for the first time he saw the dangling body.
He would have to come and fetch it later for burial, but
now he had to get Kitty to a safe place where she could
be revived. He started to walk away, not hurrying, not
daring to, but as soon as he had turned the corner, he
began to run.

'Don't die on me,' he murmured, as he ran. 'Please
don't die. Oh, why did I ever bring you to this Godforsaken place? It is all my fault.'

Telling himself that he wasn't to know how much
worse things had become since the King's execution,
that he had expected to find James easily, that she was
headstrong enough to have come without him, did nothing to ease his conscience. He had made a mess of it.
He should have put her back on the packet to England,
he should not have allowed the forger to sway his
judgement and he should have told Jean to keep her
indoors by force if necessary.

He looked down at her. She was still unconscious and
there was a dreadful bruise round her neck, but she was
beginning to breathe again in a ragged kind of way,
gulping air. 'Oh, my love,' he said, hardly aware of the
endearment. 'You are going to have a dreadful sore
throat, but thank God you will live.'

A few minutes later he turned the corner into the
market and ran under an archway to what had once been
some stables and there, to his unbounded relief, he
found his horse and cart and gently laid his burden in
the back. He had thrown Lucie's blankets over the horse
to keep it warm, and now he pulled them off, folded
one under Kitty's head and put the other over her, adding his dirty old overcoat for extra warmth.

He had a flask under the driving seat, but he dare not
try to give her anything to drink while she remained

unconscious. She was breathing a little more easily and he bent to kiss her before slipping off the back of the cart and going to the driver's seat. It was not safe to stay in Paris, he could not burden any more of his contacts with his personal problems. Nor would his superiors condone it. There was too much at stake. But Kitty must be saved and there was no time to lose.

It was not just that she was another human being needing help—it was far more than that. She had taken that hard-shelled heart of his in her small hands and cracked it wide open to reveal the core of him, the need in him, the capacity for love he had stifled for so long.

How had she done it, when he had put up a solid wall against such a happening? By being herself, he realised. There was nothing half-hearted about anything she did; that business with the guards at the barriers had proved that. Tiny as she was, she had immense courage. Her laughter was full-bodied, her anger red-hot. She was infuriating sometimes, but loyal and capable of infinite tenderness. Her hatred, he guessed, could be terrible, but her love steadfast to death. He knew it and he knew also that he loved her.

'Oh, Kitty, what have you done to me?' he murmured as he picked up the reins and the cart jolted out into the market place and made its way northwards to the Porte Saint-Denis.

Kitty felt as though her throat was on fire and her body ached with every jolt of the cart. What had happened? Where was she being taken? Where was Judith? She tried to cry out, but could not. She was beset by images of women's faces, of noise and a pounding in her ears, of her feet leaving the ground. Slowly, the horror of it all came back to her. She had been hanged and now, believing her dead, they were taking her for burial. She tried once again to move, to cry out.

'You are safe,' said a disembodied voice, somewhere above her. 'Lie still. Don't try to talk.'

She knew the voice. Oh, blessed, blessed relief!

The jolting of the cart increased until she could hardly bear it. 'I'm sorry,' he said, hearing her groan and wishing he could take her pain on himself. 'We'll soon have you comfortable again.'

They stopped at last. Jack came round to the back of the cart and picked her up in his arms as if she weighed nothing at all. She tried to speak, to thank him, but could not. He carried her into the farmhouse they had left only three days before, though it seemed like a lifetime. Up the stairs they went to the room she had occupied before, where he put her gently on the bed and covered her before turning to light a candle.

'You must stay here until you have fully recovered,' he said, his voice thick with emotion. 'Then we will talk.'

He took the candle to the window and stood passing it from side to side, before setting it down and returning to sit on the side of the bed. 'Lucie will see the light from her mother's house and know that I need her. She will be here soon. Shall I fetch you a drink?'

She managed to croak 'Please', but it hurt dreadfully and she put up her hand to her throat. She could feel the ridges left by the rope and shuddered.

He took her hand away and held it in his own. 'Don't talk. I will get you a drink of water with a few drops of laudanum in it and that will help you sleep.' He raised her hand to his lips, then got up and left the room.

As soon as he had gone and she was alone, the terror returned. Every shadow caused by the flickering candle held a menace, the sound of the wind in the trees outside the window was threatening voices. The creak of the stair was her executioner coming for her. She sat up, opening her mouth to scream, but no sound emerged. She was dumb.

And she had lost the one person she held dear, the one person who cared enough to give her life for her. Judith. Judith had tried to protect her. She had died, hadn't she? It wasn't a terrible nightmare. What had happened to her body? Had someone taken her down and buried her? Poor, poor Judith. She had not wanted to come to France but, staunchly loyal, she had been prepared to follow her mistress wherever she went, whatever mad scheme she dreamed up.

It was all her fault. All of it. Kitty flung herself face down and sobbed, thumping her pillow with a clenched fist.

'Now, that will do you no good at all,' Jack said, returning with a glass of cloudy liquid and sitting on the side of the bed to help her to drink it. 'You must stay calm.'

'Calm!' she mouthed, turning to face him. 'How can you talk of being calm? I don't feel calm. I feel angry. Angry! Angry! Angry!' With every silent word, she thumped the pillow.

'Good,' he said, grinning. 'That's more like the old Kitty. Now drink this and go to sleep. Tomorrow will be time enough to talk.'

He held the glass to her lips and she sipped it very slowly, forcing herself to swallow, but the fire in her throat made every tiny mouthful agony. He was very patient, taking the glass away from time to time so that she could recover a little, then beginning again, until it had all gone. Then he put her back on the pillows and covered her up.

'Sleep is what you need,' he said softly. 'Sleep and time to forget.' He rose to leave, but she clung to his hand and would not let it go. He smiled. 'Very well, I will stay.'

He sat and held her hand until her even breathing told him she had fallen asleep but, instead of tiptoeing softly from the room, he sat on, watching her.

There was no colour in her cheeks, or even in her lips, which made the red, mauve and yellow on her neck seem more pronounced. Her expressive eyes he could not see, but he noticed the long lashes and the finely drawn brows, the smooth forehead and the mop of dark hair framing her piquant face. One hand was flung out, the other lay in his palm, like a tiny bird in its nest. She was lovely and so innocent. It was that innocence which made her so vulnerable and so trusting, that and her courageous spirit which did not take caution or discretion into account.

He must teach her not to trust; he must teach her to doubt all men, not to rely on anyone. For her own safety, he must teach her wisdom and cunning and how to be deceitful, because a time might come when he could not protect her. And in doing so he would spoil her. It had happened to Gabrielle.

Oh, he had not corrupted his wife, others had. She had early learned to make demands and to turn to whomever would satisfy them. He didn't understand it, her parents were not like that. The *comte*, whom he had—God forgive him—vilified to his card-playing companions, was a good man and he loved the *comtesse* like a second mother. If it hadn't been for them, he would never have undertaken to find their wayward daughter, his wife, and embarked on his career as an agent.

As he sat watching the sleeping Kitty, his mind went back over the years and he was once again a young man. He wasn't old now, a mere thirty-one, but there had been so much pain and suffering, so many delusions shattered in that time that he felt ancient. Already there was grey in the hair at his temples.

But ten years ago he had been carefree and in love and staying with his mother's sister, Anne-Marie, and her husband, the Marquis de Saint-Gilbert, at their château above the village of Haute Saint-Gilbert just north of Lyons. Comte de Malincourt was their near neighbour and, during the course of that visit, he had been introduced to the *comte*'s daughter, Gabrielle. She had captivated him on sight and, before long, with the enthusiastic support of her parents, he had proposed and been accepted.

He had taken her home to England, to his father's estate in Wiltshire, but she hated it. It was too dull for her and she was not used to the strict etiquette prevailing in England. She, who was like an exotic butterfly, wanted to preen herself, to be the centre of attention, to go to balls and meet the top One Hundred, to flirt.

At first he had humoured her, spending more time in London than he ought, alienating his father, who told him he should be stricter with her, and upsetting his mother, whom Gabrielle made no secret of disliking. There had been constant friction. And then she had taken a lover. His hurt when he learned of it had penetrated deep into his soul, making him withdrawn and bad-tempered.

'I cannot see why you are in such a state about it,' she had said, when he confronted her. 'It is the natural thing to do. In France every man of any consequence has a mistress and every woman a lover.'

'This is not France.'

'More's the pity. If we were in Paris, we could have a gay time and see whom we pleased and no one would think anything of it. We should be accepted at court and visit Versailles and…' She had scolded on and on until, in order to try and save his marriage, he had moved to France, spending half the year at Malincourt with her parents and half the year in Paris. It made little difference. Until the Revolution.

Always one to keep abreast of current affairs, he had seen it coming, though not until the riots, which included the storming of the Bastille, was he able to persuade Gabrielle to return to England and then only because her parents had decided to flee the new regime and become part of that vast army of *emigrés*.

His father had several properties in London and one of these he leased to the *comte* and that, together with the proceeds from the gold and jewellery they had managed to bring out of France, allowed them to live in some degree of comfort. He had taken Gabrielle back to the family estate in Wiltshire, but his hopes that she would settle down to life in England were dashed when, less than two years later, she disappeared with a new lover. Jack had followed her to France and been arrested leaving his uncle's town villa.

It was while he was in prison that he learned that his wife had told the authorities he was a spy. At that time it had never entered his head to do anything of the kind. After all, he was half-French himself. It was only later, after his escape, when the Minister for War approached him, that he agreed to do what he could.

The danger excited him, made him forget his wife's

perfidy, and he believed he was doing some good, not only for England, but for France and all the oppressed people in that troubled country. He had tried to forget Gabrielle, to put her from his mind. Until yesterday in the Palais Royal, over a game of cards.

It was as if a door had closed on his past, but it had not freed him, because another had opened and he had been fool enough to enter it. He looked down at the slight form sleeping so peacefully, her hand in his, and wondered how he could harden his heart again, temper it like a blacksmith forging a shoe, when every fibre of him wanted to protect her, to see her safe, to hold her close to him, unchanged and unchanging, to love and cherish her.

But it was already too late. She had had her first taste of bestiality and man's inhumanity to man, and he did not suppose it would be her last. He bent to put his lips to her forehead as he heard a step on the stair which was followed by a light tap at the door. He got up to open it.

'Lucie, thank you for coming. *Ma'amselle* needs your help. She has had an unfortunate accident.' He stood aside and the girl hurried to the bed, gasping when she realised what had happened to Kitty.

'She will live?'

'Praise God, she will live, but she must stay here until she mends. Will you look after her?'

'Of course, *monsieur*.' She stopped to correct herself. '*Citoyen*. But where is her *maman*?'

'Dead.'

'Not…?' She looked down at Kitty's neck. 'Not that…?'

'Yes, I am afraid so. I do not know if she realises it

yet, but when she wakes, we must break it to her gently.'

'Oh, *la pauvre*! We must fetch a doctor.'

'No.' The word was almost snapped and he regretted it instantly. 'I'm sorry, Lucie, but it is obvious what has happened to her and the doctor would not treat her without informing the authorities. We cannot afford to be investigated. In truth, no one must know we are here…'

'But if she should die?'

'She will not die. She had already started to recover when I gave her a sleeping draught.' He smiled to reassure her. 'We will see how she goes tomorrow, eh?'

'Very well. I will watch over her. You must go to your own bed, you look exhausted.'

'I am. *Merci, ma petite*.' He dropped a kiss on the top of her head and went to his own room. Three days and nights with hardly any sleep had taken their toll, and he had hardly pulled off his clothes and flung himself on his bed before he was out to the world.

A weak winter sun was shining in at the window when Kitty woke. She turned her head and saw Lucie sitting in an armchair beside the bed. The light played on her blonde hair, turning it to iridescent gold; she made Kitty think of angels. 'Where am I?' she croaked.

'*Dieu soit béni!* You are awake. Do not try to talk. I will fetch *monsieur*.'

She hurried away and presently Jack came into the room. Lucie had evidently caught him in the middle of dressing for he was wearing black trousers and a rough shirt, but no neckcloth or waistcoat.

'How are you?' he said, sitting on the side of the bed.

'Sore.' It was no more than a whisper. 'I can't talk.'

He grinned. 'A silent woman, now there's a thing!'

He paused and looked closely at her, putting his hand on her brow. Thank heaven, there was no fever, her eyes were bright and there was a little more colour in her cheeks. 'You do know how lucky you are, don't you?'

'Yes, and I must thank you. If you hadn't come when you did I...' She shuddered. 'Judith...?'

His heart was wrenched with pity, but he could see no way to soften the blow. 'I am sorry I was too late to save her.'

'What...will...happen to her? Will someone take her down?'

'Yes. I will see that she is buried.'

'Those dreadful women. Like animals, screeching for blood...'

'They were hungry and their children starving.'

She was astonished. 'You condone what they did?'

'No, of course not, but they have been taught to hate the aristocracy as the cause of all their ills and hate dies hard.'

'They had no reason to hate us. I was pushed over. Judith tried to stop them trampling on me.'

'That was all?'

'They did not like our petticoats.'

'Petticoats!'

'Said they were too fine and we must be aristos.'

'You had them on under your rags?' If he had known that before they left Calais, he would have insisted on them being removed.

'Yes. We were cold without them.'

'You didn't give your name, or that of Faucon?' If his cover was blown, he must find a new identity and quickly.

'No.' She began to cough and he picked up a glass of water and held it to her lips. When she had swallowed a little she pushed his hand away. 'We said nothing.'

He scrutinised her carefully, deciding that being soft would not do, he had to make her realise her predicament or they would all be lost. 'Did you not realise that when I told you to stay with Jean, I had a very good reason for doing so and expected to be obeyed?'

'You did not come back.'

'I was detained. You should have waited.'

'Your friends did not want us, they were afraid.'

'Everyone is afraid. Now, in future, you will obey me to the letter, do you hear?'

She nodded. What else could she do? She was virtually his prisoner. All her money had been taken; she was penniless and entirely in his hands. She was not even sure that he had her welfare at heart. Had he even looked for her brother or simply gone about his own business, whatever that was?

'James…?'

'Your brother has disappeared.'

'You looked for him?'

'Of course I looked for him. Do you think I wanted to be saddled with a couple of silly women? There is nothing I wish for more than for him to take charge of you. I could find no sign of him.'

She could not believe that, after all she had been through, she was not to be reunited with James. 'Do you think he has been arrested? Or…' she gulped, feeling the rawness of her throat '…hanged?'

'I have certainly found no evidence of it. He may have sensed danger and decided to go home. I have yet to find out.'

'What must I do?'

'Nothing. You will stay here and get well. Lucie will

look after you, but you will not attempt to go out and, if anyone comes to the house, you will hide. Lucie will show you where. Is that understood?'

She nodded. She must have imagined his tenderness of the night before, dreamed that he had kissed her; there was nothing tender about him now. What was he up to, that there had to be so much secrecy? Was he a criminal? She knew he would not answer if she asked him, but he could not be all bad because he had saved her life. Why had he bothered, if she was such a burden to him?

'Good. Here is Lucie with some chicken broth for you. You must try and swallow it. I must go.'

'Go? Go where?'

He smiled. 'That's another rule. No questions. The less you know, the better. You won't always be dumb.'

He stood up and made way for Lucie to sit in his place. 'Be good until I return.' And, to Lucie, 'She is not to get up. If she attempts it, you are to tie her to the bed.'

Lucie smiled at Kitty. 'He does not mean it.'

'Oh, yes, he does,' he said. And with that he was gone.

Lucie sat by the bed and slowly spooned broth into Kitty's mouth until she had drunk nearly a whole bowlful, then she helped Kitty to lie down and tucked the bedclothes about her.

'Goodnight, *ma'amselle*,' she whispered. 'I will be in the next room, if you need me.'

Kitty watched her as she glided silently from the room and gently shut the door. She smiled as she heard the key turn in the lock; Lucie was going to make quite sure she obeyed Jack's command.

Chapter Five

During the next two weeks, Kitty mended slowly. The bruises on her neck, though fading, were still visible and she still spoke with a rasping voice, but her hurt went deeper than bruises and that would take longer to heal. And the longer she stayed inactive, the more time she had to dwell on her culpability.

Oh, if only Judith had been saved too! She missed the old servant, she missed her warm affection, even her scolding, and wished she had taken more notice of her. Judith's death was on her conscience and she would have nightmares about it for the rest of her life. She turned her head into the pillow and wept silent tears of remorse and misery. 'Forgive me, Judith, forgive me.'

Her confinement frustrated her and she longed to be able to dress and go downstairs, to go out and breathe fresh air, but Lucie would have none of it. '*Monsieur* said you must stay indoors,' she said firmly.

'He is a tyrant,' Kitty whispered, when her latest request was denied her.

'No, *ma'amselle*,' Lucie said, putting a tray containing a bowl of soup in front of her and handing her a spoon to feed herself. 'He is gentle and kind, but it is sometimes necessary for him to be firm. It is for our own good.'

'Do you always obey him?'

'Always.'

'When did you meet him? Is he your kin?'

Lucie laughed. 'Kin? No, I am far, far beneath him.'

'But you do love him.'

'*Naturellement*, I do. I owe him my life. Just as you do.'

'Tell me about it.'

'There is little to tell. I worked in the household of a *duc*, as a maid to the *duchesse*. They were ardent Royalists and were accused of taking part in the plot to help King Louis and his family flee the country. When they were arrested, the Duchess entrusted me with a letter to take to the Comte de Malincourt, a friend she thought might be able to help them. Unfortunately, I was searched on my way out of the château and arrested too.

'Citizen Faucon heard of it and he came to my trial and told the court I could not read or write and did not know the importance of what I had been given. He said I was on my way to deliver the letter to the captain of the guard, believing it to be my duty. They believed him and I was released.' She paused to make sure Kitty was swallowing the soup. 'It was very brave of him to stand up in public like that. He risked his own safety for me and I can never sufficiently repay him.'

'And now he has saved my life too,' Kitty croaked.

'Yes.'

'Why was it such a risk for him to defend you?'

'It is always a risk to cross the Public Prosecutor. It will be held against him if he is ever caught.'

'Caught doing what?'

'That I cannot tell you, *ma'amselle.*'

'Cannot or will not?'

Lucie blushed crimson. 'I have not asked him and I entreat you not to do so.' She took the tray with the empty bowl from Kitty and stood up. 'We have talked long enough and you must rest.'

The more Kitty learned about the enigmatic Jack Chiltern, the more puzzling she found him. The man Lucie had described was hardly the man she knew. The Jack Chiltern she knew hadn't a sympathetic bone in his body. He had saved her life but, even after that, when she thanked him, he had cross-questioned her, more concerned with what she might have told those dreadful women about him than about how she felt. And he had made no secret of the fact that he wanted to be rid of her. And yet, in spite of that, he had rescued her.

Lucie stayed in the house and occasionally her mother arrived with provisions and gossip, but no one else came to the farmhouse and, so far, Kitty had not had to resort to hiding behind the wood panelling under the stairs. It had no window and was cramped and airless; on the one occasion she had rehearsed going into it, she had been beset by a horror of the dark, something that had never bothered her before coming to France, and only just managed to refrain from screaming.

Jack's return, at the end of three weeks, was a great relief.

Lucie had allowed her to dress and go downstairs on her promise not to try and leave the house, a promise she gave willingly because all thoughts of trying to proceed alone had been driven from her by her terrible ordeal at the hands of the mob. It could so easily happen again. She was thankful Jack had made her leave her luggage at the farmhouse, so that she still had some clothes to wear.

As soon as he entered the room where she was struggling with the French in a book she had found on the shelf, she stood up, wanting to run into his arms, to tell him how pleased she was to see him and how much she had missed him, but she dare not. There was a moment of awkward silence while they stood and looked at each other, before she gave him a little curtsy. 'I am glad to see you back, sir.'

He smiled. It had not taken her long to forget their intimacy and become once more a cool young lady of manners. But also a very beautiful young lady in her green silk dress, which fitted her slim waist and flowed over her hips to almost cover her dainty shoes. She had allowed her hair to fall loose on her shoulders, held back from her face with combs, and had filled the neckline of her dress with a lace fichu, in order to hide her throat, but he could still see a little of the purple bruising.

He gave her a sweeping bow. 'Ma'am, your obedient. I hope I find you recovered.'

'Indeed, yes. You see, I can speak again.'

The slight huskiness in her voice enhanced it and he was tempted to tell her so, to admit that he found her enchanting, but it was a temptation he stifled. 'You will be pleased to know that I have news of your brother.'

'You have?' Her eyes lit with hope and she forgot their stiffness with each other. 'Where is he? Is he well? What did he say?'

'I have not seen or spoken to him, but I believe I know where he is.'

'Then let us go to him at once.'

He smiled at her eagerness; she was simply asking to be teased. 'Is my hospitality so lacking, my dear?'

'No, no, I did not mean…' She stopped, confused. 'You have been very kind and I am not ungrateful, but I do so want to see my brother again. It is why I came to France in the first place.'

'Is that so?' he said laconically, seating himself on the sofa beside her. 'Now, I thought it was something to do with a distaste for marriage…'

She coloured. 'I have no distaste for marriage, I did not want to marry Edward Lampeter simply because he kissed me.'

'Kisses mean nothing to you, then? Anyone may kiss you with impunity so long as they do not ask for your hand in marriage? I am relieved to hear that I shall not be expected to offer for you, after all.'

She stared at him, uncomprehending, making him laugh. 'Had you forgot so soon? Perhaps I should remind you.' He put a hand either side of her face, drawing it towards him. The temptation was almost overwhelming; her soft lips, slightly parted in surprise, were only inches from his. He smiled, tipped her head down and kissed her forehead before releasing her.

'Sir,' she said, refusing to admit, even to herself, that she had wanted him to kiss her, to experience again that extraordinary feeling of dizziness, of floating on air, of being moulded to his body as if they were one being, of hot sweet melting deep inside her. She wanted to know it if were real or she had dreamed it. But her behaviour on that occasion had not been ladylike and she did not want him to think she was always so wanton. 'I do not need reminding that you are not a gentleman and care little for a lady's sensibilities, and I should certainly refuse you should you have the impertinence to propose.'

He threw back his head and laughed aloud. 'Oh, well said, *ma petite*, but don't you think it is too late? You are already my wife, or had you forgot?' He paused and became serious. 'Citizeness Faucon.'

'Jacques Faucon does not exist, so how can he have a wife?'

'I have papers to prove he exists.'

'Forged.'

'You know that for sure, do you?'

'Of course I do. Jacques Faucon is not your name and, besides, you told me you were married.'

'How do you know what my name is? How do you know that, in these heathen times, a wife cannot be discarded as easily as a grubby cravat, that a marriage ceremony is necessary? If the Jacobins have their way, the Church will become defunct. They have already confiscated the assets of many churches and sold off their lands to the highest bidders.'

'I don't believe that. You are just trying to frighten me, to make me do as you wish.'

He sat back and surveyed her, looking from her dainty feet, up over yards of green silk and her poor bruised neck to her face and expressive violet eyes, which betrayed her bewilderment. Did she really believe he could be so callous? She might be grateful to him for saving her life, but gratitude was not love or trust. He had nothing to complain of; he had done nothing to deserve either.

'Enough of this banter,' he said brusquely. 'I am not coercing you into anything, but if you want to see your brother again, we have a long journey ahead of us and it were better you believed in Jacques Faucon.'

'Long journey?' she queried. 'He is not in Paris?'

'No, he has gone south to Lyons. We leave tomorrow. Be ready.' He paused to pick up a handful of her silk skirt and rub it between finger and thumb. 'As Citizeness Faucon.'

They set out at dawn, travelling in the old coach. Kitty, dressed in the common dress of a *sans-culottes*, sat on a cushion provided by Lucie. A rough blanket was tucked about her legs and there was a warm brick on the floor at her feet, though the balmy air was showing the first signs of spring. Her remaining clothes had been packed into her basket and were stowed away under the seat on which she sat.

'If we are stopped, do not speak,' Jack said, as he shut the door. 'I do not want a repeat of your performance at the Paris *barrière*.'

'Supposing I am asked a question?'

'Then groan. I shall say you have a contagious fever. It might be enough to make inquisitive people keep their distance.'

'How far do we have to go?'

'Three hundred miles.'

'Three hundred!' She was aghast. 'How long will that take?'

He grinned. 'At six miles an hour, you work it out.' He turned from her to make a final check of the harness. 'And don't forget the poor horse has to be rested regularly and we have to sleep.'

She stuck her head out of the window as he climbed on the driver's seat. 'Couldn't we go post chaise?'

The question seemed to afford him a great deal of amusement; he chuckled but did not answer as he flicked the reins. 'Walk on, Samson, my beauty.'

Kitty sat back on her cushion as they jolted down the lane to the road. They had hardly gone a mile when he turned off it again to avoid going through Paris.

Kitty did not want to go to Paris; she never wanted to see the place again, but three hundred miles in this bone-shaker was going to be an appalling journey and she would be black and blue after one day, let alone…how many? She shut her eyes, doing the arithmetic. How many miles a day? How many stops and for how long?

Even in March, the days were still short; they could not start out until it grew light enough for horse and driver to see or they would stumble into the huge pot-holes and ridges which were a feature of the roads. And darkness fell soon after four, earlier on an overcast day, that meant eight or nine hours, not counting rest periods and if the poor horse did not need them, she surely would. Why, they would be lucky if they made thirty miles in a day. Ten days, probably more.

No, she would not believe it; he was teasing her again. That was the trouble with him, he changed so quickly. One minute he was being brutally frank, the tyrant, the next he was the courtier, laughing and teasing her, both equally annoying. There was a third side to him, which she had glimpsed once or twice, and that was the thinker, the quiet man, the man who had sadness and pain in his eyes; the man he kept hidden beneath the veneer of the other two.

They turned off the road into a wood at mid-day and he lit a fire to warm them and heat a little soup that Lucie had packed for them. There was also half a loaf and some cold chicken wrapped in a clean cloth. The fire was welcome and Kitty huddled on the ground beside it, warming her frozen hands and toes, while the horse munched its way through a handful of hay and some mouldy carrots. An hour later Jack hitched up the horse and they set off again.

Just as Kitty was wondering if they were going to sleep under the stars, they pulled up in the courtyard of an inn. Jack jumped down and came to the door to help her alight. 'Now, guard your tongue,' he murmured in an undertone. 'I do not think we are in any danger, but it is as well to be prepared.'

He did not take her arm, nor show any particular concern for her, as he strode ahead of her into what she could only describe as a hovel. But it was cleaner than she expected and as soon as Jack produced good hard coinage, the innkeeper and his wife were all smiles.

'Our best room, of course, citizen. Come with me,' the landlord said, picking up a lamp and leading the way through a brick-floored parlour and up some rickety stairs to a landing, where he opened the first door he came to.

'Fresh linen on the bed this very morning,' he lied, putting the lamp on a table and going over to the hearth to set light to a few sticks. Straightening up, he grinned at Kitty and then at Jack. 'Don't suppose you need a bedwarmer.'

Jack laughed, not so much at the man's crude joke but at Kitty's look of dismay. 'I'd say no, but we have been on the road some time in bitter weather and the citizeness has terrible cold feet, which she delights in putting on my back, so a hot brick would be appreciated.'

'Very well, citizen. And do you want food?'

'Naturally we want food. Bring a tray up here, the best you've got. And a bottle of wine.'

The man left, closing the door behind him.

'If you think I am going to share a room with you—' Kitty began as soon as he had gone.

'Only the nobility can afford the luxury of separate quarters,' he said. 'Would you have these good people think we are aristos?'

His use of the word aristos served to remind her of what had happened in Paris and she shuddered. Surely the whole countryside was not infected by this madness? 'You did not have to say we were married.'

'Our passports say we are, you know that. How else can I protect you? A woman alone, and not just any woman, but a very young and beautiful one, would fall prey to the first lecher who knocked on her door. And standing on your dignity would avail you nothing.' He came over and took the blanket and shawl from her to throw them on a chair, standing for a moment with his hands on her shoulders and looking down into her upturned face.

Her eyes were bright and her cheeks rosy with cold; her lips were slightly parted and the pink tip of her tongue protruded between her teeth. Did she have any idea of what she was doing to him? Did she know that her mixture of hauteur and innocence was having a profound effect upon him, turning him into a quivering mass of indecisiveness and desire? He was rapidly losing the initiative.

He dropped his hands to his sides and took a deep breath to regain control of the situation. 'Now come and sit by the fire and warm yourself. It is not necessary for us to fight.'

He pulled a chair close to the meagre blaze and motioned her to sit. 'I told you before and I shall tell you again, I have more important things to do than seduce an unwilling chit. We share the room and that's an end of it.'

She had seen that look in his eyes again, the look of pain and doubt, as if he were undecided whether to take her into his confidence or not, but before she could say anything the innkeeper returned with a tray of food and a hot brick wrapped in flannel. Jack took both from him and thanking him, ushered him out again.

'Now, eat,' he commanded, pulling a small table close to her chair and setting the tray on it. He put the brick in the bed and returned to add another log to the fire before bringing up another chair for himself. The meal was only a thin stew, with a few grisly pieces of meat, some onions and carrots, accompanied by cabbage and a couple of tiny potatoes, but it was nourishing in its way and she knew they would not even have had that if Jack had not given the couple more money than they could earn in a month.

He poured the wine which was surprisingly good and they ate and drank in silence. She wanted to ask him what his business was and, if it was so important, why was he taking time to escort her on this journey? Why wasn't he concerned about his wife? Shouldn't he be searching for her? Unless she was in Lyons too, or somewhere on the way. Was James even in Lyons? She had only Jack's word for it.

So many questions buzzing round in her head, but she knew it was no good asking them. He told her only what he wanted her to know. Besides, she was feeling replete and sleepy, but unwilling to admit she wanted to go to bed. 'I worked it out,' she said.

'Worked what out?'

'At six miles an hour with stops we shall cover no

more than thirty miles a day. We shall be on the road for ten days at least.'

'Two weeks would be nearer the mark.'

'And we go all the way like this?'

'Like what?'

'Plodding along all day with you on the driving seat and me rattling round inside and the nights spent…' She spread her hands to encompass the room.

'If we are lucky.'

'If we are lucky!' she repeated. 'You call this miserable existence lucky? I should hate to encounter ill-luck.'

'So should I,' he said laconically. 'A broken axle, perhaps, a lame horse, bad weather, brigands…'

'Stop! Stop! I really do not want to know.'

He smiled. 'If you had known what was ahead, I'll wager you would never have left home, would you?'

She looked at him with her head on one side, pondering the question and he found himself holding his breath for her answer. 'No, for I would not then have been the cause of Judith's death and I can never forgive myself for that.'

He supposed it was the kind of answer he should have expected from her. She said nothing of her own ordeal, or the discomfort she was being forced to suffer, the poor food, the filth, his overbearing manner. 'You should not blame yourself,' he said. 'She chose to come with you.'

'She was loyal and my stepmother would have turned her out of the house in any case, so what choice did she have? And it was my decision to leave Monsieur Clavier's, not hers.'

'You could as easily blame me for taking you to Paris. I should have forced you to return to England.'

She smiled mischievously. 'Do you really think I would have gone? It seems to me I gave you no choice either because, in spite of your efforts to prove the contrary, I do believe you have some gentlemanly feelings…'

He inclined his head, amusement in his brown eyes. 'Thank you, ma'am.'

She stood up, trying not to let him see how nervous she was. 'Now, I think I must put that to the test. I am going to bed.' She went over to the four-poster and removed a blanket and a pillow which she dropped into his lap. 'It will be warm by the hearth. I bid you goodnight, sir.'

He scrambled to his feet and watched her clamber on to the bed and draw the curtains round her, dislodging a thick film of dust which made her cough. They had obviously not been drawn for a very long time and she was lucky they did not fall down about her head. He thought about going to help her but such a move would undoubtedly be misunderstood.

He heard the bed creaking as she endeavoured to undress on it and then there was silence.

'Goodnight, my dear Kitty,' he murmured, putting out the lamp before taking off his coat and boots and stretching himself on the hearthrug in shirt and trousers and pulling the thin blanket over him.

Kitty had removed her skirt and blouse and lay down in her shift and petticoat, but in spite of her fatigue she could not sleep. She was acutely aware of his presence in the room. The fire went out and the wind began to rattle the window panes and creep into the cracks around the door; she could hear the inn sign creaking as it swung to and fro. The moon rose and cast long shadows on the curtains that surrounded her. She felt closed in, unable to breathe and at the same time shivering with cold.

She pulled the curtains to one side so that she could see the window. Clouds were gathering, obscuring the moon. Tomorrow, there would be rain. The brick at her feet lost its warmth and she pulled it out and put it on the floor, glancing between the bed hangings at the huddled form on the hearthrug. He must be even colder than she was. She lay back on the pillows and shut her eyes, trying to empty her mind of all that had happened, so that she could sleep. She was so tired…

Her own screams woke her. Woke Jack, too. He rushed to her side, pulling aside the curtains and sitting on the bed to hold her in his arms. 'Hush, hush, *ma petite*, you are safe. I have you safe. Look, there is no one here but me. Hush, hush…'

She clung to him as her screams subsided into sobs and the sobs into long heaving breaths, as she tried to throw off the nightmare. It had been so real, so terrifying. She was being buried alive in a dark cellar with hundreds of dead bodies. They were all about her, mangled, grotesque. She saw Judith's face, her mouth and eyes wide open. There was a door and James stood by it, looking for her, but she could not move, could not cry out to let him know she was there, alive, not dead like everyone else.

'That's better,' he said, stroking her hair. 'Try and go back to sleep.' He laid her back on the pillow and pulled the blanket over her, but she continued to shake. 'You are cold.' He fetched the blanket she had given him and tucked it round her.

'No, no,' she murmured. 'You will freeze.'

He smiled and climbed in beside her, taking her shivering body into his arms and holding her close against him. 'We will share. Go to sleep. No more nightmares.'

His voice was so soothing, the warmth of his body so comforting, she forgot to be afraid. A tiny voice in her head reminded her that what they were doing was scandalous in the extreme, but the voice had no strength and was lost among the screeching of the demons of her nightmare. She was tired and afraid and he comforted her. She put her head on his shoulder and risked shutting her eyes. The nightmare did not return and she slept.

When she woke again, dawn was breaking and rain was beating against the window pane. Had she dreamed that Jack Chiltern had lain beside her, that he had held her in his arms and soothed her? Or was that a dream too? She turned her head. The imprint of his head dented the pillow beside her, but of Jack Chiltern there was no sign.

She sat up in a sudden panic. His boots and coat had gone. He had abandoned her, gone on without her. She scrambled out of bed and reached for her skirt and blouse just as the door opened. He came in bearing a tray.

'Good morning, sleepy head,' he said, smiling. 'I thought you would never wake. Now, come and have breakfast, we must be on our way as soon as you are ready.'

It was all so very normal.

That day and night were the first of many, all very similar. Sometimes it rained; sometimes the sun shone; sometimes they made only half a dozen miles a day because the poor old horse could do no more. When that happened, they had walked beside it, talking in desultory fashion.

Without once mentioning his wife, he spoke of his parents and his boyhood which had been spent in England, of the countryside, the hunting and fishing with which he had filled his leisure, of his liking for books and learning and his assessment of the political situation. He talked of France under the *ancien régime* which he seemed to know just as well as England, and the changes brought about by the Revolution.

'Theory and practice do not always go hand in hand,' he said on one occasion. 'Equality when applied unequally does not work. The new regime was supposed to have addressed the problem, made things more even, but the rich still escape while the poor still pay. They pay taxes to the state, taxes to the church, taxes to their *seigneur*. The cost of the intervention in the American War was bad enough, but now France is at war with half of Europe and the cost in money and lives is crippling. The country is all but bankrupt.'

She smiled. 'You care, don't you?'

'Of course I care. Ardent patriotism soon turns to fanaticism, and fanaticism to despotism in the hands of powerful men, especially when the supreme authority is weak.'

'You mean the King?'

'Yes, the King. He was made the symbol of repression and it was easy to incite the poorer sections of the community into believing he was the author of all their ills.'

'Now he is dead, has anything changed?'

'No, of course not, so they turn their attention to the Queen and anyone seen to sympathise with her.'

'They will never execute her, surely?'

'Who knows?'

'Poor woman.'

'As you say, poor woman. If England were to win this war…' He stopped, realising he was getting dangerously close to confiding in her and that would be bad for her safety. 'It's beginning to rain again and Samson has had his rest, so into the coach with you.'

She had returned to the vehicle and he had climbed on to the driving seat again, and they had continued their bone-shaking journey. But she was slowly beginning to understand him, and in that understanding there was a flicker of something more. Of love.

During the day she could set aside the terrible memory of Judith being hoisted up to the top of the lantern; during daylight hours, she could pretend there was nothing wrong, but when night came, when she went to sleep, the nightmares returned and then she was glad that he slept in a chair in the same room or across the foot of the bed.

Hearing her cries, he would wake her and murmur softly and lay beside her and both would sleep. She no longer argued against sharing a room with him. If they derived comfort and warmth from each other, that was good. She was as chaste as the day she left the vicarage, though she doubted if anyone would believe it. But England seemed far away and the proprieties she had been brought up to observe hardly seemed relevant.

They travelled almost due south, passing through the forest of Fontainebleu, favourite hunting ground of kings, on through Sens, with its tall cathedral and half-timbered houses, to Auxerre and Avallon, set on a promontory jutting out over the river valley along which they meandered, as if they had all the time in the world, then through forests, stopping to rest beside lakes, where Jack caught fish for their mid-day meal.

Sometimes he snared a hare to supplement their diet of onions, peas, beans and cabbages and whatever they could glean from the hedgerows. Bread was in very short supply and very dear.

The days became a little warmer and the bare fields changed to sloping vineyards, each overlooked by its château, some quite small, others as big as castles. Beaune gave way to Chalon-sur-Saône, then Tournus and Macon, and still they journeyed on, following the banks of the river, sometimes hemmed in by towering cliffs, at other times gentle rolling hills, dotted with little villages.

The people they met on the roads and on the river barges pretended little interest, but Kitty was sure that they were watched and their presence commented upon. Occasionally they met soldiers on the march and Jack pulled off the road to let them pass. But even then the violence of Paris seemed a long way off; the gentle pace they had maintained for the benefit of an old horse also served to calm their own separate conflicts and produce a kind of euphoria.

But as they neared the city of Lyons, Jack fell silent and Kitty began to think more and more about her brother and what lay ahead. What would James say to her? What was he doing in France that prevented him from going home? He had always been headstrong, even more so than she was, so had he become involved in revolution or counter-revolution? Why Lyons?

It was nearer three weeks than two when they stopped at Villefranche-sur-Saône, capital of the Beaujolais region, and next morning turned off what was euphemistically called the high road on to one that was even worse. Here the land was marshy and dotted with lakes, home of thousands of wild birds: waders, herons, birds of prey. Their pace became even slower.

'Why are we going this way?' she asked when he stopped the carriage at mid-day. 'Is it a short cut?'

'No, not a short cut, but beautiful, don't you think?'

'We have made a detour in order to admire the scenery?'

He smiled, fetching out the bread and cold chicken which had cost him a small fortune at the hostelry they stayed at the night before. 'No, this is the only way.'

'To Lyons?'

'No, to our destination. You will soon see...'

'But you said we were going to Lyons.'

'Later, perhaps. After I have made certain inquiries. Now eat up, we will soon be there.'

After they had finished their meal they set out again and began to climb into the hills. To save the horse, they both got down to walk. The road became steeper and more broken and Jack began to fear for the carriage, as it jolted out of one pothole into another. There was a single roadmender half-heartedly throwing rocks into the worst of the holes and even as they passed him, he stopped and sat down on the side of the road to drink from a flask, watching them out of sight.

Halfway up the hill they came to a village, surrounded by a broken wall. At the gate Kitty turned to look about her. The view over the valley below was breathtaking: rocky outcrops, stands of trees, shimmering lakes and terraced vineyards.

'Our destination,' Jack said, pointing at a large château which overlooked the town from the tree-clad hills above it.

The old carriage rumbled over the cobbled streets of the little town with Kitty and Jack walking at the horse's head. It seemed a typical hillside community, with lopsided wooden houses, a church with a very tall spire, a mill, a town hall, a fountain in the middle of the central square and an inn with a stableyard. She could not imagine many wayfarers passing through; the only road out of it, apart from the one climbing up from the valley, seemed to lead to the château.

'What is this place?' she asked. 'And who lives at the château? Is James supposed to be here?'

He smiled; never content with one question, she must always ask several at a time. 'The village is called Haute Saint-Gilbert and the château is the home of my mother's sister and her husband, the Marquis and Marchioness de Saint-Gilbert, or I should say the *ci-devant* Marquis and Marchioness, since titles have been abolished and he is simply a citizen like everyone else. And, yes, we may very well find your brother here.'

'What is he doing here?'

'You must ask him that.'

As they climbed the last steep hill of their long journey, she began to wonder what Jack would do next. Would he hand her over to her brother and leave her? Six weeks before she had not wished for anything else, but now she realised she would miss him dreadfully. He had become necessary to her existence and without him she would crumble to dust and be borne away on the wind.

He had kept her sane when nightmares troubled her; he had provided her with food and warmth, had entertained her with discourse and laughter, instructed her on the countryside, pointing out places of interest. He had been her guide on her very own Grand Tour. And now it was coming to an end.

He had protected her from prying eyes, lied gallantly to ensure her safety as well as his own and, if he had sometimes been tyrannical, it was a tyranny of love not hate. She loved him. She knew hardly anything about him and yet she loved him. He was married and yet she loved him. Her footsteps slowed as she realised the enormity of her discovery and the hopelessness of it.

'Come, I would have thought you would be all eagerness to be there,' he said, stopping to wait for her to catch up.

'Of course I am,' she retorted. 'But this slope is so steep I hardly know how to climb it.'

'Nonsense! You have walked up far steeper ones in the last three weeks.' He reached out to take her arm. 'Here, let me help you.'

She wrenched herself from his grasp, unable to bear his touch for fear of giving herself away. 'I'm all right.'

He looked sideways at her, wondering what had come over her. She was ill at ease, walking with her head down, as if she did not want to look at him or speak to him. He sighed. 'What have I done wrong now?'

'Nothing.'

'Then I wish you would look more cheerful. Your brother may see us coming and will surely think I have been ill-treating you.'

'Don't be silly. Why should he think that?'

'You have a face like thunder and I do believe I could strike a tinder from the sparks in your eyes.' He stopped and took her chin between his fingers and thumb and forced her to look at him. 'Or are they tears?'

'Of course not. Please release me.'

He dropped his hand and pulled on the horse's harness. 'Come, Samson, just a few more yards and your work is done, then you may rest as long as you want.'

Kitty looked up as he spoke and realised they were within a stone's throw of the château, every bit as imposing at close quarters as it had been from the village below. It looked like a fairytale castle with steeply sloping roofs and several turrets and a huge oaken door which stood open to reveal a paved courtyard and a fountain. Jack led the horse and cart through it.

A door opened to one side and a young lady flew out of it and ran towards them. 'Jack! Jack!' He stood with his feet apart, holding out his arms and she flung herself into them. Laughing joyously, he picked her up and swung her round and round, revealing a frou-frou of lace petticoats and silk stockings, while Kitty watched, her heart growing as heavy as lead.

This must be his wife. She was so young, hardly more than eighteen, and Kitty's notion that he had not talked about her because he did not care flew away. He had not spoken because he cared too much to share his thoughts with a mere stranger. This lovely girl was petite and pretty and beautifully dressed in pale aquamarine silk, with ribbons in her very pale hair.

Kitty became acutely conscious of her rough peasant skirt and blouse and the darned shawl which she had draped about her shoulders. And, unlike the girl's satin pumps, her shoes were so thin that even the smallest stone imprinted itself on the soles of her feet. She could not bear to look and turned away to pat Samson's nose.

'Oh, Jack, you do not know how I have longed to see you again.' Kitty could turn away, but she could not shut out the sound of the young lady's voice. 'But how did you manage it? Are you going to stay this time?'

'Questions, questions, questions,' he said, setting her back on her feet. 'Why are women so full of them?' Reminded of Kitty he turned to her, only to realise she had disappeared. 'Where is the pesky woman?'

'You mean the *citoyenne*. Why, she went round to the back of the carriage. I must say, Jack, it is the most dilapidated vehicle I ever did see. And as for that animal…' Her laughter pealed out, making him smile.

'He brought us safely from Paris,' he said. 'Three hundred miles, as Kitty will vouch if I could only persuade her to come out of hiding.' He went round the carriage and found her trying to pull her basket out from under the seat where it was wedged fast. 'Leave that,' he said, taking her hand. 'A servant will see to it. Come and meet Nanette.'

'Nanette,' he said, drawing her forward. 'This is Miss Kitty Harston.'

'Kitty Harston,' she repeated in astonishment. 'You mean Jamie's sister?'

'I do, indeed.'

She stared at Kitty, taking in her rough clothes and tangled hair, obviously doubtful as to the truth of the young woman's identity. 'But I thought you were a peasant. Whatever are you doing here?'

'Now, that is hardly a welcome, *ma petite*,' Jack remonstrated. 'We have come a long way and we are dirty and tired…'

'Oh, please forgive me, Miss Harston. I was so taken aback I forgot my manners. And Jack has forgotten his, too, for he has not introduced me. I am Nanette de Saint-Gilbert.' She smiled at Jack. 'And for my sins I am Jack's French cousin.'

'His cousin.' The day was overcast but it seemed as

though the sun had come out and flooded the courtyard with its warmth. This lovely girl was not Jack's wife.

'Yes. You do speak French, do you not?'

'A little.' Kitty curtseyed. 'How do you do, *ma'amselle.*'

'Come in. Come in. A bath and a meal first, I think. Papa and Mama are out visiting, but they will be back directly, and we will save the story of your journey until they arrive and we can all hear it together.' She took Kitty's arm as she spoke and led her into the house.

'*Mon frère…?*'

'You have just missed him. Jamie went to Lyons this morning. There is to be a meeting tomorrow.'

'When do you expect him back?' Jack asked, as he followed them into a vast marble-floored vestibule with an enormous fire which burned a log as big as a tree trunk.

'I don't know. The day after, perhaps. He was a little vague.'

Jack groaned. The man was as elusive as a butterfly. What was he up to? What meeting? If he was stirring the mutterings of discontent into more rebellion, he must be stopped. It was too late to do anything tonight and he was dog-tired. Tomorrow he must find him and make him understand that people who went off at half-cock without proper orders were a danger to themselves and everyone else. James must take Kitty home.

Nanette clapped her hands and servants appeared from everywhere. One was despatched to see to the fires in bedrooms, another to make up the beds, two others to fetch hot water and another to summon the cook for new instructions. The Revolution did not seem to have touched this out-of-the-way place; everything spoke of opulence. The furniture, the hangings, the carpets, the huge fires, the myriad of crystals in the chandeliers, the paintings on the walls, the carved oak staircase, the long windows, all spoke of great wealth.

Kitty was led upstairs to a huge bedroom which had a magnificent view of the town nestling on the hillside. From here she could also see that there was another road down the mountain, small and winding and hidden for most of its length by trees.

Servants bustled in to fill a bath before the fire, which was already warming the room. Kitty suspected that it was kept alight and only needed stirring up and more fuel added.

'Take your time,' Nanette told her, as a male servant arrived with her basket. 'Let me have the gown you mean to wear, I will have it pressed for you.'

'Thank you.' Kitty, who had very little choice in her basket, picked out a short-sleeved dress of blue muslin, with a deep frill at the hem and a fichu of white lace to fill its low neck. She handed it to Nanette, together with a fine lawn petticoat trimmed with lace, the same undergarment she had been wearing in Paris. She shuddered as she touched it, remembering again the humiliation of having it flung over her head, but pulled herself together and smiled at her young hostess.

'You don't know how much I have been looking forward to being clean and civilised again.'

'I suppose that reprobate cousin of mine insisted on you dressing like that? It really is too bad of him.'

'I believe it was necessary.'

'Then you shall tell me all about it later.' She turned for the door with the clothes. 'I admire your courage, *ma'amselle*. I am quite sure I should never have endured it. Marie will help you dress and conduct you downstairs when you are ready.'

The water was hot and scented with jasmine. Kitty soaked herself for nearly half an hour, until every vestige of grime from her journey had been washed away. The maid washed her hair and she sat before the fire to dry it, musing on the events which had brought her here. Less than two months before, she had been sitting in a bath and having her hair done before dressing for the Viscount's ball.

Young and naive, she had set out in a mood of excitement, looking forward to the dancing and the supper, of meeting one or two local eligibles, perhaps even the man of her dreams. He would be handsome and gallant and fall in love with her on sight. Instead she had been kissed by Edward Lampeter, whom she had known since childhood and who was definitely not the man her fantasies were made of.

It was strange how something as innocent as a kiss could lead to this. A château in the middle of France in the company of a married man. She had no money, only two dresses and a filthy skirt to her name and that name tarnished forever. Would she, given her time over again, have stayed at home?

No, a thousand times no. If she had stayed she would be betrothed to Edward by now, her future mapped out for her and she would not have met Jack. Chiltern or de Saint-Gilbert or Faucon, it did not matter; she loved him whatever his name. But she did have two regrets: Judith had died needlessly and Jack was married. Both gave her nightmares.

Marie, the maid Nanette had assigned to her, returned with her petticoat and dress and laid them on the bed. 'Shall I brush your hair, *ma'amselle*?' Her voice impinged on Kitty's reverie and she shook her sad thoughts from her. She must think of happy things, of

James and their coming reunion. He was obviously staying at the castle and expected back so it would not be long now.

She sat in her shift and petticoat while the maid did her best with her hair, which was inclined to be wayward and would not stay where it was put. Since Judith had cut it, it curled all over her head like a mop. 'Do you wish for powder?' the servant asked. 'It might help it to stay down.'

'No, thank you. A ribbon band will suffice.'

Her reflection in the glass revealed a much thinner Kitty Harston than the one who had set out on what she had so naively called high old adventure, but it suited her, made her look older. She supposed she had matured. In a few short weeks she had changed from a schoolgirl into a woman. She stood up and allowed herself to be helped into her gown, then slipped on some pumps which Judith had packed for her and picked up her fan. 'I am ready.'

Chapter Six

Kitty was conducted downstairs and along a wide corridor to a large room which overlooked terraced gardens, just beginning to show the green shoots of spring. It was luxuriously furnished, making her wonder again how it had escaped the ministrations of the *sans-culottes*.

At first she thought she was alone, but a slight sound made her turn and she saw Jack standing by a bookcase with an open book in his hand. He had shaved and changed into black superfine breeches with white silk stockings and buckled shoes. His black velvet coat had diamond buttons; his jabot of fine lace cascaded over his embroidered blue waistcoat and ruffles of lace fell over his wrists. His hair, washed and brushed to a black sheen, was unpowdered and held back by a velvet ribbon. She was surprised that he had such finery in his small valise. Did it mean he meant to come here all along?

He bowed formally. '*Ma'amselle.*'

She curtsied. '*Monsieur.* I may call you *monsieur* now and not citizen?'

'You may call me Jack, as you have been doing for

the past few weeks.' He put the book back on the shelf and walked towards her, surveying her from her dainty feet to her mop of dark curls and smiled. 'The cygnet has become an elegant swan and I am overwhelmed.'

It was true. He had always thought her beautiful in a gamine sort of way, an innocent, but now she took his breath away. Here was no schoolgirl, but a woman of startling attractions. The oval shape of her face, the expressive eyes, the firm mouth and clear-cut brows, the heavenly curved body filled him with desire.

He had not been unaware of it when he held her in his arms each night, trying to keep her warm, to comfort her when nightmares invaded her sleep, but it was easier to think of her as a child. He could only thank God for the rough clothes, the lack of hot water to wash, the cold, and her fear of the bad dreams that had brought out the gentler side of his nature. Why had she come into his life when she had? The timing of it was all wrong. What future could they have?

'Kitty…' He took a step towards her, just as the door opened and Nanette came into the room, and whatever he had been going to say remained unsaid.

Nanette, innocently unaware that she had interrupted anything, crossed the carpet and took both Kitty's hands in her own and held them out to look at her. 'Why, you are quite lovely,' she said. 'Jack, how could you bear to disguise her in that horrible garb she arrived in?'

'It had to be done,' he said. 'Paris is a hotbed of revolutionaries. No one is safe.'

'So Jamie told me, which was why he decided to come back with Papa after his visit to Paris last year.'

'And found the delights of Haute Saint-Gilbert so beguiling he forgot he was supposed to meet me in Paris,' Jack said. 'It was damnably inconsiderate of him.'

'He said there was plenty of time,' she said, blushing and looking down at the toe of her slipper, peeping out from the hem of her gathered satin skirt. 'He did not expect you so soon and he was not to know his sister would come looking for him, was he?'

Jack smiled, noticing the flush in her cheeks. 'Oh, I see. That is the way the wind blows, is it? And what does my illustrious Uncle Louis think of that?'

'He is perfectly at ease with it. James is the grandson of an English viscount, after all, and he is a very presentable young man.'

'With no prospects.'

Kitty could not let that go. '*Monsieur*, I protest. Prospects are not everything, if two people are in love. He will come into something from our grandfather, even if it is not a great deal.'

'I was not referring to material wealth, so much as his penchant for hurling himself into every adventure that comes his way with no thought for the outcome,' Jack said; then, to Nanette, 'Where is he now? What is this meeting all about?'

Nanette shrugged. 'I do not know.'

'You think he is in danger?' Kitty asked. 'Oh, I don't think I could bear it if anything happened to him.'

'What is going to happen?' said a booming voice from the door.

All three looked round to see a portly man in a square-cut blue frockcoat, short brocade waistcoat and cream cashmere breeches. His hair was long and heavily powdered.

'Papa, look who is here,' Nanette said. 'Jack has brought Jamie's sister to stay with us.'

'His sister, eh?' The Marquis advanced into the room

and stood facing Kitty before inclining his head towards her. *'Enchanté, ma'amselle.'*

Kitty curtsied. 'My lord.'

'Hush, child, there are no titles now. I am citizen along with everyone else.' He turned to Jack and held out his hand. 'Good to see you, boy. How goes it in Paris?'

'Bad, I'm afraid. Anarchy. Hangings and beheadings and likely to be worse before it is better.'

'That is precisely why I keep my head down. I give the peasants most of what they want and they leave us alone, it is as simple as that.' He paused. 'You were speaking of that pup Harston, I believe?'

'Yes. Miss Harston has travelled all the way from London to find him and now it seems he has gone off on some errand of his own. She is concerned for his safety.'

'Oh, he is safe enough under my patronage. He has only gone to his club.'

'And what club would that be? It wouldn't be counter-revolutionary, would it?'

The Marquis laughed. 'Now, you know me for a patriot, Jack. Would I countenance a counter-revolutionary under my roof?' He turned to take Kitty's hand and pat it. 'Now don't worry, my dear, he will be back tomorrow and you will be reunited with him. But I am curious to know why you found it necessary to venture so far in search of him.'

'Here is *maman*,' Nanette said, as her mother came into the room, saving Kitty from having to reply immediately. 'Mama, this is Miss Kitty Harston.' She giggled and pointed at Jack. 'And this is citizen Jacques Faucon, a perfect stranger to me.'

The Marchioness, unlike her husband, was very tall

and thin, and made taller by the two feathers which she wore on a band in her hair. The hair itself was thick and dressed in fat round curls. Her brown taffeta was striped horizontally with red satin ribbon. A white silk shawl covered her shoulders and upper arms. She wore a quizzing glass on a ribbon about her neck and now picked it up to examine Kitty.

'How do you do, my dear. You are very welcome. As for you…' She turned to Jack. 'Still playing at charades, nephew? What was it last year? A colonel in the… What regiment was it? I forget.'

He grinned and went to kiss her on both cheeks. 'It was the National Guard, Aunt Anne-Marie.'

'And now you are dressed like a turkey cock. Such finery in this day and age. Dear me, you are taking a risk, are you not?'

'I have changed since I arrived, Aunt. You would not have had me at your table dressed as a *sans-culottes*, unshaven and dirty.'

'No. I do not believe in this universal lowering of standards. France was always a civilised country and I deplore what is happening to her. But I believe supper is ready, so we will adjourn to the dining room and you can tell us all about it.' She offered her arm to her nephew and he escorted her in to supper, while the Marquis followed between the two young ladies.

The food was better than anything Kitty had tasted since leaving England, but it was certainly not a banquet. 'I am sorry for such poor fare,' the Marchioness said. 'But even here, we have been beset by shortages and it does not do for our servants to report to those who govern us that we live a life of luxury. We have had to tighten our belts.'

'It is quite delicious,' Kitty murmured, tucking into

roast chicken in a light creamy sauce and several kinds
of vegetable. If this was belt-tightening, what was it like
in the old days?

'Now, Jack,' the Marquis said. 'Tell us everything.
How did Miss Harston meet you and persuade you to
bring her here?'

While they ate, Jack told the tale very simply, saying
nothing about their habit of sharing a room, making
their journey sound almost commonplace. Kitty was
quizzed about her reasons for leaving home and, though
she tried to explain, she sensed their condemnation of
her conduct for which she could hardly blame them.

They did not understand about her stepmother and
she didn't think they believed that nothing had happened between her and Jack, especially as she blushed
crimson whenever she mentioned that journey. He had
done nothing but hold her, but if he had kissed her
again, caressed her as a lover, she might very well have
allowed her own burgeoning passion to get the better
of her. Young ladies of quality were not supposed to
feel passion, were they?

But he hadn't made any advance at all. Oh, she knew
he loved his wife and guessed that he was not the sort
of man to take his marriage vows lightly but, apart from
that kiss on board the cross-Channel packet, he had
given no indication that he found her desirable, that he
had even been tempted. His compliments were always
teasing and not meant to be taken seriously. He looked
on her as an overgrown child and had kissed her to
teach her a lesson. The knowledge did nothing for her
self-confidence.

'And you lost your maid,' Nanette said. 'It must have
been dreadful. However did you manage to dress?'

'Dressing was not the problem—after all, I could

only wear peasant clothes. The worst of it was the manner of her death. I am afraid it still gives me nightmares.'

'*Ma pauvre,*' Nanette murmured. 'No wonder you wanted to find James. He will be here tomorrow or the day after and will be very surprised to see you, I think.'

Jack smiled. James would be astonished and, if he guessed aright, not particularly pleased. Having to take his sister home would curtail whatever he was up to, political or personal.

'And you, Jack,' his aunt put in, 'what are your plans? Will you spend some time with us?'

'I think I will go into Lyons tomorrow and bring James back,' Jack said, smiling at her. 'The sooner he takes his sister home the better.'

Kitty's heart sank. He wanted to be rid of her after all; though she loved her brother dearly, he would be no substitute for the man she really loved. A married man. She must never allow herself to forget that.

He had gone by the time she rose next morning and he did not come back that night. Although her host and hostess were polite and pretended to make her welcome, she felt undercurrents of disapproval, of tension. She was sure they would be glad when she left. If only Jack had taken her with him, they could have shared whatever danger was out there…if danger there was. In the isolated château above the peaceful village, it was difficult to imagine there was conflict all around them.

The following day Nanette suggested a walk and Kitty was happy to agree. She felt stifled in the house and decided a little fresh air might make her feel better.

They put on hats, coats and half-boots and set off up the slope behind the château into the forest.

The days were becoming longer and warmer. The scent of hyacinths filled the borders near the house; early clematis was already covering the walls of the château and the bougainvillea and jasmine were in bud. On the slopes, the vines were green and down in the valley the fields were beginning to reveal shoots of corn, peas and beans.

'You know,' Kitty said when they had been walking in silence for several minutes. 'I never did know how Jack and James came to know each other. I thought James was in Italy. Is that where they met?'

'No, it was in Paris last year. Jamie told me about it.' She took Kitty's arm as she spoke. 'He is very resourceful and brave, you know.'

'Jack?'

She laughed. 'Jack, too, but I meant Jamie. He saved Jack's life. Didn't Jack tell you?'

'No. I didn't even know he was in France last year. I met him in London and assumed he had been there some time. He did speak of his home in Wiltshire and I thought…' She stopped. She had already made too many false assumptions about Jack Chiltern and here was another proved wrong.

'Oh, he comes and goes all the time. I am not quite sure what he does, it is better not to ask, but I think he has been helping *emigrés* to escape. He was caught last year, did you know?'

'No.'

'He was denounced and the Guard went to arrest him at our town villa in the rue Saint-Honoré, where he had been staying with Papa. Papa had gone to Paris to see the King and speak to citizen Danton. He thought he might act as an intermediary but the King was arrested…'

'What has that to do with my brother?'

'Jamie was in the street when Jack was brought out of the house. He told me he was on his way to visit him. He had an introduction from a mutual friend and he thought Jack might show him the sights. He also intended to write a first-hand account of what was happening under the Revolutionary Government for the English newspapers.'

It was typical of her brother to discount the fact that the city was full of unrest and violence and seize on what he saw as an opportunity to make a name for himself. 'Then what? Did James rescue him?'

'Not right away, there were half a dozen guards and they were all armed. He followed them to the Conciergerie prison and later bribed a guard to lend him his uniform. When Jack was brought out to be taken to his trial, Jamie said he had been ordered to take charge of the escort.

'He pretended to treat him roughly and knocked him to the ground. Then, when he hauled him up again, he whispered who he was and cut his bonds with a knife he had in his belt. Before they reached the Palais de Justice, they overpowered the other two guards and dived into the river. I believe shots were fired, but neither was hit and they crawled out half a mile downstream.'

'Goodness, what a tale! I wonder why Jack did not speak of it?'

'I expect he found it difficult. You see, the woman who denounced him was his wife, Gabrielle.'

Kitty stopped walking and turned to face Nanette, her

face betraying her shock. 'Oh, no! How dreadful! Surely she would not do such a thing?'

'I think Jack is convinced she was forced into it. You see, Gabrielle's father, the *comte* de Malincourt, was one of the *ci-devant* King's most useful courtiers and was privy to a great many of his secrets. After the Revolution began in eighty-nine, he was in danger of arrest and Jack persuaded him to take his family to England. They lived in one of the Earl of Beauworth's properties in London.'

'Earl of Beauworth?'

'Jack's father.'

'His father is an Earl?' Kitty gasped.

'Yes, did you not know?'

'No, he told me his name was Jack Chiltern.'

'So it is. Chiltern is the family name. He is Viscount Chiltern. His name is John, but as that is also his father's name, he is called Jack by the family.'

'I had no idea,' Kitty said. So the mysterious Jack Chiltern was of noble birth. Why was she surprised? Shouldn't she have guessed? She had called him arrogant, but that was how he had been brought up, to command, to lead, to stand no nonsense from those below him and that included her. 'And is he really your cousin?'

'Yes, that is true. Mama and his mother are sisters. Aunt Justine went to live in England when the Earl married her. He wasn't the Earl then, of course, his father was still alive. He inherited the title when Jack was a boy and then Jack, who is an only child, became the Viscount. Is that not the way of English nobility; the son takes his father's lesser title?'

'In some cases, yes. But I never heard anyone call

Jack…' she paused to correct herself '…his lordship by his title.'

Nanette smiled. 'It is not a good idea to admit to being an aristocrat in France at this moment, especially an English one. I think you had better forget I told you. It is dangerous knowledge.'

'I shall certainly say nothing. I would not for the world put him in danger. But if his wife was in England, how did she betray him?'

'Gabrielle was abducted by someone from our Embassy in London on one occasion when she was visiting her parents. She sometimes used to leave Jack at home on their country estate in Beauworth and stay with them in London. I think she found country life a little dull.'

'Abducted? But why?'

'Well, nothing was said officially and I do not think the Revolutionary Government would ever have admitted they had a hand in her disappearance, but I suppose they thought they could hold her hostage to force the *comte* to return to France and stand trial. Naturally, Jack went after her. Papa said they must have freed her on condition she led them to him.'

'And James saved him. I am very proud of my brother for that. But what happened then?'

Nanette shrugged. 'I don't know. Papa deemed it prudent to leave Paris and return home and James came with him. He feared he might be arrested for his part in Jack's escape and he also wanted to write about the counter-revolutionaries in this part of France. We heard nothing of Jack and assumed he had taken Gabrielle back to England.'

'No, he told me he thought she was in France. I assumed he was still looking for her.'

'Oh, then that accounts for him not coming back last

night. He would have gone to Malincourt to see if she had gone to her old home. It is only ten kilometres from here. But I should be surprised if he found her there. No one lives there now and the land has been sold off in small lots.'

'He loved her very much, then?' The words were wrung out of her, though she could not keep the huskiness from her voice. She tried pretending it was the result of the attempted hanging, but she could not deceive herself.

'Oh, yes. You should have seen them when they were first married—so close, they had eyes only for each other. He showered her with gifts and even lived in France rather than England because she didn't like the English climate, but the Revolution changed all that and they had to return to England. How Gabrielle came to fall into the clutches of the man at the Embassy, I do not know.'

Kitty felt wretched. Nanette's revelations had helped her to understand the man beneath the rough exterior, but left her feeling desolate. His love was for his wife. His careful protection of her on their long journey was no more than a heightened sense of chivalry. When he rescued her from those bloodthirsty women and looked after her, when he warmed her with his own body, when he paid the exorbitant prices demanded for food and lodging for her, he had been doing no more than repay the debt he owed her brother for his life. A life saved for a life saved.

'He is a wanted man, then?' she said. 'No wonder he took such great care to play the *sans-culottes*.'

Nanette laughed. 'And made you play it too. Oh, Kitty, what adventures you have had. I think you are very brave. I know I should not have been able to do it.'

'Now we are here, what do you suppose he means to do?'

'Has he not told you?'

'No. He has undertaken to reunite me with James, no more. My brother and I have still to leave the country.'

'True, and it will be even more difficult now. In the last few weeks, there have been even more repressive measures passed by the ruling committees in Lyons. They are so afraid of counter-revolution they have ordered the National Guard to arrest anyone they consider suspect and that includes anyone without a passport.'

'Oh, but I have one of those.' Kitty laughed in spite of her low spirits. 'In the name of citizeness Kitty Faucon. Jack keeps it with his.'

Nanette stared at her with her mouth open in surprise, then she laughed delightedly. 'Oh, how clever of him! But it is doubtless forged?'

'Yes, but it served me well whenever we were asked for it.'

'You had Jack with you then.'

'Yes, but James will be with me on the return journey.' Although she spoke with confidence, she knew James was not Jack and his French was only a little better than hers. Without Jack the journey would be doubly difficult. Without Jack she would be miserable, even if there were no danger at all.

'Yes, Jamie must go with you.' Nanette's voice was wistful.

'Oh, you must think me very selfish,' Kitty said, taking Nanette's arm, as they picked their way over fallen pine needles. 'Of course, you do not want him to leave.'

'Oh, I do. And he must,' Nanette cried. 'I think he

has become very involved with politics here and that could be very dangerous. There are counter-revolutionaries plotting to overthrow the regime and restore the monarchy and he goes to their meetings.'

'Is that where he was going when he left here?'

'Yes, I think so. He says it is only so that he can write it all down to make a book, but no one is going to believe that. If they catch him, they will say he is spying. I am very afraid for him. You must make sure he leaves with you.'

'You could come with us.'

'I would not leave my parents. We are in no danger as long as we do as we are told. Papa has been forced to give nearly all his money to the poor and waived his seigneural dues. He is accepted as a good patriot.'

'Poor Nanette,' Kitty said softly. 'You are torn between them, aren't you?'

'Yes, but I know where my duty lies. And I have always been a dutiful daughter.'

Kitty laughed suddenly. 'And I have not. And look what has happened to me.'

'I did not mean that as a criticism of you, Kitty. You have no parents living and we are very different in character, are we not? I have not half your courage and independence.'

'Nonsense. You have not yet been tested, that is all.'

'Then I hope I never am.' She paused. 'Now, I think we have gone far enough, don't you? Let us turn for home. Perhaps they will both be back.'

Jack returned in the middle of the afternoon without James. He looked tired and was not in the best of tempers. 'The silly young fool has gone off to rally the other sections and communes to join the federalists,' he told Kitty and Nanette. They had seen him coming from an upper window and had gone down to the hall to meet him. 'He is asking for trouble. They will never unite, they differ too much about what they want to achieve.'

'Someone ought to let the world know what is going on,' Kitty said. 'If he wants to write about it, then he needs to be in among them. It doesn't make him a conspirator.'

'Write about it!' he scoffed. He had been riding hard and his scuffed boots and long coat were covered in caked mud. He had been looking forward to a bath and was not in the mood to be cross-examined. 'Stirring up the populace with rumour and plots and inciting them to rise against their elected rulers will achieve nothing and will only bring the wrath of the National Assembly down on them.'

'Is that what he is doing?' she asked, becoming alarmed for her brother's safety.

'So I am led to believe. They are too disorganised to succeed and it will only result in the chaos we have seen in Paris.'

'I am surprised at you,' Kitty said, a little waspishly. 'If they need organising, why are you not doing it? People listen to you. You are—'

'I am an Englishman and it is not my business,' he interrupted her. Better she should think him indifferent than know the truth. The less she knew, the safer she was. 'Nor should it be your brother's. He is interfering in what does not concern him.'

'I do not understand you,' she said. 'When we were in Paris, I was sure you were a Royalist, now I begin to wonder…'

'The King is dead, that is a fact. And the country must be brought to peace. James has been in the country less than a year, how can he understand? This is not England. It is nothing like England and it is useless to try and impose English thinking on French people who have been sorely tried over a great many years. And they are afraid.'

'At least James is trying.' She didn't know why she was arguing with him when in many ways she agreed with him. It was not what she wanted to do. She wanted...she wanted him. She loved a man who loved his wife and loved his duty even more; there was no place in his life for her. England and home suddenly seemed very desirable and very far away.

'Very trying,' he said laconically.

'You are in a very disagreeable mood,' Nanette said. 'Have you been to Malincourt?'

He looked at her sharply. 'What made you say that?'

'I thought you might have gone there to look for Gabrielle and that has made you miserable.'

'Gabrielle.' There was a ragged tone to his voice which betrayed his emotion; he was not as cold and hard as he would have them believe. 'She is not at Malincourt. Now, if you will excuse me, I must change.' He bowed to both girls and left them looking at each other in bewilderment.

'I told you, didn't I?' Nanette said, as soon as he had gone. 'Jamie is involved with the counter-revolutionaries. Oh, I wish he would come back, then Jack would persuade him to leave.'

'And what about Gabrielle? Would Jack go without her?'

'I don't know. If he has no idea where she is...'

'In that case he must be worried to death,' Kitty said.

Jack's worries had nothing to do with his wife, they were for Kitty. He sat in the hip bath which had been brought up to his room and took stock of a situation which was rapidly getting out of hand.

He was half-French, half-English, and he hated this war, but not so much as he loathed the despots who had taken over his beloved France and made it into a place of fear and reprisal. When he told Nanette and Kitty that he wanted peace, he had been telling the truth, but not peace at any price, not if it meant destroying everything that was great and good.

He had been instructed to see that James returned to England before he clumsily upset everything, but obeying that was secondary to his orders to scout out the strength of the Royalist faction, to find out what they needed and which of the leading men could be relied upon to welcome British intervention, if it were offered.

Admiral Hood was in the Mediterranean with the British fleet and he was successfully blockading the port of Toulon and preventing essential food stuffs, including the desperately needed grain, from reaching the people. How far were they prepared to go to obtain those supplies? Would they welcome an invasion for bread to put in their children's mouths?

And he had no orders at all about Miss Kitty Harston. Kitty. She was rapidly undermining his ability to think dispassionately, to function as an agent. What should have been his last concern had become his first. He loved her.

In spite of his promise to himself never to let another woman rule his heart, to stick rigidly to what he conceived to be his duty, he had succumbed to those deep violet eyes and inviting mouth. But, more than that, he loved the person she was, bright, independent and thoroughly infuriating.

When he first met her, he had thought of her only as a spoiled child, used to having her own way, protected from the evils of the world to such an extent she could not recognise danger even when it was thrust under her nose. To a degree that was right, but she was far from unintelligent and she had learned quickly. Now he knew he could trust her in a tight situation and she would not panic; there had been enough sticky moments on their journey to convince him of that.

And every day he had grown closer to her, admired her more, chided her less, and every day he had been tempted to tell her that he loved her. But he could not. Once the words were out of his mouth, she would change, just as Gabrielle had changed. She would become the tyrant and he would be like clay in her hands. He could not afford to lose control. If she were arrested and let it be known, however inadvertently, that he loved her, they might use it, use it as bait as they had used Gabrielle. Except his wife had co-operated willingly.

On the other hand, could he rely on James to take Kitty safely home? James would turn aside whenever the opportunity for fresh adventure showed itself. His presence among the counter-revolutionaries proved that. Did James think he led a charmed life and nothing could touch him? He was in for a rude awakening if he did. He might very well forfeit his life. And Kitty's.

The bath water was becoming cold and he heaved himself out of it and towelled himself dry. He must finish his business, find James and take them both south to Toulon. There were allied sympathisers there who would help them to join the British fleet.

Dressed once more in respectable breeches and stockings, a clean white shirt and neckcloth and striped waistcoat, he shrugged himself into a frockcoat and went down to join the ladies. Kitty was alone in the withdrawing room.

'Nanette not here?' he queried.

'No, my lord...'

'Oh, it's my lord now, is it? What happened to Jack?'

'I don't know. He has gone. He disappeared when Nanette told me who you really are. I had no idea you were Viscount Chiltern and the son of an Earl. Why didn't you tell me?'

'Would it have made any difference if I had?'

'No, I suppose not,' she said slowly. She would still have fallen in love with him.

'Then, I beg of you, forget it. Titles are never mentioned in France unless they have *ci-devant* in front of them.'

'One time,' she translated. 'No, there is nothing of the past about you.'

He laughed and took her hand to kiss it, sending shivers of desire coursing through her. To hide her confusion, she turned away from him just as the door opened and the Marquis joined them.

'My boy, there you are. Tell me the latest news...'

Kitty became increasingly concerned for her brother over the next few weeks. According to Jack, he had been seen in one place, heard of in another, was reported to be riding south, then north, then west to the Vendée where there were other counter-revolutionaries. 'Mind, it might not be James,' he told Kitty one day when they were walking in the garden with no other company but each other.

Neither was prepared to speak of what was in their hearts. To do so would have set off an avalanche of emotions which would engulf them and leave them gasping, unable to continue the roles they had set themselves. Keeping their relationship on an impersonal level was the only way they could survive.

It was almost midsummer and the flowers in the untended garden were a riot of colour: red geraniums, mauve bougainvillea, bright yellow mimosa, heavily scented jasmine. The uncut grass was parched and brown, and the roses a tangle of thorns and spilled petals. Kitty could imagine it in its heyday before the gardeners had disappeared.

'He is not using his own name,' Jack went on. 'And I have only a description which is vague to say the least.'

He did not add that there was a price on the Englishman's head and the people were so poor that they would denounce anyone for a precious loaf of bread.

'Does he know I am here?' Kitty asked him. 'Have you been able to send a message to him?'

'I dare not. It is impossible to know whom to trust.'

'But he is safe?'

'I have heard nothing to the contrary.' Which was an evasive answer, but the only one he was prepared to give.

'He will come back to Nanette, I am sure. He loves her. Love is the greatest force of all, don't you think?'

He smiled wryly, looking down into her upturned face and forcing himself not to succumb to the urge to kiss her again, to enjoy the taste of her lips, the feel of her clinging to him as she had done that first time. 'And naturally, you know all about it.'

'I…' She stopped, unable to go on.

'Love is a tyranny,' he said. 'It commands obedience, it stifles free will, it makes a man act irrationally.'

'How cynical you are,' she said, wondering why he was so vehement about it if he loved his wife so dearly. 'But I do not think you mean it.'

'Oh, I do, believe me, and I have more important things on my mind than love. If I cannot find James in the next two days, we must leave without him.'

'Why? What has happened? Are we not safe here?'

'For the moment, but the situation is changing all the time and we shall soon have outstayed our welcome. I cannot put my uncle at risk. He is not a man who enjoys risk, which is why he has obeyed all the edicts of the Revolutionary government in return for being allowed to keep his home but...'

'That might change? Is it because of what James is doing?'

She was extraordinarily perspicacious, he decided. James was stirring up a hornet's nest and the outcome, if the bees buzzed too noisily, would be civil war. He dreaded that.

'No, not altogether. I have heard that General Dumouriez has been driven back from the Netherlands and instead of rallying his army for a counter-attack, he tried to persuade them to march on to Paris and restore the monarchy. Louis's young son is still held in the Temple prison, you know; he is the rightful king. But the troops refused to follow him and Dumouriez has fled to the allies. His desertion has started a wave of anti-Royalist agitation.'

'Is that not good?'

'No. A Committee of Public Safety and a Revolutionary Tribunal have been set up in Paris to prevent any more dissension. I hear the guillotine is becoming increasingly busy.'

'But that is Paris, not here.'

'Like a plague, it will spread. Representatives have been despatched throughout the country to make sure its decrees are obeyed and enforce the conscription of all able-bodied men into the army. Soon they will be combing this district and our presence here will not remain a secret much longer. Any strong young man not in uniform will be suspect.

'Already there is a brand new guillotine in Lyons ready to execute the so-called enemies of equality, hoarders, capitalists, members of the nobility and priests who refuse to conform.' He smiled wryly. 'Not to mention Englishmen and women.'

'You are worried on my behalf?'

'Naturally I am. Until I find your brother, you are my responsibility.'

'How can that be? I forced myself on you. It was not your choice.'

'What would you have me do?' he asked, his mouth lifting in the ghost of a smile. She was the most provocative woman he had ever met. 'Should I have left you to hang? Should I abandon you now?'

'You could.'

'Don't think I haven't thought of that,' he said grimly. 'But I must also consider my uncle and aunt.'

'I am sorry,' she said. 'Nanette told me the Marquis has already forfeited his title and his dues as a *seigneur* in order to appease the local government. She said they were safe as long as they did as they were told.'

'Perhaps they are, but we are not helping by being here.'

'You are suspect?'

He smiled grimly. 'Jack Chiltern may be. Jacques Faucon is a true patriot.'

She giggled. 'Are you still using that ridiculous name?'

'Of course. It is what keeps us safe. For the moment.'

'Does anyone know Jacques Faucon is staying here at the château?'

'No, I do not think so. I live in a labourer's cottage on the far side of the estate and make a living rearing pigs and growing cabbages.'

'But then who am I? How did I arrive here?'

'You are simply a visitor, a relative staying with the family. My uncle brought you back with him from Paris last year.'

'I see. He brought a young lady back, not a man.' She laughed suddenly. 'I could say I came disguised as a boy—my brother and I are alike.'

He was forced to smile, though the situation was serious. 'I sincerely hope you are not thinking of repeating your playacting performance at the Paris barriers, my dear.'

'No, I have learned my lesson. But do you think we might be questioned?'

'It is always possible.' He reached for her hand, making her shiver with pleasure. His touch always affected her like that, but he seemed totally unaware of it. 'While you are here, you are not citizeness Faucon, but Catherine Gilbert, a distant cousin of the Marquis, do you understand? It is why I keep your passport. If it was found in your possession...' He stopped.

'I understand. I know nothing of Jacques Faucon. I have never heard of him.'

'Good. I am leaving now for a last look for James. I should be back in two days. Be ready to leave.'

There were visitors to the château the day after he had gone: six men in grubby pantaloons and red caps with tricolour cockades pinned to them. They had muskets in their hands and pistols in their belts. Kitty kept herself hidden while they spoke to the Marquis, the Marchioness and Nanette and, although they left soon afterwards, apparently satisfied with the answers they had received, they served to reinforce what Jack had said. There was danger everywhere.

She stood on the gallery above the vestibule as the Marquis and his wife watched them leave. 'She can't stay here,' he said, turning to come back into the house. 'She'll have to go. We should never have let Jack persuade us to take her in. We have to think of our own skins…'

Kitty did not wait to hear any more. She ran to her room, changed into her old peasant skirt and packed everything else in her basket; Nanette would come looking for her soon and she must make haste. She scribbled a letter to her host and hostess, then went down the back way to the stables and hitched Samson to the old carriage, thankful that Jack had taught her how to do it while they had been on the road and had even allowed her to drive along some of the better roads.

Carefully she drew out of the yard and started off down the steep, winding hill. This was the most dangerous time because in some places the road could be seen from the château and from the town and she was not sure how far the guards had gone. But she passed no one except the lazy roadmender who sat beside his heap of stones, smoking a clay pipe and surveying the scenery as if filling holes was the last thing on his mind.

Remembering the alternative road she had seen from above the château, she decided to take that. It was more wooded and less open to prying eyes and with luck she would join the main road in the valley without being seen. From then on, she would have to say she had come direct from Paris. Her destination was... Where could she possibly be going? Italy. If she could cross the border, she would be safe.

But what about James? And Jack Chiltern? Jack was resourceful enough to survive, especially when he did not have her to hinder him. He would be glad she was no longer his responsibility and he could go and search for his wife with a clear conscience.

She did not consider how and when she would eat, where she would sleep, what she would do for money. She had not used any of her own since Jack had taken charge of her; he had even returned the sovereign she had left with the Claviers, saying it was useless. But it was gold, wasn't it? Someone must accept it. And she had a pearl necklace her grandfather had given her—that might fetch something.

The road she had taken was even worse than the other one, steep and twisting, and she sat on the driving seat, hanging on for all she was worth, allowing the old horse to pick his own way down. She shouldn't be here, she should never have come, never allowed Jack Chiltern to bring her here. It was a wild goose chase. He had no idea where her brother was and even less idea of how she felt.

She loved him. Hopelessly. She hated him, too, for making her love him. She hated France. She hated this dreadful flannel skirt which made her itch, hated the horrible red cap. She pulled it off and flung it into the trees. She hated the women who had killed Judith, a kind gentle soul who had never done anyone any harm. She hated her brother for disappearing, Edward Lampeter for kissing her.

It was that kiss that started it and another which had

enslaved her. Jack had said love was a tyrant; well, he was right there. She felt so helpless and lonely and so angry, she was weeping. Tears cascaded down her face, as the old carriage rumbled on. She did nothing to wipe them away, was hardly aware of them.

Immersed in misery for which she could blame no one but herself, she plodded on until she suddenly became aware that the track had widened; lying by the side of the road was a pair of iron gates, pulled off their hinges and flung into the undergrowth. She scrubbed at her tear-streaked face with the edge of her skirt and urged Samson on, but then she caught sight of the name interwoven in the scrolling of the gate: Malincourt. Looking to her left, she saw a weed-encrusted drive at the end of which stood a château.

Curiosity quenched her anger. She turned and went in past the gates. Nanette had been right; the house was much bigger than the Saint-Gilbert château. Its turrets soared above the surrounding trees; it must have once been very grand. But now weeds and overgrown shrubs had encroached almost up to the building itself.

Every window was broken, the great front door missing and the walls smoke-blackened. She stopped and climbed down, hitching the horse to an overgrown lilac bush. Picking her way over broken glass, roof tiles and smashed furniture, she stepped into the hall. It was black with soot and littered with debris and she could see the darkening sky through its roof. There wasn't a whole piece of furniture, a picture or an ornament left. She supposed they had been looted.

No wonder Jack had been in such a miserable mood. It was enough to break anyone's heart. She turned to go, to leave the place to its ghosts, but it was growing dark and she could not continue without the risk of toppling the horse and carriage into a pothole or turning it over the side of the road down the steep mountainside. She would find a corner to sleep in and go on in the morning.

The stable at the back still had its roof and it was big enough to hide the horse and the carriage. There was a little straw there, too, and a trough of water, but no hay. Sensibly she had thought of that; the inside of the coach, besides her basket, contained a few armfuls of hay and some carrots which she had taken from the Saint-Gilbert stables. The horse was fed, but she remained hungry. Stealing food for herself had not occurred to her.

She looked after the animal and was about to make herself comfortable in the straw when a sound disturbed her. She whirled round to find herself face to face with a man in the garb of a *sans-culottes* who blocked the doorway. He carried a musket which he was pointing at her. She froze.

Chapter Seven

'She's in here, citizen Santerre,' he called to someone behind him. He stepped forward and walked round her as three more men entered.

'Who...who are you?' Kitty managed to ask, not daring to move, although her knees were shaking so much she was afraid they would let her down.

'We ask the questions,' a second man said. The cockade on his cap had a gold edging and she supposed that was a sign of authority. 'You are under arrest.'

'*Pourquoi?*'

'That we will discover when you have been questioned. It is enough that you are suspect. Come with us.' He grabbed her arm and dragged her out into the open where two more men waited on guard. It appeared they had arrived on foot; she supposed they were the men she had seen at the château. They must have looked back and seen her leave and followed her.

They harnessed the horse to the carriage again and bundled her inside. Two climbed in with her, two sat on the driver's seat and two more walked either side of the horse's head to guide it in the dark. And thus they arrived in Lyons just as dawn was breaking.

If Kitty had not been so immersed in her own seemingly insurmountable problems, she might have been able to admire the view from the steep cliffs above the city of Lyons. They were breathtaking. Lyons lay below them at the confluence of two rivers, the Saône and the Rhône, a sprawl of old and new, low red roofs, a church spire here and there, open tree-lined squares.

It was France's second city and, according to Jack, had always prided itself on its independence from the central government, but now all that was changing. Paris was dictating policy.

Jack. Had these men been looking for Jack when they found her? Jack Chiltern or Jacques Faucon? Did they think she would betray him? If so, they would be disappointed. She was alone now and, whatever she did, she must not implicate him or say anything to endanger the Saint-Gilberts. She must remember what Jack had told her. She was an innocent visitor. She had simply been out for a drive and was drawn to the deserted château out of curiosity.

She knew there were huge holes in her story that any good lawyer would probe, but she would have to trust to luck. She could protest her innocence, pretend to be younger than she was, perhaps a little simple. Would that do?

She did not need to force the tears that ran down her cheeks as the old carriage bumped down the mountain track, on to a lower road and into the old town, through its warren of narrow streets and alleys, to a small square lined with elegant old houses built for the town's rich bankers and silk weavers.

Years ago Kitty remembered her mother speaking of Lyons silk and showing her a lovely puce-coloured gown. What had happened to the silk weavers since the

Revolution? she wondered. Had they, like Jack's uncle, embraced the new regime or had they aligned themselves with the counter-revolutionaries?

Her captors, who smelled of sweat and drink, offered no conversation at all and seemed relieved to hand her over to the warder of the town prison when they arrived at its doors a few minutes later.

Here she was taken to a cell and locked in to await interrogation. She did not struggle; it was better to seem bemused. Her trial was the place to act the innocent. She would have a trial, wouldn't she?

Although the room was small, it was crowded. Men and women jostled for places to sit against the walls or stood to breathe what little air came from the tiny barred window. It was unbelievably hot and Kitty could feel the perspiration running between her shoulder blades, making her clothes stick to her.

One woman, dressed almost identically to everyone else in the cell in black skirt and red peasant blouse topped with a shawl in the ubiquitous colours of the Revolution, edged up to make room for her on a narrow bench. 'Another one for Madame Guillotine,' she said cheerfully. 'What are you accused of?'

'I don't know.' Kitty smiled wanly, trying not to retch from the stench which assailed her nostrils. 'They said I was being arrested on suspicion of being a suspect, which doesn't make sense, does it?'

The woman cackled. 'To them it does. You don't come from round here, I can tell by the way you speak. Up north, was it?'

'Yes.' No sense in saying she was English. In fact, the less she spoke the better. 'What are you accused of?'

'Hoarding flour. Two kilos I had in my cupboard.

Two kilos and me with ten mouths to feed. And my husband conscripted into the army.'

'Oh, that is terrible. Surely they will not condemn you for that?'

'I sent my eldest to fetch the *curé*. He'll speak up for me. I've done my share for the Revolution, they know that. I am hopeful.'

Kitty, who had no one to defend her, was not so sanguine of her own chances. She had had one taste of revolutionary justice already, she certainly did not want another. But this time she was not being tried by rioting women but a court of law. Surely her accusers would realise their mistake and set her free?

A very small plate of food was brought to everyone later in the day, but Kitty had no idea what the time was, except that the light was fading. The food was cooked in oil which was rank and she could not swallow it. There was nothing to lie on, nowhere to be comfortable, and she spent the night sitting on the bench with her back against the wall. Sleep was impossible.

She tried to pass the time thinking of summer in England, of her childhood and her mother, but that made her sad. She tried to think of what she would do when she returned home and that led to wondering if she would ever go home and made her sadder still. She listened to the woman beside her chattering until the *curé* came and the prisoner was released. Others in the cell were crying, others singing loudly and raucously to cover their fear.

Dawn came and the prisoners began to stir and scratch, making Kitty itch too. Some thin gruel was served to them, but it was greasy and tasted foul. As with the meal the night before Kitty gave hers away.

One by one, the prisoners were led out to be tried. One by one they came back, crying, screaming or numbly silent. It was late afternoon and Kitty was just beginning to think that she would have to spend another night in uncertainty, when her turn came.

She was marched to a large hall where three men, dressed in unrelieved black, sat at a table on a dais. At a table below them was another man whom she supposed was the clerk to the court: he had pen, ink and papers on the table in front of him. There was a dock and a public gallery, but she soon discovered that was as far as the system went in following normally accepted legal procedure.

Her jailer pushed her into the dock. 'Citizen Judge,' he said, addressing the man who sat in the centre of the three on the dais. 'This citizeness refuses to give her name and carries no passport. She was found looting at the Château Malincourt. Also she had stolen a horse and carriage, the carriage being that of the *ci-devant comte* de Malincourt, with the arms painted over. She was also carrying English gold coins.'

The judge peered down at her. She was weeping copious false tears and looking at her feet. 'What do you say to that?'

Kitty did not know what to say. The horse and carriage were not hers and to say where she had come by them would implicate Jack. As for the money, that was perhaps the most damning evidence of all. This was not suspicion of being a suspect, this was real evidence and she had no answer that would satisfy them.

The crowd began to shout. *'Traître! Traître! À la guillotine!'*

The clerk to the court shouted for silence and, when order had been restored enough for him to be heard, the judge spoke to Kitty. 'You are condemned by your own silence. Guilty! The sentence is death.'

That was too much. The tears were miraculously dried by anger. 'Am I not to be allowed to say anything in my own defence?'

'You were caught red-handed,' the judge went on. 'You have no defence. Take her away.'

The whole bizarre business had taken less than five minutes and she was dragged out and returned to her cell to await execution. It had happened so quickly, she thought it must be one of her nightmares, but after a few minutes back in the cell, the reality of her situation swept over her like a huge black cloud.

So this was the end. Was the guillotine quicker and more merciful than hanging? She was going to lose her life miles away from home, and no one would know what had become of her. Not her uncle, or James. Not even Jack. She had refused to give her name. She was going to die unknown and unmourned. Jack would never know how much she had loved him, or why she had decided to leave the château when he had told her not to. But at least she had not implicated him. He was safe.

'Damn it all,' James said for the hundredth time. He was riding up the winding road towards the Château de Saint-Gilbert beside Jack. The two men were wearing nondescript black clothing and were riding scrawny mounts which plodded along, as much affected by the heat as the men who had been riding all night and most of the morning.

James continually removed his tricorne hat to wipe

the sweat from his brow with his sleeve. He was a good-looking young man with short dark curls, brown eyes and a ready smile, features which young ladies found attractive and which he often used to charm his way out of trouble. And he seemed to invite trouble. How he had survived as long as he had was a mystery to Jack.

'Are you sure it is Kitty?'

'Of course I'm sure.'

'But I cannot imagine her running away. She's always been a dutiful little thing, wouldn't say boo to a goose...'

'When did you see her last?'

'Oh, it must have been three years ago, maybe more. I didn't go home very often when I was at Cambridge. Didn't like the old stepmama, don't you know. Then I went off on the Grand Tour and stopped off in Paris on the way home. You know all that.'

'I was only pointing out that she was a child when you last saw her, but she's a woman now. And a woman with a mind of her own.'

'Dangerous, that,' James mused. 'Women with minds of their own.'

'Quite. Which is why she must be got home as soon as possible.'

'You brought her. You take her home. In fact, I think you should. There'll be an almighty scandal.'

Jack turned in the saddle to look at the young man. Was he really as callous as he sounded? 'Don't you care?'

'Of course I care. She's m'sister, after all. But to bring her all this way unchaperoned...'

'I would not have done if you had stayed in Paris as we arranged.'

'The place got too hot for me.' He laughed. 'Now, I've got rather fond of your little cousin and…'

He stopped speaking as they approached the front of the château and the door was flung open. He dismounted as Nanette came running down the steps and threw herself into his arms. Jack, still sitting his horse, watched with a wry smile, wondering why Kitty had not also come out of the house to greet them.

'Oh, I am so pleased to see you safe, Jamie,' she cried. 'But now Kitty has disappeared.'

Jack was off his horse in an instant. 'Disappeared? When? What happened?'

'It was after the gendarmes came…'

'What did they want?'

'Something to do with capitation tax. They had heard we had a visitor. Papa told them what you said, that Mama's cousin's daughter, Catherine Gilbert, was staying with us for a week or two, but would soon be leaving.'

'And—' He could hardly contain his impatience. 'Did they see Kitty?'

'No. She stayed out of sight, but when they had gone I went to find her and she had disappeared. She left a note for Papa…'

Jack did not wait to hear more. He left the two young people to make their own way into the house and hurried to find his uncle.

'What's this about Kitty going off alone?'

The Marquis shrugged. 'Gone. Taken the old horse and carriage. Left a letter thanking me for my hospitality. Signed it Catherine.'

'That's all?'

'Yes.'

Jack squashed his mounting exasperation in favour of

action. Kitty must be found before she got herself and everyone else into more trouble. He turned went straight out of the house and remounted. There was only one road down the mountainside, discounting the track that went past Malincourt; she would not attempt that with the old top-heavy carriage.

Halfway down the hill he encountered the roadmender, shovelling stones into the potholes. 'If you're looking for the English *ma'amselle*,' he said without bothering with a greeting, 'she went down the old road.'

'The old road?' Jack drew up beside the man. 'Are you sure?'

'Yes.'

'God in heaven, she'd never make it. We'll find her at the bottom of the ravine.'

'No, she made it,' the man said laconically. 'With a little help.'

'Help—what do you mean?' His heart was thumping in his throat and he had to force himself not to go rushing off at half-cock.

'The local National Guard found her and escorted her down. Took her to Lyons gaol.'

'They arrested her?'

'Yes. Your cover's blown, old man. It's time to beat a hasty retreat.'

'Not without Kitty.'

'But they'll know everything by now. Who you are, what you are, what you know.'

'She knows nothing except my name.'

'And that's enough. Jack Chiltern was the man who engineered the escape of the Malincourts and that coach was last seen thundering along the road to Calais with the National Guard in hot pursuit. Now it's back at Malincourt and even these dimwits can add two and two.

Jack Chiltern is back in France...' He left the end of
the sentence unfinished.

'I'll lay odds she won't talk.'

'Then you've more faith in her than I have.'

'I'm going into Lyons. I've got to get her out.'

'You'll be putting your own head in the jaws of Madame Guillotine.'

'Then I die with Kitty. You can take the despatches
back to England.' He fetched a bundle of papers from
the capacious pocket of his frock coat and handed them
down to the roadmender.

'What are you going to do?'

'I don't know until I get there. If I succeed, I'll meet
you at your cottage and take those back.' He nodded at
the papers.

'You're mad, you know that, don't you?'

Jack laughed, wheeling his horse round. 'Tell James
to meet us at the cottage.' And with that he was gone.

Kitty heard the key grating in the lock and the door
opened. 'Where is the English bitch?' the turnkey demanded.

The woman next to her poked her in the side. 'I think
he means you.'

Kitty tried to stand. Her legs felt boneless and there
was a knot of pain in her stomach that almost doubled
her up; she did not know how she was going to walk.
She forced herself upright and stepped forward.

'Come with me,' the jailer said, grabbing her arm and
pushing her in front of him. 'This way.'

She shrugged him off to walk unaided. At least she
could die with dignity. Her shoulders went back and her
head went up. I am not afraid, she said to herself. Then,
aloud, 'I am not afraid.'

He laughed.

Outside in the street a horse and cart stood ready to convey her to the guillotine. Beside it stood Jack, looking very fierce in his red cap and dirty old greatcoat. Shocked to the core to see him, she stumbled and would have fallen if the jailer had not taken her arm again.

'She's all yours, citizen,' he said, pushing her towards Jack who gave her a look which told her to say nothing. Not that she could have uttered a word; she was too bewildered. Was Jack planning on a rescue from the very jaws of the guillotine? Oh, what a terrible risk. Especially when she had been at such pains not to involve him. But, oh, how glad she was to see him!

None too gently he grabbed her from the jailer. 'My thanks, citizen, though why I should bother my head with her, I do not know.'

'You're welcome. And if I were you I'd beat her for wasting everyone's time.'

'That I will do,' Jack said, grinning at him. 'Good day to you, citizen.' He picked Kitty up and heaved her into the cart with no more care than he would a sack of potatoes. 'Get in there with you, woman. And be quiet.'

He climbed up on the cross bench and Kitty felt the cart jolt into motion. 'Keep down,' he muttered in a low voice. 'The people will not like being deprived of their spectacle.'

They moved agonisingly slowly. Unable to see where they were going, she lay in the bottom of the cart, and gave thanks for her deliverance. Once again, Jack Chiltern had saved her life. But the risk to himself was enormous. Why had he bothered?

They left the town behind; she could no longer see buildings between the cracks in the side of the cart and the smooth road had become a rutted track, she could tell by the added jolting. Still she dare not lift her head. There were trees blotting out the sky now and she wondered if they were going back to the château of Saint-Gilbert. She ought to tell him what she had overheard; there would be no welcome there, she was sure.

'Jack, you must not—'

'Save the talking for later, madam,' he said so brusquely she felt it was wise to obey.

Half an hour later, he turned to look over his shoulder at her. She was crouched in the cart, looking crushed. He wanted desperately to soothe her, to comfort her, to tell her that he would go to the ends of the earth for her, but that would only make her think she could twist him round her little finger and behave with even less circumspection. It was too risky. 'You can sit up now, if you like.'

She scrambled up beside him and impulsively took his arm. For a moment he looked down at her and then put his arm about her shoulders and pressed her to him. His bulk and warmth enveloped her like a comforting mantle and she laid her head against his chest and allowed herself the luxury of feeling protected. He was her bulwark, strong and steadfast, and she needed someone like that. But sometimes she needed a little tenderness, too, and he did not seem able to provide that.

'Thank you,' she said, looking up at him. He was looking straight ahead, almost as if he were embarrassed by that simple show of affection.

'For what?'

'For saving my life again. Once more I am in your debt and I don't know how to thank you.'

He removed his arm and took up the reins in both hands again. 'You could try doing as you're told.'

She drew back from him and looked into his face, expecting thunderous looks to match his words, but there was no sign of anger, only a quiet desperation. 'I know. I am truly sorry. But I didn't know what to do. I couldn't stay at the château. I had to leave.'

'Why?'

'To protect you.'

'Protect me!' He laughed. 'How could you possibly protect me?'

'By relieving you of a responsibility you find onerous and because you were right, we had outstayed our welcome. Men came to question your uncle after you left; after they had gone I heard the Marquis say you should never have brought me to them and he had to think of the safety of everyone else. I dared not wait for you to return.'

'I half expected it. But my uncle satisfied them, I dare say.'

'I think so, but then I thought of the risk my presence was causing them and you and so I decided to leave.'

'And where did you think you were going?'

'To Italy. I thought if I could cross the frontier...'

'Without me? Without your brother?'

'You could not find him. And the longer you searched, the greater the risk.'

He grinned. 'You may set your mind at rest. Your brother is safe.'

'Why didn't you say so before?' she cried, eyes bright with eagerness. 'Where is he? Where did you find him? He's not in trouble, is he?'

'No more than he was before, but he will not leave

Nanette and has gone back to the château to try and persuade her to come with us.'

'Oh, no! He'll be caught, just as I was.' She paused, suddenly realising that no one at the château could have known she had been arrested. She had refused to give her name. And if that were so, how had Jack known where to look for her? 'How did you know where to find me?'

'You were seen leaving.'

'Oh, I was followed. I guessed as much. Those men were the same ones who had been at the château. They found me in the stables at Malincourt.'

He twisted in his seat to face her. 'What, in the name of all that's holy, were you doing there?'

'I was looking for somewhere to sleep for the night and I saw the gates and decided to go in.'

'The place is in ruins.'

'Yes, it must be very sad for you,' she said gently.

'Sadder for the *ci-devant comte* de Malincourt.'

'Yes, to be sure. Did you know that coach had once belonged to the *comte*?'

'Yes. We used it when we escaped the first time. We hid it in the barn of a deserted farm near Calais when we embarked for England. I remembered it when I needed a conveyance to get us to Paris.'

'You didn't want to take me to Paris, did you?'

'Of course not. But as soon as you knew your brother was there, you were determined to go, with or without me. I could not allow you to run into danger, which you surely would have done had you gone alone.'

'And then I did, in spite of your care. Oh, how angry you must have been that I had disobeyed you.'

'Not angry,' he said softly, remembering how he had felt when he had seen her hanging from the lantern.

'There was no time for anger and afterwards…' He shrugged and flicked the reins across the horse's back, though, if he were honest with himself, he did not want it to go any faster. He was content for the moment just to have her safely by his side again.

When he had learned that she had been arrested, it had taken all his self-control not to dash after her and make a scene in the courtroom. He had pictured her in a crowded cell and then put up before the court and all the onlookers baying for blood like so many thirsty hounds. His first task had been to discover how much was known about her and what she had been accused of and then to devise a plan.

'And then I went and did it again,' she said. 'How did you manage to save me this time? That jailer handed me over to you without a qualm. He was laughing.'

He smiled crookedly. 'I used the same story that worked before. I told them you were my foolish wife, a complete scatterbrain. You were in the forest gathering firewood when you came upon the old coach. It had obviously been abandoned and so you came home and fetched the horse and harnessed it up and brought it to our cottage.'

'How clever of you. They obviously believed you.'

'Yes, I said I had told you to put it back where you found it, that we could be in grave trouble if we kept it.'

'But what about my English sovereigns?'

'You found them hidden in the coach. We quarrelled when you wanted to keep them. You went off in a temper while I was working in the fields and I did not know you had gone until a neighbour came and told me you had been arrested.'

'I am so sorry, but the more I realise all the risks you have taken to rescue me, the more I wonder why.'

He threw back his head and laughed. 'I should have thought that was self-evident, you keep putting yourself in need of rescuing.'

'I am grateful, of course I am, but that doesn't answer my question. You did not need to do it. I have no claim on you.'

He smiled slowly. The claim she had was unbreakable; it tied him to her with bonds stronger than chains. He would die for her. 'Let us say I must and leave it at that, shall we?'

'Because of James?'

'James?' He was puzzled. 'What has he to do with it?'

'He saved your life when you were arrested last year. Maybe you thought you owed it to him.'

'Who told you about that?'

'Nanette.'

'My goodness, you did have a pretty little coze about me, didn't you? What else did she say?'

'That you had been betrayed. Is it true?'

'You could say that. Did she say why and by whom?'

'By your wife. Nanette said she was forced into it.' She looked up at him, waiting for his comment but the only reaction was a slight twitch in his jaw and a tightening of his hands on the reins. He obviously still found it difficult to talk about. 'It is a terrible situation to be in, being so frightened you say things you don't mean.'

'True. But you did not, did you? You were not so frightened that you confessed all you knew. That was very brave of you.'

She must have been terrified and he would not have blamed her if she had spoken out, but as soon as he got to the court and started telling his cock-and-bull story, he knew she had remained silent. And he had been so proud of her when he saw her emerging into the sunlit street with her head high. Gabrielle had not even been under duress and, in any case, what she had told the prosecutor had been a tissue of lies.

'I know very little.'

'Enough. I shall have to devise a way of making you safer.'

'How?'

'I shall think of something.'

He fell silent, as if cogitating on the problem, and Kitty used the opportunity to look about her. They were climbing steadily along a dusty track. The sun beat down and the heat shimmered on the distant hills. Either side of them were terraced vineyards with people hoeing between the bushes. It was too soon to be gathering grapes, but they hung in clusters on the stems of the bushes, small and green. She wondered if the harvest was going to be good and hoped so for the people's sake.

As they approached a crossroads, she noticed a man sitting on the ground beside a heap of stones which had been collected from the fields. He was eating a hunk of black bread, but stuffed it into his bag and rose as they approached. She gasped when she saw it was the road-mender.

'Jack, that man…' She nodded in his direction.

He laughed and pulled the horse to a halt. 'It is my good friend, Thomas Trent.'

'Your friend?'

'Yes.' He reached out and shook the man's hand. '*Bonjour*, Thomas.'

'*Bonjour, mon vieux.* Did you have any trouble?'

'None at all. This, as you have no doubt guessed, is *citoyenne* Kitty Faucon, the bane of my life. Kitty, may I introduce Captain Thomas Trent.'

The captain smiled and climbed up beside her. '*Bonjour, citoyenne.* I am glad to make your acquaintance and only sorry you had to wait so long for rescue.' His English was perfect and she realised, with a little sense of shock, that he was an Englishman.

'You knew? Was it you who told Jack I had been arrested?'

'Yes.'

'I am glad you were there.' She smiled. 'You seem to be everywhere.'

He laughed, but made no comment. Jack set the horse off again, turning right and making for a stand of trees on the hills above the vineyards. She wondered where they were going, but did not dare ask.

Now there were three of them the intimacy she had shared with Jack was gone and she regretted its passing. For a little while he had seemed relaxed, willing to talk. He had almost dropped his guard. Almost. Now it was back again, as impenetrable as before.

'Anything to report?' he asked the roadmender.

'No. I gave James your message.'

'Any sign of the gendarmes?'

'No, but they cannot be far away.'

'Do you think they will be looking for us?' Kitty asked.

'Perhaps.'

'But if they believed Jacques's story…'

'They would still follow it up.'

'Then James is in danger. Jack, we must warn him. Where are we? How far is it to your uncle's?'

He laughed. 'You see, Thomas, what I have to contend with? She can't help herself, you know. As soon as she scents an adventure, she must rush headlong into it...'

'It's no more than you do,' she retorted.

'I never rush headlong anywhere,' he said, laconically. 'I stop and think first.'

'What are you thinking now?'

He smiled. 'I am thinking that somehow, God knows how, I must cure you of your impetuosity.'

'That's not what I meant. I was speaking of warning James.'

'Oh, that,' he said calmly. 'You must leave that to me, my dear. After all, there is nothing to connect Jacques Faucon and his erring wife with the *ci-devant* Marquis de Saint-Gilbert. Is there?' He turned to look at her, requiring confirmation that she had said nothing to her captors.

'No, I suppose not. If it was Monsieur Trent and not the gendarmes who saw me leave.'

'Quite.'

'But you told me to forget Jacques Faucon, to deny all knowledge of him.'

'That was while we were at my uncle's, where I expected you to stay. Your flight changed everything. We have left there now and nothing we say or do must lead anyone back there, you understand?'

'Yes. I would not for the world betray his hospitality.' She was a little hurt that he had even thought that she might, but, remembering what Gabrielle had done, she could understand why.

'Turn left here,' Thomas said, as they reached the edge of the woods. 'The track is rough, but the cart will make it if you are careful.'

It was an understatement. It took all Kitty's efforts to

retain her seat and several times she grabbed Jack's coat sleeve to save herself as they bumped their way between the trees. The only consolation was that they were now out of the sun and it was cooler. After several more concisely given directions they reached a clearing and there before them was a tiny cottage, dappled in sunlight.

They stopped in front of it and the Captain jumped down. 'Here we are, safe as houses.'

Jack climbed down and turned to Kitty, holding out his hands to help her. 'Come, my dear. This is as far as we go for the moment.'

She grasped his hand and jumped straight into his arms. After the relief of being rescued and sitting so long on the hard bench, she felt weak at the knees and unable to stand.

He held her for a moment longer than he needed to, savouring the feel of her small body against his, wishing he could claim it, to make love to her, to tell her she need never be afraid again. But that was foolish; they had a long way still to go and heaven knew what dangers still faced them. If only he could keep her safe. He had to, whatever it cost. She was dearer than life to him. He bent to put a kiss on her untidy curls and then released her.

'Come inside,' Thomas called to them from the door.

The little cottage was very primitive, having only one room downstairs, with a lean-to addition at the back, but it was clean and warm and the food Thomas prepared, though simple, was good and hot. Jack would not allow her to speak until she had eaten her fill, by which time she was feeling decidedly sleepy, although it was barely dusk.

'Did you sleep last night?' Jack asked, smiling at her.

'No. There was no room to lie down and too much to think about.'

'Then it's time you went to bed.' He reached out his hand towards her.

'But what about James...?'

'Leave your brother to us. Come along.'

It had been a long day. She had lived through terror and isolation even in the crowded cell, had felt herself slowly giving up hope. And then there had been the immeasurable relief at seeing Jack waiting for her, followed by that bone-shaking ride which had numbed her bottom. And meeting Captain Trent and eating and drinking while the two men talked generalities and never once mentioned their plans. It was all too much.

She took Jack's proffered hand and allowed him to lead her across the room to a narrow staircase which led up to the loft. 'Up you go.'

He followed as she climbed the stairs. There was only one room which contained a narrow bed and very little else. She stared at it, then turned to face him, noticing how tired he looked. His face seemed grey and the lines about his mouth and on his forehead were more pronounced, though his eyes still seemed able to see deep into hers and winkle out whatever thoughts she might be trying to keep hidden.

And the thoughts she were trying to hide were shameful. She wanted him to sleep with her, to hold her and make love to her, and she knew if they shared a bed again, it would happen. Since they had been at the château, they had behaved correctly towards each other, putting on a semblance of gentility with their good clothes, bowing and referring to each other by their titles and avoiding being alone together. Which was as it should be, she told herself, but it put a distance between them.

'You may have the bed,' she said. 'You need it more than I do. I shall go downstairs. There is a settle…'

She turned to go down but he grabbed her arm, forcing her to face him. His own emotions were so ragged, he could only control them with levity, by teasing her; he could not handle tenderness, not now, not yet. 'No. You will have my friend Thomas wondering what sort of a wife you are if you cannot be pleased to see me after the ordeal you have endured.'

'You are despicable!' Why, after all the time they had been together, she should choose this particular moment to think about propriety, she did not know.

'You would rather I had left you to the mercy of Madame Guillotine?'

'No, of course not. I am grateful for your timely rescue, but that doesn't mean I am prepared to…to…' She stopped because he was doubled up with mirth. 'What are you laughing at?'

'My poor dear Kitty, we travelled three hundred miles and spent—how many nights was it?—on the road, often in the same bed, what is so different now?'

She wanted to say, Because now I know I love you, because now I know that what I want most is to be your wife in reality and not just pretend, that if I lie beside you, I should surely give myself away. Because you are married and love your wife and I could never respect a man who betrayed his wife with me, however much I loved him. And because you are a nobleman and I am nothing, a nobody. Instead she said, 'That was an expediency for the duration of our journey—'

'Which is not yet ended. In fact, this is less than

halfway. The second half will, I hope, take us back to England.'

'Us? You mean you are coming too?' She could not keep the pleasure from her voice.

'Yes.'

'And we go on as before?'

'How can we? Things are different...'

'Yes,' she said. Did he mean different in the same way that she meant it? 'Tomorrow, James will come and...'

'And what will James do? Will he be able to make everything right again? James says he loves Nanette and wants to take her to England.'

'She told me she would not leave her parents,' she said.

'Then James might want to stay here.'

'It is too dangerous.'

'Love conquers all, you said that yourself, or something very similar.'

She looked up at him then and he thought his heart would burst. She was extremely pale; there was no colour in her cheeks and there were dark smudges beneath her eyes and tears glistening on her lashes. He reached out and wiped them away with the back of his forefinger.

'What are you trying to tell me?' she asked. 'That I have been on a wild goose chase? Do you think I don't know that? I know I never should have come. I know I should have turned back at Calais. Judith would still be alive if I had. And even after you rescued me the first time, I could have said I did not want to go on to Lyons. It was not too late to turn back.'

'Yes, it was. There was no one to accompany you,

not even Judith, and I could not return with my mission
unaccomplished…'

'Intelligence gathering?'

'Yes,' he admitted. 'Finding James seemed to be the
only solution.'

'And now you are telling me it was not?'

'I am telling you that, for me, there was no alternative. From the moment you stepped ashore at Calais,
our lives were inextricably linked.' He smiled wearily.
'Call it fate, if you like.'

He possessed himself of her hands and drew her to
sit on the bed beside him. 'Now, let us have no more
teasing because I want to talk to you very seriously and
I want you to understand.'

'I am listening.'

'Play-acting is all very well here in France where we
are not known and where everyone is more concerned
with their own lives than with propriety, but what hap-
pens when we return to England? Had you thought of
that? You have spent days and nights in my company
unchaperoned—what do you think that will do for your
reputation and how will your grandfather, the Viscount,
react, do you suppose? Will he cut James off? Will he
turn your uncle from his living?'

'He would surely not punish them for something I
have done?'

'Mud sticks, my dear.'

'Oh, that is so hypercritical. And it isn't fair. James
has done nothing wrong. And neither have we.'

He smiled. Was she being deliberately naive? 'Will
anyone believe that?'

'Perhaps not, but as I have no intention of going
home, not to Beresford…'

'Then where will you go?'

'I shall find somewhere. You need not concern yourself about me.'

'No? What do you think I have been doing these past six months?'

'Six months? Is it as long as that?'

'January to July. I am sure it must seem a lifetime to you…'

'No, it seems shorter.' She spoke softly, not daring to look up at him. 'You have looked after me so well, I hardly noticed the days passing.'

'Some would say otherwise. Some would say I had ill used you.' He knew he should have found some other way, he should not have insisted on her playing his wife, or on sharing a room. The first night he had done it to drive home his message that she was not safe alone, which was true. The second night, he had sat in a chair by the hearth, listening to her tossing and turning and crying out in her sleep. Once, he fancied she had called his name. And he had answered her, gone to take her in his arms, to comfort her, sleeping beside her. He had known what he was doing; she had not.

'Jack, please don't make it sound sordid when it was nothing of the sort. What you did was good and chivalrous…'

He laughed harshly. 'Chivalrous! Chivalrous to share a room, sometimes a bed…'

'You did it for my protection. I had nightmares…' She shuddered. 'You have no idea how bad they were. Thanks to you they are far less frequent now and not half as frightening.'

'For heaven's sake, don't make me into some kind of saint. I am nothing of the sort.'

'Jack, I am very tired. Please tell me what all this talk is leading to.'

'A way out of our dilemma,' he said, stroking the back of her hand idly with his thumb. 'You could marry me. I mean a real marriage, not this charade we have been playing.'

'Marriage!' She was so startled she pulled her hands from his and gaped at him. He had the grace to look sheepish. 'Are you mad? Or is bigamy accepted in this Godforsaken country now?'

'Bigamy?'

She laughed shrilly. 'Had you forgotten you are married? I believe her name is Gabrielle. Nanette told me all about her. She said you were devoted to each other.'

'Gabrielle is dead,' he said flatly. 'She died last year.'

'Oh.' She was so shocked she could not go on, but pulled herself together quickly. 'I didn't know. Oh, Jack, I am so sorry. Please forgive me.'

'There is nothing to forgive.'

'When did you find out? How did it happen?'

'She went to the guillotine. I learned of it while we were in Paris. Now we will talk of her no more.'

'Of course. I can see it is a painful subject. But how can you talk of marriage to me? You do not love me and…'

'What has love to do with it?' he broke in before she could force a confession out of him. How could he tell her that ever since he had saved her from that hanging, perhaps even before that, the one thing he had wanted was to make love to her? That his desire that been overwhelming and could only be controlled by teasing her or being harsh with her?

He wanted to marry her, to have her legitimately in his bed. And James, hearing how they had come this far without a chaperon of any kind, had insisted on it. 'My sister is an innocent,' he had said when Jack finally caught up with him two days before. 'She doesn't understand that she can never go back to England unmarried. You must make an honest wife of her.'

Jack did not need to be told; it had been occupying his mind for some time and the solution he had offered was the only one. It was also the one he most wanted. She was looking at him now, hurt and puzzlement in her lovely eyes, and a dash of anger too. He could hardly bear it.

'Is this another tease?'

'No, far from it. I am in deadly earnest.' He retrieved her hand and lifted it to his lips. 'I'm sorry, my dear, that was not the most romantic of proposals, but you must know me by now. I am not a romantic man, and the circumstances are hardly conducive to tender declarations. Perhaps if we were in England…'

'If we were in England,' she snapped, 'I would not even entertain such a proposal.'

It was such a set-down, he gave up the struggle to redeem himself, but neither could he withdraw the proposal. 'Then let us come to an amicable agreement,' he said brusquely. 'We will marry tomorrow. Thomas will fetch the *curé* and he and James can be witnesses. And though I do not hold with breaking marriage vows, I shall raise no objection if you decide to ask for an annulment after we arrive safely in England.'

She was staring at him as if he had run mad and he supposed he had, mad enough to think they might be able to find happiness together in spite of the circumstances. 'Think about it,' he said, getting to his feet. 'Think about the alternatives and give me your answer tomorrow.' Then he bent to kiss the top of her head and left her.

He joined his friend downstairs. The roadmender was

sitting by the hearth, smoking a clay pipe, but knocked it out on the fender when he saw Jack. 'All is well?'

'I think so. What do you think happened to James?' Jack asked, taking a seat at the table. 'He should have been here hours ago. Do you think there's trouble up at the château?'

'Could be. After all, the guards know you are related to the Marquis and if they think you are in the area...'

'By me, you mean Jack Chiltern, not Jacques Faucon?'

'Either. The two will be connected before long. You can't afford to hang about waiting for someone who may never come.'

'Kitty won't go without him. Not willingly.'

'Then you'll have to make her. Marry her or something.' Thomas stood up and pocketed his pipe. 'I'll take the horse and see if I can find out what is happening. If I ride over the top of the hill, it should only take a couple of hours. But whether I come back or not, you must leave at dawn.'

He went from the room, leaving Jack with his elbows on the table and his head in his hands. It had been a nerve-racking day and he was exhausted. So was Kitty and he should have waited until they had both had a good night's sleep before proposing to her. He had handled it very badly, stressing the practical arguments instead of opening his heart to her. 'I am not a romantic man.' He grimaced as he remembered his words.

It would serve him right if she turned him down.

Chapter Eight

Kitty was exhausted, mentally and physically. She lay on the hard bed, her head buzzing with everything that had happened to her since her precipitous and unthinking flight from the rectory: the poverty and dirt and, worst of all, Judith's death, which had robbed her of a good friend as well as a chaperon, and now a proposal of marriage which, as Jack had pointed out, was far from romantic.

Just how much did it mean to him? It seemed extraordinary that he should be prepared to sacrifice his future happiness, perhaps even his inheritance, for her sake. He did not even like her; he found her a nuisance, a responsibility he would rather be without.

She could not forget what Nanette had told her about how Jack behaved towards Gabrielle, how close they had been, how he had done all he could to please her. It was almost as if she were talking about another man, not the Jack she knew. Could the loss of his wife have changed him so much, that he was harsh and uncaring about every other woman he met?

And yet he had offered to marry her, to try and mitigate the scandal. He was so deeply immersed in his grief for his wife that he did not consider it much of a sacrifice. But she did. She must say no. She must take the consequences of her own actions and face the shame when they returned to England.

But, oh, how she loved him! She knew that beneath that harsh exterior there was a man who could feel deeply, who could put someone else before himself, who was honourable. After all, there had been countless occasions when he could have forced himself on her and had not. She smiled wryly to herself in the darkness—not much force would have been needed because she loved and wanted him.

His touch, however fleeting, sent shivers down her spine, and she longed to dispel that look of pain she sometimes saw in his eyes. Could she make him forget Gabrielle with her own love? Could she make him love again?

If she said yes, then it would be a genuine commitment on her part to make the marriage work and hope that in time he would come to love her. If she failed, if he continued to be cold and hard, then she would be trapped in a loveless union because she would not go into marriage with the intention of ending it if it went wrong. Dare she chance it?

She fell asleep, dreaming of pale English skies, of gentle rain in summer, of the peaceful countryside and the placid pattern of life there, of friends and family. If she could find that again, she would never again long for adventure.

She woke suddenly before dawn to the sound of horses and voices. Scrambling from her bed, she hurried to the tiny dormer window, but it was in the slope of the roof and she could see nothing. She turned back, pulled on her clothes and crept down the stairs. Jack was fast asleep in a chair at the table, his head on his folded arms. She shook him. 'Jack, someone's coming.'

He was awake in an instant and on his feet. 'Stay there.'

He went outside. She could hear voices and then laughter and the next moment the tiny room was full of people: Jack and Captain Trent and a man she had not seen before, besides Nanette, who was hanging onto the hand of another young man.

'James,' Kitty cried, flinging herself at her brother. 'You're safe.'

'Of course I'm safe, silly.' He grinned at her and held her at arm's length. 'My, how you've grown! If you didn't look so horribly like a peasant, I'd say quite the lady.'

'The disguise was necessary,' Jack said, defending her. 'But you may take my word for it, she is quite the lady.'

James turned to him. 'And are you going to make an honest one of her?'

'James!' Kitty remonstrated. 'Don't be so tactless.'

'Sorry,' he said quickly. 'But it is better to be blunt, don't you think?'

'It is none of your business.'

'Oh, but it is. I am your brother and in the absence of our guardian…'

'Shut up, James,' Jack said sharply. 'Kitty left home because she did not want to be forced into a marriage and here you are, only five minutes reunited, trying to do the same. Let her make up her own mind.'

'Well, she had better make haste. The Marquis has betrayed us all…'

'My uncle? I can't believe that.'

'He has,' Nanette put in. 'The guards came back and I heard him talking to them. They seemed to know you were in France. It had something to do with the *comte*'s carriage and knowing we were related…' She paused. 'Papa told them all about Jacques Faucon and what James was doing, everything. He did not need to, he could have pleaded ignorance.'

'Have they arrested him?'

'No, because he convinced them he intended to hand you over. He told them they could find you at Malincourt.'

'But we are not at Malincourt,' Kitty said.

'We are not far from it,' Jack said. 'We had better make a move.'

'We have time for a wedding,' James said, nodding towards the fourth man. 'The *curé* is prepared to conduct the ceremony.'

'You take too much upon yourself,' Kitty said. 'I have not agreed.'

'You may do as you please,' James said. 'But I do not intend to stir unless Nanette and I are married. Not for the world would I expose her to the kind of scandal you will be subjected to if you return to England unwed.'

'Oh, I am sorry, I did not think of that.'

'No, that is just your trouble,' her brother said. 'You never stop to think—'

'And you always consider the consequences of your actions, do you?'

'Children! Children!' Jack laughed. 'Do not quarrel over it, for I declare you are as bad as one another.' He turned to Nanette. 'Is it your wish to marry James?'

'Yes, it is.'

'It means leaving your parents and your home. You may not see them again for a very long time…'

'I know, but Papa betrayed James and you and Kitty, who is so brave to follow her heart. Even if he is afraid to lose his house and lands as the *comte* de Malincourt did, it is no excuse. You are my cousin and James is my own true love. I have aligned myself with you.'

'So be it.' Jack turned to the priest. 'Will you marry the young couple?'

'With pleasure, *monsieur*.' He smiled and corrected himself. 'I mean, *citoyen*.' He opened a canvas bag he carried with him and began to take out his vestments.

'Can it be done here?' Kitty asked. 'Will it be legal?'

'The place is unimportant, *citoyenne*,' the *curé* said. 'It is as binding as a marriage solemnized in church. And as I now have no church, I must serve my God and my people wherever I can.'

Jack took Kitty's hand. 'Well, my dear, do we follow their example?'

She looked up into his face and it seemed as though there was a new softness there. His eyes were searching hers, asking for understanding, and her heart swelled with love. She wanted it, wanted it in spite of all the arguments against it. Arguments did not count. Risks did not count. What mattered was what she felt deep inside her. There was no doubt there. He had said love conquers all and, though he had been teasing as usual, she had a feeling he did believe it. She must put her faith in that.

'You really mean it?' she asked.

'I do not say things I do not mean.'

'Then tell the priest to make it a double wedding.'

It was far from the wedding of her dreams. She was not in her uncle's church with its high-vaulted roof and multi-coloured altar window. She was not wearing a lavish gown and costly jewels loaned to her, or perhaps even gifted to her, by her grandfather. There were no flowers, although the priest had brought out some incense and the tiny room was filled with its heady scent, almost overwhelming her. And the ring Jack slipped on her finger was his signet ring and much too big. But none of that mattered because she was giving herself to the man she loved.

He kissed her when it was all over, kissed her for the first time as her husband, and it was a joyful and sensuous sensation, but a little constrained by the knowledge that they were being watched. She did not care. They had the rest of their lives together. He might talk of annulment, but she would never ask for it. As far as she was concerned, this marriage was going to last into eternity.

There was time for nothing else. The *curé* packed up his bag and departed, riding an ancient mule. The horse was reharnessed to the cart which had brought Kitty from the prison and brought to the door. Kitty and Nanette said goodbye to the Captain who was staying behind, then climbed into the back with their meagre luggage and a parcel of food.

Jack and James, who had remained behind in the cottage, reappeared in the uniform of French cavalry officers, resplendent in dark blue double-breasted jackets with rows and rows of silver frogging and heavy silver-fringed epaulettes. Their breeches, tucked into shining leather boots, were tightly fitting and set off muscular thighs. They each wore a sword belt and a pistol and a shako with the regimental insignia on the front. The girls gaped at them and then began to laugh.

'Oh, you are the very top of the trees,' Kitty said. 'The handsomest of heroes.'

'*Vraiment épatant*,' Nanette said, giggling. 'Truly stunning. *Magnifique.* I am overcome with admiration.'

James grinned and punched Jack on the arm. 'There, my friend! We have made a conquest each.'

Jack smiled and made no comment as he shook the roadmender by the hand and took his place on the driving seat. Laughing, James climbed up beside him and they were off.

Thus they journeyed the whole of the day, taking byroads and cart tracks. Sometimes Nanette sat beside James while he drove and Jack joined Kitty in the cart, sometimes she sat with Jack on the driving seat. Sometimes they walked.

In some ways it was like their journey from Paris except that she had been reunited with her brother and, what was more important, she need no longer worry about the impropriety of sharing this strange nomadic life with Jack. He was truly her husband now. She began to look forward to the night with a mixture of trepidation and eager anticipation.

They passed through the ancient Roman town of Vienne without stopping and by dusk had reached Roussillon where they drew up outside an inn. It seemed untouched by either the Revolution or the war, but they all knew appearances could be deceptive and were on their guard.

Going ahead of the others to reconnoitre, Jack approached the inn with caution. If anyone asked their business, they had agreed to say they were going to Toulon. The men were going to rejoin their regiment defending the city against the British navy and their wives had every intention of following them. Once there, they could discard the uniforms and make contact with the men who could take them out to the British fleet.

The innkeeper welcomed them if only because they paid him with a gold *louis d'or*, the equivalent of two English sovereigns, and far more acceptable than the paper *assignat*. He prepared his two best rooms and produced a meal of chicken and fish, with leeks and potatoes, a basket of fruit and a bottle of wine. There were no other guests and they sat over the repast for two hours, but Kitty could see that James was wriggling with impatience to have Nanette to himself; in the end, he could contain himself no longer.

'We have an early start tomorrow,' he said, smiling at his wife. 'I think it is time to retire.'

She rose willingly and took his hand. Jack, too, was on his feet. He watched them pick up a candle from a side table, light it and leave the room before he turned to Kitty. 'Well, my dear, shall we follow suit?'

Without waiting for her answer, he went to light a second candle and stood by the door. Suddenly she was nervous and afraid. She looked across at him, her eyes mutely appealing. He smiled and held out his hand. 'Come, my dear.' His voice was gentle.

She went to him and slipped her hand into his. Together they climbed the stairs to their room.

Once in their bedchamber with the door closed, he seemed to hesitate, uncertain what he should do. He had offered her an annulment and he supposed that was what she wanted. To share her bed would be construed as consummation, even if he managed to refrain from touching her. It was ironic that what had been acceptable when they were unmarried could not be countenanced now.

What he wanted most was to be a proper husband to her, to love, honour and cherish her to the end of their days. Why had he never told her so? Because he was afraid of rejection, of being spurned, because he hoped she would change her mind about the annulment when they reached England. In England he could woo her as a man should woo the woman he loved, unhampered by rough living and danger, which made people say and do things they did not mean.

'You go to bed,' he said, putting the candle down on a chest. 'I must see to the horse.'

She was bewildered. He had never been irresolute before, he had always known exactly what to do. Surely the presence of his ring on her finger hadn't changed that? It ought to have made it easier for him to share her bed, not more difficult. 'But the hotel ostler has done that,' she said. 'Why go out again?'

He smiled, but it was a smile that did not reach his eyes. They were blank, almost as if he had deliberately shut her out. 'You did not think I should be so unfeeling as to assert my rights, did you?'

'Unfeeling?' Her own heightened sensitivity, her mental preparation for the night to come, her disappointment, made her so angry she was almost shouting. 'Yes, you are unfeeling. You play with people, do you know that? You treat them as if they have no more feelings than a piece of furniture. Do this, do that, don't do this, don't do that. Get up. Be quiet. Go to bed. Did it ever occur to you to wonder how I felt about it all?'

He stared at her, completely taken aback by her outburst, as she was herself. She had not meant to let fly at him, especially not tonight, their first night of marriage. She did not understand herself, let alone him.

'I did not need to wonder,' he snapped. 'You made

it abundantly plain. I was conveniently to hand when you needed an escort. I was there to shield you from the grimmer realities of life, rescue you, even to marry you to prevent scandal…'

Instead of telling him that he meant far more than an escort to her, which would have defused the situation, she seized on his last unflattering statement. 'That was your idea, not mine. I would have continued as we were.'

'And I could not. The world would never believe we had not become lovers in the months we have been together. For your sake…'

'For my sake! Are you sure you are not thinking of your own reputation?'

'You are surely not suggesting I coerced you into marriage in order to—' He stopped. He hadn't done that, had he? 'Oh, no, my dear, nothing was further from my thoughts. You cannot annul a marriage that has been consummated, you know.'

'And you think it makes me feel better to know that I am so unattractive I cannot compete with a dead wife.' It was not her speaking, she told herself, it was the little green god of jealousy and she hated herself for it.

'Leave my wife out of it.' He did not want to talk about Gabrielle; she had no part to play in the present situation.

'Why should I? You evidently cannot.'

'God, woman, what do you want from me? You are the most trying, the most provoking, the most…' He grabbed hold of her shoulders. 'I am not a saint. I cannot stand much more of this. Look at me, damn you.'

She tilted her head to look at him. His dark eyes were pinpoints of steel flashing in the light from the candle flame. His jaw was rigid, his mouth grim. For the first time ever, she began to feel a little afraid of him. 'Let me go, you're hurting me.'

Her mouth was slightly open, almost inviting him to do his worst. 'Heaven help me,' he said, lowering his mouth to hers in a bruising kiss.

It went on a long time. She beat her hands on his chest but he simply wrapped his arms about her, imprisoning her and taking the breath from her body. His mouth explored hers, setting up sensations in her belly she could not control. Every fibre of her was shouting its own needs, making her respond, making her lean in to him, to feel his heartbeat, his strength subjugating hers; she wanted him. She stopped struggling.

He picked her up and carried her to the bed, flinging himself down on top of her. Holding her down with the weight of his own body, he lifted her skirt and parted her legs. 'You want proof I am not made of stone, do you? You shall have it.' He undid the buttons on the flap of his pantaloons and began to thrust into her. He did not look into her face, did not see the pain and horror there; he was too intent on releasing months of frustration and anger.

Afterwards came the remorse, the burning shame, the knowledge that he had spoiled everything that had been good about their relationship, the trust they had always had in each other. He would never forgive himself, so how could he expect her to forgive him? He turned towards her, not knowing how to make amends.

She was lying on her back looking at the ceiling, silent tears streaming down her face. How tiny she was; small pointed breasts, slim thighs, little feet. He had great strength and he had used it to subdue her. He had taken something which was precious as life to him and crushed it savagely.

'Oh, God, what have I done? I didn't mean it, I didn't mean to hurt you. I was out of my mind.' He reached out to wipe the tears away, but she knocked his hand from her.

'Kitty, I am truly sorry.'

'For what? For acting like the tyrant you are?' She gave a cracked laugh. 'Am I supposed to complain when my husband takes only what is his by right?'

'But I had no right to hurt you. I beg you to forgive me. It will never happen again, I promise you.' He tried again to reach out to her.

She turned her back on him. 'Go away.'

After a moment, he left the bed and she heard him fumbling with his clothes, then he was gone, taking the guttering candle with him.

She pulled off the ring and flung it into the darkness in the corner of the room and sobbed in total despair. There was no love in him, there never would be for her and she had made the greatest mistake of a life already over-full of mistakes. She had thought she could make him love her. How conceited, how foolish she had been!

She had wanted him to make love to her, would have given herself happily and willingly if he had asked it of her. He did not need to be cruel. It was the mention of his wife that had triggered it and that was her fault. And now she must live with his contempt.

She rose next morning, her eyes, heart and feet as heavy as lead, and sat looking in the cracked mirror above the dressing table, then smiled crookedly at her reflection. She had not slept and she looked terrible.

Would James guess what had happened? Would Nanette notice? She could not bear the thought of their pity.

Turning her basket upside down, she began flinging clothes this way and that. Judith would have packed some rouge and powder, she was sure of it; she could not have known they would not need these essential requisites to a lady's toilette. Grabbing the little pot, she returned to the mirror and coloured her cheeks and lips. It made her look a little less wan, but could not disguise the misery in her eyes.

Five minutes later, dressed in her blue muslin, she made her way downstairs. James and Nanette were sitting at the breakfast table, gazing into each other's eyes and smiling dreamily. Their night had obviously been all they had hoped for.

'Kitty, good morning,' James said, rising. 'Come and have some breakfast. I just saw Jack, he said you wouldn't be long. He's gone to give orders about the horse.'

'Yes, he told me,' she lied.

She sat down but she could not eat. Her mouth was too dry to swallow. She gulped coffee. She must behave normally. She must not let them see that her wedding night had been a disaster. She smiled. 'Well, you two seemed pleased with the world this morning.'

'Why shouldn't we be?' James said, smiling at Nanette. 'We are as happy as two lovebirds can be. We can face anything so long as we are together, rain, wind, rough seas, even Madame Guillotine, it doesn't matter. Don't tell me you don't feel the same.'

'Of course I do,' she said, just as Jack came into the room to join them.

He walked over to Kitty and bent to kiss her cheek. 'Good morning, sweetheart. You looked so peaceful, I let you sleep, but we must not be long before we move off.' His voice was perfectly normal—he was much better at playacting than she was, she decided.

'I am ready when you are,' she said, surprised that he had not suggested she should change into the peasant costume. After all, that's how he liked to have her. Well beneath him, under his control. 'My basket is packed and only needs fetching from the bedchamber.'

'I'll get it, my love,' Jack said. 'You go and get in the cart. It's ready at the door.'

James had already brought Nanette's bag and his own valise downstairs. He picked them up and led the way into the street. Unwilling to be parted even by a couple of feet, he settled himself in the cart beside Nanette, leaving Kitty to climb up on to the crossbench to wait for Jack. He joined them five minutes later, put Kitty's basket and his own small bag into the cart and jumped nimbly up beside his wife.

'Right,' he said with false cheerfulness as he picked up the reins. 'Let's be off.'

She noticed he was wearing his signet ring. It was why he had been gone so long; he had noticed she was not wearing it and had been searching the room for it. He would take that as a sign that the marriage was over before it had ever begun. He was too proud to ask her forgiveness again and the future looked bleak indeed.

The horse was younger and stronger than old Samson, and they were able to cover many more miles a day than they had from Paris to Haute Saint-Gilbert. And, as they were so far from the capital and in pro-Royalist country, there was less danger too. But Kitty could not appreciate that; she was so overcome with misery, she could think of nothing else.

Jack treated her with the utmost courtesy, worrying

about her comfort, running little errands for her, speaking gently, doing everything a considerate husband should do for a wife. Except love her. At night, he slept in a chair or huddled on the floor of whatever hotel, inn or deserted cottage they chose for their night's lodging, while she occupied the bed alone. He had said it would not happen again and he meant to keep his word.

Each morning he rose, apparently refreshed, and went to see to the horse, to pay the innkeeper, to shop for food for the day, leaving her to her toilette. James and Nanette, immersed in each other, knew nothing of the anguish they both suffered. Life for them was good and, now that they were out of the district of Lyons, they did not even worry about the danger or the Reign of Terror beginning far to the north.

They followed the river bank to Tournon, with its granite hills and steep vineyards, and from there climbed a tortuous road with breathtaking views. At its highest point they could see Mont Blanc in the east and Mont Ventoux to the south.

On they went, through Valence and then Montelimar, where they were caught in a violent rainstorm which turned the tiny stream which ran through it into a torrent of swirling water. They stopped here, earlier than they might, in order to take shelter and dry their clothes.

Sitting in the porch of an empty villa, looking out at the brilliant flashes of lightning, listening to the thunder reverberating through the hills, they chatted of other storms in other places. And that led on to tales of home, summers in England. Kitty, listening to Jack speaking of his home, was filled with longing. Would it ever be her home too? Would his father and mother welcome her? Did she even want to go there under the circumstances?

She did not know, was not sure of anything any more. Her high-flown plans to make her marriage work, to make Jack forget his dead wife and learn to love the one who was alive and wanted and needed him, would come to nothing. Vanity, that's what it had been. Conceit. Pride. And now she must pay the price.

She must live with the tyrant love. She did not know whether she wanted this journey to end, so that she might know what fate he had in store for her, or whether she wanted it to go on and on, that she might never have to face it.

Their progress southwards continued in brilliant sunshine the next day and James sang snatches of *The Beggar's Opera* as they went. Nanette joined in, trying to learn the English words, making him laugh. They were so happy, it hurt Kitty to watch them. She dare not look at Jack for fear he could read the envy in her eyes, and he would not look at her, for the guilt was still with him.

Why had she provoked him on their wedding night, taunted him about his wife? That had been the crack which had burst the dam. All his hurt and frustration, all his iron self-control, had come spilling out. It was not Kitty, he had wanted to hurt, but Gabrielle. Gabrielle who had spurned him, who had wanted him dead so that she could impress her lover, had injured his pride. His pride had retaliated, had punished Kitty whom he loved beyond reason.

How could he explain that to her, when she would not even speak to him, except in the day-to-day polite discourse of passing acquaintances? And at night, when they should have been opening their hearts to each other, they did not talk at all. Nights were silent tor-

ment. But he could not blame her. He had brought it
on himself and must pay the penalty: her contempt.

When they moved into Provence they felt a distinct
rise in temperature. As the old cart with its single plodding horse took them through the little town of Orange
with its ancient Roman theatre and steep terraces, the
north was left behind. The days were hot and even the
nights too warm for comfortable sleep.

The sky was a deep blue, the light very clear, putting
the white houses with their red roofs into sharp focus.
Oleander and bougainvillea climbed over walls. Cicadas
screeched, a hawk swooped and rose with a tiny mouse
in its claws; and they could smell the wild thyme, the
rosemary and lavender growing on the roadside verges.

After a night spent in yet another country inn, they
continued through a rocky countryside dotted with vineyards and olive groves and on to Avignon, which had
been Papal property until two years before when the
Revolutionary government had appropriated it.

James, who was sitting in the back of the cart with
Nanette, began to sing again.

—Sur le pont d'Avignon,
—L'on y danse, l'on y danse;
—Sur le pont d'Avignon
—L'on y danse tous en rond.

Laughing, Nanette joined in and then Jack, who was
driving, accompanied then in a surprisingly good tenor
voice. Kitty stole a glance at him. Was he as relaxed as
he seemed? Had that dreadful night left no mark upon
him at all?

They turned away from the river and, at the end of a

long day, came to Aix-en-Provence with its narrow medieval streets. Soon they would reach the sea and then would come the difficult part of their escape, moving from land to water and persuading Admiral Hood to take them on board. After that, their return to England was in his hands. Not even Jack could influence it.

Wanting them to have a good view of the bay and its shipping before going down into the town of Toulon, he took them through a spectacular gorge overshadowed by huge rock formations and up a steep hill at the top of which he stopped. They climbed out and stood looking down at the bay of Toulon sparkling beneath them. It was crowded with shipping, none of it able to move because of the British ships that blocked the entrance to the bay. They could just make them out on the horizon.

'What a sight!' James said.

'Let's hope they don't decide to lift the blockade before we get out to them,' Jack said.

'How are we going to do it?' Kitty asked. 'All those ships. There must be hundreds of French sailors in the town with nothing more to do than catch spies and traitors.'

'Then we shall have to avoid them,' Jack said, as if it were the easiest thing in the world. 'Come on, back in the cart. In a few hours we shall have no more need of it.'

They rumbled into the town and Jack, who seemed to know where he was going, drove the cart along the twisting old streets and stopped at a blacksmith's forge. 'This tired old nag needs new shoes,' he said to the farrier, a big burly man in a leather apron, who came out to meet them.

'Now why should he bother with new shoes?' Nanette whispered to Kitty. The two girls were sitting in the cart with their legs dangling over the back. 'We don't need the horse any more.'

Kitty shrugged, knowing how Jack operated. He seemed to have contacts the length and breadth of the country, knew who could help him, whom to avoid. She recognised a password when she heard it.

She was right. Half an hour later they were all seated in the back parlour, eating a hastily cooked meal of fish, listening to the blacksmith telling them the latest situation in impeccable English.

'The town is being systematically starved into submission,' he said. 'Nothing is coming in by sea and nothing comes down from the north because Paris commandeers what there is. There is talk of surrender. Admiral Hood's launch comes almost daily to offer terms and the local government is on the point of accepting.'

'Can you get me aboard the launch when it comes next?' Jack asked.

'Get *you* aboard!' James exclaimed. 'What about us?'

'It will have to be arranged,' Jack said. 'Four extra passengers in a small launch would not go unnoticed by the port authorities.'

'That is true, Mr Harston,' their host put in. 'If his lordship goes first, something can be arranged. Though how you expect to get to England once aboard, I don't know. There are no plans that I know of to lift the siege.'

'Despatches have to be sent home regularly,' Jack said. 'We go with the despatches.'

'You too?' the blacksmith demanded. 'Do you not stay behind and continue your work?'

'I have done what has been asked of me. Now I must take my wife home.' He looked at Kitty as he spoke, smiling a little crookedly. His wife! What a mockery! 'We have not long been married.'

'Is that so? Then may I offer my felicitations to you both.' He looked from Jack to Kitty as he spoke, forcing her to smile and bow her head in acknowledgement.

'It is the same for us,' James said, reaching across the table to take Nanette's hand. 'I cannot wait to get out of this barbarous country and return to my home-land. Begging your pardon, *monsieur*.'

'Oh, you do not have to spare my feelings, Mr Har-ston. Now, I will go and find out when the Admiral's launch is expected and let us hope he has not given up trying to negotiate. You must wait here and you'll oblige me by staying indoors.'

They wiled away the time by playing whist, at the end of which James had lost several guineas. 'I don't mind in the least,' he said when Jack commiserated with him. 'Unlucky at cards, lucky in love. I know which I would rather be.'

Kitty stole a glance at Jack, who was gathering up his winnings, but he did not look at her. She had lost too, so the old saying could not be true. Her luck was abysmal on both counts.

Towards evening the blacksmith returned to tell Jack to be ready to leave the following morning. 'I told the bo'swain in charge of the launch that you had important information which you would only impart to the Ad-miral himself.'

'That is true.'

They listened as he explained how Jack was to be smuggled aboard while the launch was tied to the quay, waiting for the Admiral's party to return to the flagship.

Once on board it was up to the Admiral whether he helped them or not.

'You mean he might not?' Kitty asked, her hopes plummeting again. 'Surely he would not leave us here to fend for ourselves? Supposing he won't let Jack come back for us?'

Jack smiled crookedly. 'Why, I do believe my loving wife cannot bear to be parted from me.' He rose from the table and took her hand to kiss it, making her shiver with desire. She hated herself for her weakness. 'You don't know how gratifying that is.'

James gave him a curious glance and then laughed in an embarrassed way. 'Are you surprised? You have hardly been married a se'ennight. I know Nan would feel the same if I went off on my own.'

'Of course. Leaving Kitty, even for a minute, breaks my heart. But you know how I like to tease.' Jack's little show of temperament was over almost as soon as it had begun, but it left Kitty feeling more uneasy than ever, if such a thing were possible. It seemed there was to be no expunging of that dreadful wedding night from their memories.

She freely admitted she had been as much at fault as he had, but she had not been able to tell him so because he made sure he was alone with her as little as possible and, when it could not be avoided, he discouraged conversation by pretending to be busy with other things, or asleep, or so deep in contemplation that she could not interrupt him. Gone was their earlier affinity—now they could not communicate at all.

Not wishing to intrude on James and Nanette, she spent the waiting time alone, pacing up and down their room or sitting in the corner of the forge, away from the heat of the fire, pretending to read. Most of the time she was mentally rehearsing conversations with Jack, conversations in which she was open and eloquent in explaining her feelings and he listened attentively and told her how much he loved her. All fantasy.

He returned late the following afternoon with the news that a boat would be sent secretly at dead of night to pick them up at a little cove further along the bay and take them directly to the sloop which was due to sail for England, just as soon as the wind was favourable. The blacksmith would guide them along the top of the cliff and show them a way down. After that it was up to them to make the rendezvous on time.

With Kitty and Nanette wearing dark clothes and hoods, provided by the blacksmith, and the men in naval coats with no embellishments, they set off at dusk, following the bulky shape of the blacksmith. By the time they reached the tortuous path which led from the cliffs to the beach, the moon was up, lighting their way.

The blacksmith pointed. 'Down there. *Bon chance, mes amis.*' Before anyone could thank him, he had melted away, making no sound.

'Look!' James said, pointing out to sea. 'There's a small craft, rowing out from that ship. We must make haste.'

They scrambled down. Jack went first, stopping every now and again to help the ladies over a difficult piece of ground, leaving James to bring up the rear. Several times they dislodged loose scree which went tumbling down, making a noise that sounded loud in the silence of the night. They waited to see if any sentries had been alerted, then continued down.

Once on the beach, they made for the water's edge,

standing with their feet in water, ready to jump into the rowing boat which was only a few feet from the shore. 'Chiltern?' queried a voice from the boat as the oars were shipped and one of the rowers jumped out to pull the small craft inshore.

'Yes. All present and correct.'

'In with you then, quick as you can. If this night's work becomes known to the local citizenry, it might well foil the negotiations.'

They needed no second bidding, but waded knee-deep to scramble into the boat. The rowers had dipped their oars almost before they were safely aboard and Jack had to be hauled in by James as they began to pull away again.

Twenty minutes later they were among the British ships and making for a sloop on the outer edge of the fleet. A rope ladder was flung over the side and caught by Jack as they came alongside. He turned to Kitty, holding out his hand and smiling reassuringly. 'Up you go, my dear. James will be right behind you.'

Now was not the time to have qualms, to have doubts about her fitness or wonder whether she might fall. Now was the time to grit her teeth and climb. She took a deep breath and began, one rung at a time, while Jack steadied the swaying ladder from below. She could hear James's heavy breathing as he followed her. As her head reached the top, many hands reached out and unceremoniously hauled her on board.

James came next, then Nanette, sobbing because she had almost slipped and had looked down to see the sea, inky black below her, and lost her nerve. Only Jack, climbing almost over her to steady her, had kept her going. But now all four were aboard.

'I'll take you down to the Captain's cabin,' one of

the sailors said, as Kitty and Nanette shook out their skirts and patted ineffectually at their hair.

They followed him down the companionway and were soon being ushered into the Captain's presence, a young man with untidy blond hair and very blue eyes.

'Edward!' Kitty and James exclaimed in unison.

He laughed. 'The last person you expected to see, eh? I have the honour of commanding this vessel, His Britannic Majesty's sloop, *Lady Lucia*.' He bowed with as much of a flourish as he could manage given the size of the cabin and the number of people in it.

To Jack he offered his hand. 'Good to see you again, my lord.'

'And I you. May I present my cousin, Nanette.'

'My wife,' James announced proudly.

Edward bowed to her. 'My felicitations, ma'am. I hope I may make you comfortable.' He turned to Kitty. 'And you, Miss Harston...'

'Lady Chiltern,' Jack corrected him.

'Is that so?' Edward looked from one to the other with amusement. 'Then may I wish you happy?'

'Thank you.' Kitty said, her voice slightly too brittle to be natural.

'Who would have thought when I last saw you that it would all turn out so well?' Edward said, beaming at her. 'I must say, I am vastly relieved. I often wondered if I was right to help you escape. I would certainly have thought twice about it if I had known where you intended to go.'

'Did my uncle know it was you?' she asked.

'I do not think so. He never said, though I have seen little of him since because of my naval duties. War keeps a man from home, you know.'

'Quite,' Jack said cryptically. 'Kitty's debt to you will be repaid just as soon as we reach home.'

'Pray, think no more of it,' he said. 'It was a gift, and if it has made Kitty happy, then I am content.'

Kitty did not reply and neither did Jack. There was nothing they could say. The silence stretched uncomfortably.

'I shall look forward to hearing all about your adventures tomorrow.' Edward said, smiling round at them all, making Kitty wonder if he had detected the strained atmosphere or whether it was her imagination. 'Now, I am afraid duty calls. We are sailing at once. The intelligence I have for the War Department cannot wait. The second lieutenant will show you to your quarters. This is a ship of war and not built for passengers, so the accommodation is somewhat spartan. On the plus side, we are fast and will have you in Portsmouth in no time.'

Portsmouth. England. Kitty viewed the prospect with mixed feelings. Not for the first time she began to wonder about her uncle and stepmother. What had happened in her absence? How was little Johnny? What would be said about her marriage? Would she be forgiven? Had her uncle received her last letter sent from Calais? Seeing Edward Lampeter again had brought it all home to her, long before she had expected to face it.

James seemed unconcerned when she found him alone, looking over the ship's rail at the oil-dark sea. She had delayed going down to her cabin, knowing Jack would be there. On board ship there were no horses to see to, no provisions to buy, no more despatches to write. They could not escape each other and the tension between them was tearing her to shreds.

'There will be no scandal,' James said. 'Why, you

have made a catch, don't you know that? Married to
the Earl of Beauworth's heir. You won't be living at
home any more, will you? You will be with your husband in Wiltshire. Alice won't be able to say a word
against you. You have come up trumps. Edward did you
a good turn.'

Her brother would not have said that, she told herself,
if he had known the truth. She had gambled and lost
and all because of one wrong move. 'I am not so
sure…'

'What are you saying? You love Jack, don't you?
You are not sorry you married him?'

'No, no, of course not. I was thinking of the manner
it came about.'

'Oh, you will soon live that down, don't worry. Jack
will be there to protect you from gossip. And so will I.
If anything is said, I shall tell everyone I was with you
the whole time. Now, go to bed.' He kissed her cool
cheek. 'Goodnight and God bless.'

Only partly soothed, she went down to her cabin.
Jack was in the upper bunk, apparently fast asleep. She
undressed in the dark and crept into the lower one.

He heard her settle down, wondered whether to ask
her where she had been, but decided against it. It might
provoke another argument, she might say it was none
of his business and he could not bear that.

They rose next morning to a calm sea and warm sunshine. After breakfast they went on deck where they met
James and Nanette. Chairs were found for them and
they sat down to a day of idleness. James was looking
forward to taking his bride home and, confident that his
reports of life in Revolutionary France would be ac-

cepted by a publisher, was full of plans to become a writer.

He had given Kitty his manuscripts to read and that furnished her with an excuse not to join in the general chatter. How could she talk of the future when she could see no further than the end of each day?

Towards noon, Edward joined them. 'All's well,' he said. 'We're on course in a good following wind, so now I have a little time to hear all about your adventures. How difficult is life in France these days? One hears such dreadful tales of the guillotine and rivers of blood. Surely they have been exaggerated?'

'Not knowing what accounts have reached England, it is difficult to say,' Jack said. 'Our own experiences were hair-raising enough. Kitty still bears the scars of an attempted hanging.'

'Good God! I beg your pardon, ladies, but that has really shocked me. How did it happen? How did you two come to be together in France? Surely that was not coincidence.'

'It was,' Kitty said, and told him how she had met Jack on board the packet, how Judith had died and her own ordeal. 'Jack looked after me, until we joined James,' she said.

'The last time I was home, my father told me that your uncle had had news of you,' he said. 'He knew you had gone to stay with the Marquis de Saint-Gilbert; your stepmama even boasted of it.'

'How could he possibly have known that? The last time I wrote was from Calais.'

'I wrote to him from Paris,' Jack said. 'I had intelligence to send, and enclosed news of you and told him where we were going, so that he would not worry about you.'

'Why didn't you tell me?' she demanded. 'I could have written myself.'

He smiled enigmatically. 'I could not tell you I was in touch with London, could I? It would have contravened all the rules of espionage and put you in very grave danger if the despatches had been intercepted. It was all done in code. By the time we reached Haute Saint-Gilbert, it became too difficult to send word overland, so I am afraid your uncle does not know we are married. That is something we shall have to tell him when we arrive, my dear.'

It was the longest speech he had made to her since their wedding night and the most exasperating. Long after Edward had left them to return to his duties, she went over and over it. Why had he taken all that trouble? The risk must have been enormous. Nanette said she thought he had been helping aristocrats to escape, but it was much more than that.

Wherever he went, he was known. There was the couple at Calais, the Claviers, Thomas Trent, the blacksmith and others along the route. And there had been times when he left her at their lodging in the evening, telling her to go to bed and not wait up for him. She imagined him relieving the boredom of escorting her by drinking and gambling. Sometimes he had called for pen and ink and wrote far into the night. Despatches. Letters to her uncle.

And there was Gabrielle. He had learned of her death in Paris and yet he had kept it to himself, bottled it up. Why could he not have confided in her? Why, oh, why had he married her?

Chapter Nine

Edward was right; the *Lady Lucia* was fast. Five days later they docked in Portsmouth with nothing to complain of but a little rough weather in the Bay of Biscay. The formalities were soon concluded, they said goodbye to Edward and stepped ashore, back in peaceful England at last.

Jack hired a coach to convey them all to his home where James and Nanette were to stay overnight before proceeding on to London. It was taken for granted that Kitty would remain at Chiltern Hall when James and Nanette left. Why wouldn't she? She was Jack's wife and, however brutal the circumstances of it, the marriage had been consummated.

She was filled with apprehension and misery, wondering what the Earl of Beauworth and his wife would think of their son's new wife. She looked like a peasant, had lived like one for so long she was even beginning to think and behave like one: ill clad, rough and unmannerly.

Both the gowns she had taken with her were torn and dirty, her stockings were full of holes, though she had tried mending them. She had no hat and her hair, a little longer than when Judith had cut it for her, stuck out like a bush. How could she face her new in-laws like that?'

Jack smiled when she ventured to express her concern. 'My dear, clothes mean nothing. You are who you are whatever you wear and my parents will understand. Nanette is also dishevelled and as for James and me...' He spread his hands, laughing at his disreputable appearance in black trousers, second-hand naval jacket and a plain tricorne hat. 'Hardly the stuff of gentlemen, are we? We are not returning from just a grand social occasion, but an adventure of epic proportions.'

An adventure, she thought, an adventure of my own making. Did I once envy James his independence? Did I really long to test my mettle in new experiences? Did I once wish I were a man? How foolish of me! Now I shall be labelled a hoyden and, if it had not been for Jack Chiltern, it would be much worse. She sighed. There was nothing to be done but brave it out.

'What you need, what we all need, is a bath and a good meal and a day or two to recuperate,' he went on. 'After that, you can go shopping for your immediate necessities in Winchester and, later, you can go to London and buy whatever fripperies take your fancy.'

Not one word about how he was going to explain their marriage so soon after he learned about the loss of his first wife, not one word about an annulment, or how they were going to go on, when they were so obviously not going to suit.

Chiltern Hall was a huge mansion set in acres and acres of parkland and reached by a private road lined with ancient elms. It had hundreds of windows and almost as many chimneys.

'Home,' Jack said, as the coach came to a stop outside the porticoed main entrance. He opened the carriage door and jumped down almost before the wheels had come to a stop and ran up the steps just as the door opened and a footman appeared.

'My lord! Oh, her ladyship will be so pleased to see you safe. She is in the blue parlour.'

'Oh, no, she is not,' said a female voice in a slight French accent. Kitty, who was being helped from the coach by James, looked up to see a woman, of perhaps a little over fifty, run and throw her arms about Jack. She was slim and elegant in a round gown of dark blue silk trimmed with bands of coloured ribbon. Her dark hair, with hardly a trace of grey, was piled high, on top of which was perched a tiny lace cap from which floated more ribbons. 'When did you get back? Oh, I am so glad to see you safe.'

She caught sight of the trio on the gravel beside coach. 'Who are these people?'

He smiled. 'Mother, here is Nanette. You remember her, don't you?'

'Nanette! *Quelle surprise!* Of course I remember you. Come 'ere, child, let me kiss you. Why, it must be seven or eight years since I saw you at Haute Saint-Gilbert. You are quite grown up. I am so pleased to see you safe. Is my sister with you? And the Marquis?'

Nanette curtsied and kissed her aunt. 'No, Aunt, Papa would not come, he feels his place is at home. *Maman* would not leave him.'

'No, she would not. But you are 'ere and for that I give thanks.'

Nanette turned towards James. 'Aunt Justine, this is my husband, James Harston.'

James swept an elegant bow. 'Your obedient, my lady.'

''Arston? Are you not the young man who saved my son in France?'

'It was fortuitous that I was in the right place at the right time, my lady.'

'Then you are doubly welcome.'

Jack reached out to take Kitty's hand and draw her forward. The gentle pressure of his hand, the warmth of his smile, made her insides melt, as they always did whenever he touched her. It was pleasure and torment together, heightening her sense of isolation and loss, feeding her desire. If he took her violently again, she would welcome it, welcome any sign that he wanted her for his true wife. If that was what the marriage bed was all about, so be it. But she could never tell him that.

'Mother, this is James's sister, Kitty. She is my wife.'

'Wife?' She looked from one to the other in confusion. ''Ow can she be? Gabrielle…'

'Gabrielle is dead, Mother. She died over a year ago.'

'Oh. Then I am sorry for it, but to marry again so soon…' She sighed. 'But I suppose you know what you are about.'

Did he? Kitty wondered as she curtsied. 'My lady, my presence must be a shock to you and I am sorry for that…'

'Oh, Jack is always giving me shocks. I am used to them,' Lady Beauworth said. Her smile was so like Jack's and her eyes were so like reflections of her son's that Kitty found herself warming to her. 'You are welcome. Come in and tell me all about it. But first some refreshment.' She led the way as she spoke.

'No, Mother,' Jack said. 'First a bath and clean clothes and then we can think of refreshment.'

'Of course,' she said. She turned to the footman. 'Fletcher, fetch Mrs Gordon.'

When the housekeeper arrived, crying with pleasure to see Jack safely home, her ladyship issued instructions one after another; fires were to be lit, water heated, beds made, food prepared. Servants ran hither and thither, obeying her commands, and, in no time at all, Kitty was in a vast bedroom being helped out of her filthy clothes and into a scented bath by her ladyship's own maid, Susan, whom she had brought with her from France when she married and who had never managed to get her tongue round the English language.

An hour later, with her blue gown cleaned, mended and pressed and her hair looking surprisingly neat after being washed, brushed and dressed, she ventured downstairs. Now she could converse with her hostess in a civilised fashion, to try and reverse what must have been a very poor first impression.

Her mother-in-law had taken the news of Gabrielle's death very calmly. It was almost as if she had half-expected it. And not a word of censure, only a warm welcome for her new daughter-in-law. If she and Jack had married in normal circumstances, if they had loved one another, she could be very happy here.

She was even more sure of it when she met the Earl of Beauworth, who was an older version of Jack, still very handsome though his hair was white. At dinner he questioned Jack carefully about the situation in France and what he had learned, especially about the situation around Lyons, his wife's former home.

'I hear Toulon has surrendered to Admiral Hood,' he

said. 'And the revolutionary government has ordered every able-bodied man into the army. Do you suppose that is the beginning of the end of this dreadful business?'

'No,' Jack said. 'I am convinced it will be worse before it is better. The revolt in the Vendée and Lyons has the government worried. They have tried to stir up more anti-Royalist hatred and ordered all the tombs and mausoleums of the kings to be destroyed. The bodies of Louis's ancestors have been dragged out and tipped into a lime-filled common grave. And the Queen has been taken to the Conciergerie and reduced to the status of a common criminal.'

'Oh, the poor, dear lady!' the Countess cried. 'And what of the Dauphin? Oh, but 'e is not the heir anymore, is 'e? 'E is the King. 'As 'e gone with her?'

'No one thinks of him as King; he is simply another Capet. By all accounts he was separated from his mother some time ago. He is still in the Temple, being brought up as a good *sans-culottes*.'

'Poor child. 'Ow can the world allow it? 'Ow can Britain stand by and do nothing?'

'We are doing what we can,' the Earl said. 'Now, tell us how you came to meet Kitty.'

This was a far happier subject and they listened with rapt attention as Jack gave them the facts in his dry, impassive voice. 'I know it was perhaps not ideal that we had to travel so far unchaperoned,' he said. 'But, until I learned of Gabrielle's death…'

'Yes, how did she meet her death?' his father asked.

'She went to the guillotine,' Jack said, his voice devoid of emotion. 'Denouncing me did not save her.'

'And have her parents been informed?' the Earl asked, while Kitty digested this piece of information.

Why had Jack never told her the manner of his wife's demise? It must have made it doubly difficult to bear. No wonder he had been so crusty.

'No, it is not something I could convey in a letter,' Jack said. 'I have decided to go with James and Nanette tomorrow and see them.'

'Tomorrow?' Kitty queried. 'But I thought…'

'It is not something that can be postponed, my love,' he said, speaking gently. 'They deserve to know the truth face to face. I will not be gone long and Mother will look after you until I return.'

'Of course,' her ladyship said. 'We will send for my dressmaker and have 'er make up some gowns, and then go into Winchester and shop for everything else. Then I shall show you all over the estate. We'll go riding and visiting in the phaeton. Will you like that?'

'Yes, very much. Thank you.'

'No need to thank me. You are my daughter now and it will give me great pleasure. You must 'ave a maid. Rose is a good girl and she 'elped me when Susan was indisposed last year. She will suit you very well, I think. I will send 'er up to you when you retire.'

Jack took his leave the very next day, kissing her goodbye at the front door with every appearance of tenderness. 'I will be back,' he said, looking into her violet eyes and wondering when the sparkle would return to them, when he would once again see the humour and spirit of her shining from them. It was his fault they had disappeared; perhaps absenting himself from her for a time might bring the roses back into her cheeks.

'Mother, you will look after her, won't you? She has been through so much and is very tired.'

'Of course, she shall have everything she needs and

wants. Now, off you go. And God bring you swiftly back.'

He climbed into the family coach with James and Nanette who had already said their goodbyes. They were taking a letter from Kitty to her uncle and step-mother, telling them of her marriage and asking their forgiveness.

She waved them out of sight and then turned back to her mother-in-law, who put an arm about her shoulders and smiled. 'Now, Kitty, you are not to grieve. 'E is only going to fulfil an unpleasant task and will be back before you know it.'

'What will your friends and neighbours think of me?' Kitty asked the Countess, two days later, when they were enjoying a ride in the phaeton. The estate was very extensive and covered parkland, pasture, woods, several farms, the river bank where the fishing was exceptional and the whole village of Beauworth. The weather was dry and warm and the workers were in the fields cutting the corn.

'They will love you, why should they not?'

'But they knew Gabrielle and that Jack loved her...'

'Jack was a fool.' It was said with such vehemence Kitty turned to look at her in surprise.

'I'm sorry, I don't understand.'

''As Jack not told you?'

Kitty smiled. 'He is hardly going to admit being a fool, is he?'

The Countess smiled. 'No, I suppose not. But 'e should 'ave said something instead of leaving you to think it was a happy marriage.'

'Nanette seemed to think it was. She said Jack was devoted to Gabrielle.'

'What does Nanette know of it? She only saw them together very briefly at the start of the marriage when she was only a child. And Jack would never complain. 'E is very good at 'iding his feelings, but that does not mean 'e does not feel deeply. Only we who are close to 'im know how much she made 'im suffer.'

Suffering. She had detected that in his eyes on several occasions. 'What did she do?'

'She was a virago, a taker. She gave nothing. Poor Jack tried to satisfy her, but the more 'e gave, the more she demanded. She would not live 'ere, said it was too dull, quarrelled with me, made Jack quarrel with me too…'

'But it is Jack's home,' Kitty exclaimed. 'And it is so beautiful and so peaceful, I cannot think how anyone could dislike it.'

'She did not want peace, Kitty, she wanted excitement. She could not live without it and turned to anyone who could give it to her. She loved risk…'

'She gambled?'

'Yes, and not just with money, Jack could have borne that in moderation. She gambled with 'is love, made 'im live in France and, when the war came and the family was forced to flee, she spent more time with 'er parents in London than 'ere.'

'It was from there she was abducted, wasn't it? Nanette told me she was kidnapped by someone from the French Embassy.'

'Abducted!' Her ladyship gave a short bark of a laugh. 'Jack told his cousin that, I expect. 'Is pride. No, Kitty, you should know the truth. The man was her lover. She ran off with 'im back to France. Her parents were distraught, as you can imagine, and they persuaded Jack to go after 'er, to try and bring 'er back. She be-

trayed 'is whereabouts to the Revolutionary government
and 'e was arrested for 'elping the *comte* de Malincourt
to escape the year previously.'

'That was when my brother saved him.'

'Yes. Jack came back without Gabrielle, but 'e was
a changed man. His former sunny disposition turned to
bitterness and anger. 'E could not settle to anything. 'E
offered his services to the government as an agent and
made several trips to France. Whether 'e was still looking for 'er, I do not know.' She sighed heavily. 'I was
desolate every time 'e went, afraid 'e would never return.'

'Why did he never tell me all this?' Kitty asked. 'It
would have explained so much.'

''E is a proud man, *chérie*. And you must not tell
him of this conversation. 'E would see it as betrayal.
No doubt 'e will tell you 'imself in time.'

'It does not matter. Now you have told me I understand.' She could understand why he found it so difficult to love, to give his heart to someone else. When
he came home, she would make a special effort to be
loving, to make him see that he could trust her and she
would not fail him.

'I am so pleased 'e 'as found you,' her ladyship said,
squeezing her hand. ''E deserves a little 'appiness.'

Kitty stared down at their two hands, one heavily
ringed and the other with none at all, wondering if she
ought to tell this dear, kind lady that the marriage was
no more than one of convenience, that her husband disliked her and that, if it had not been for that one terrible
night, it could have been annulled. She looked at her
and smiled wanly, but remained silent.

'I can see you are still tired after your ordeal,' her
ladyship said. 'We will forgo our visits today and go

'ome so that you can rest. And, Kitty, I know Jack could not buy you a proper wedding ring, but I think you ought to wear one. I will find one for you, until Jack comes 'ome and can buy you one.'

Kitty could hardly thank her for the tears which choked her.

A week passed in which she grew closer to her mother-in-law, learned the names of all the servants and was accepted by them and bought a wardrobe of new clothes, more than she needed or felt she ought to have, but the Countess would not listen to her protests. 'You must dress befitting your rank, my dear,' she said. 'There is no question that Jack can afford it. And it will please me.'

She gave in and allowed the Countess to help her choose gowns, pelisses, cloaks, undergarments, shoes, boots, shawls, even things like fans and feathers and jewellery. 'Of course, you will one day come into the family jewels,' she told Kitty. 'But, for now, I think a few pearls and simple gems will suffice, don't you agree?'

'Most assuredly I do. I am not used to so much.'

'But you deserve it for making my son 'appy.'

Kitty felt a fraud. She had not made Jack happy. He had shown no sign of being happy. Oh, he did not show his aversion to her in front of his parents or anyone else, but she knew it was there and it broke her heart.

Three days later, a letter arrived from her uncle. It was a long and loving letter. Jack had been to visit them and explained everything. They approved of the marriage and of course she was forgiven and the sooner she paid them a visit the happier they would be.

James and Nanette had arrived and were looking for a home in London. They had been most graciously received by Viscount Beresford, who had helped to find a publisher for James's account of his travels in France, and now James was planning other works.

'Jack has been to see Uncle William,' Kitty told Lady Beauworth.

'Well, naturally 'e would,' her ladyship said. ''E would want to obtain your guardian's blessing, even if it is a little late, and 'e would want to smooth the way for you to go 'ome for a visit. I would have expected nothing else from 'im.'

The letter and Lady Beauworth's comments cheered Kitty immensely and she began to look forward to making a visit to her old home. But not before Jack returned. Surely he would not have gone to see her uncle if he did not mean to remain her husband?

She began to watch for him every day. He would come home and they would make a fresh start. If she wanted her marriage to work, she must fight for it. She would risk a rejection and tell him she loved him, offer herself to him, tell him she asked nothing of him, but his good will. Love had blossomed from much less.

Her hopes were dashed when a letter arrived from Jack. She was in the breakfast parlour with her ladyship, when a servant brought the mail on a silver salver. The Earl had already left the house for the stables. One of his mares was foaling and he was particularly anxious over it.

Kitty turned the letter over in her hand, puzzled that Jack should write to her when he was expected home any day. But he wasn't coming home, she discovered when she broke the seal and began to read.

'Jack's gone back to France,' she gasped. 'Oh, why did he do that? I can't believe the War Department would make him go again.'

'Oh, *ma chérie*, I am so sorry,' her ladyship said. ''E was always doing that to me, rushing off without a by-your-leave, but I never thought 'e would do it to you. It is most inconsiderate of 'im.'

'And it's dangerous,' Kitty said. 'If he's caught…'

'Oh, you must not think of that. 'E will not take risks, not now 'e 'as you to come 'ome to. We must be patient.'

But patience was not one of Kitty's strong suits. She endured two days of idleness and then announced she was going to London. 'I must find out why he went,' she told Lord and Lady Beauworth. 'I need to know what is so important that none but Jack may be trusted with it. It isn't fair. He has already done enough.'

His lordship looked from Kitty to his wife, a question in his lifted brow. She nodded.

'I think I should also like answers to those questions,' he said. 'I will accompany you. They will be more forthcoming with me at Horse Guards than with you. We will set off tomorrow.'

'Take Rose to look after you,' Lady Beauworth said. 'I will go and tell 'er to pack.'

On Jack's instructions, the coachman had returned with the empty coach two days previously and it was soon made ready for the journey, with grooms sent ahead to arrange for changes of horses along the way.

The next day Kitty left her mother-in-law and Chiltern Hall, wondering if she would ever see them again. Jack had obviously decided to absent himself so long as she was there and she could not be so selfish as to deprive him of his home. Her grand plans to welcome him back with love and forbearance, to be a proper wife to him, had fallen about her ears. There would be no reconciliation.

She sat in the corner of the comfortable coach, staring out of the window, hardly noticing the countryside they passed. Her mind was filled with Jack, going over and over things he had done and said on their travels through France, remembering the way he had protected her and made it possible for her to return to her home with her reputation intact. Her eyes filled with tears.

'Oh, my dear, do not grieve,' his lordship said. 'He will come safely home.'

She fumbled for a handkerchief in the pocket of her gown and scrubbed at her eyes, unable to tell him the true reason for her tears. 'Yes. I am sorry.'

'Nothing to be sorry for,' he said, patting her hand. 'We will soon be there and then perhaps I can persuade the War Minister to recall him, eh?'

They stopped only to change the horses and have something to eat, and arrived at Beauworth House in Hertford Street late the same night. The Earl kept a number of servants there even when he was not in residence and their rooms were soon prepared and a meal put before them.

'Tomorrow I shall go to Horse Guards,' his lordship told her, as they ate. 'You will want to visit your uncle and stepmama. Take the coach. I can hire a chair.'

'Thank you, my lord,' she said, wishing Jack could have been there to accompany her. She needed his support. But visiting her old home would take her mind off what might be happening at Horse Guards.

* * *

It certainly did that. She dressed in the finest of her new gowns, a pale lemon silk with a deep fringe at the hem and a wide yellow-and-amber striped sash at the waist. The narrow sleeves ended in a deep frill and her shoulders were draped with a gathered scarf pinned above the cleft of her breasts with a large ornamental brooch. It was one Lady Beauworth had persuaded her to buy in Winchester and was only moderately expensive. Her hat had a tall crown and was trimmed with curling feathers. An amber-coloured pelisse, satin pumps and fine yellow kid gloves completed the outfit.

She smiled to herself as the Earl's carriage drew up at the rectory door. That would set her stepmother in a flurry and she would be dashing about giving orders about how her illustrious caller was to be received, not realising who it was.

Kitty was unable to suppress a smile when she saw the thunderstruck look on the maidservant's face when she opened the door. 'Miss Kitty!'

'Lady Chiltern,' Kitty corrected her with a smile. 'Would you please tell my uncle I am here.'

'Yes, miss—I mean, my lady.' The door was flung wide. 'I'll fetch him. Don't go away.' And she went running off to the rector's study, quite forgetting to show Kitty into the presence of Mrs Harston.

Alice, unable to contain herself in patience, came out into the hall to see an elegant young lady dressed in the height of fashion, standing alone peeling off her gloves. 'Oh, forgive me, ma'am. Where has that stupid girl gone? She should have brought you straight to me. Servants these days are so useless, one is in despair of finding one who knows what is expected of her. Do come in. Oh…' Her voice faded in shock as Kitty turned to face her. 'It's you.'

'Yes, Stepmama, it is Kitty. And Annie has gone to fetch Uncle William.'

'Oh, then you had better come into the drawing room. He will be down directly, though you are lucky to find him in. He is more often than not at Beresford Hall. Your grandfather has asked him to catalogue the library, you know.'

She led the way into the drawing room. 'As you see, nothing has changed. Sit down. When your uncle comes we will have tea. I must say, you have done very well for yourself. How did you manage to persuade Viscount Chiltern to take you on, I wonder? You had nothing to commend you. I never would have believed it if I had not met his lordship himself.

'Such a gentleman,' she went on, giving Kitty no opportunity to reply, not even when Annie came in with the tea tray and set it on the table at her side. She waved the maid away and continued without pause. 'He and the Reverend spent a long time closeted together in the study, though what they had to talk about, I cannot imagine. There could be no question of a dowry. You had left home, cut yourself off...' She looked up as the Reverend came into the room. 'Ah, here is your uncle.'

Kitty rose and ran to her uncle, dropping him a full curtsy. 'Uncle William.' She was too choked to go on.

'Get up, Kitty, do. And give your uncle a kiss.'

He was holding out his arms. She flung herself into them. 'Oh, Uncle, it is so good to see you again. I am truly sorry if I hurt you. Please say you forgive me.'

'Of course I forgive you. You are my niece, though why James should write to you of his problems and not to me, I do not know. And to swear you to secrecy! I have given him a very great scold.'

Kitty had no idea what he was talking about, but dare not say so. 'Oh, but you should not blame James.'

'No, for some of it must be put at the door of young Chiltern. Spies, agents, I never heard the like. If James needed money for his clandestine work, why did he not ask me for it? He should have known you would have to borrow it.'

She was beginning to see daylight. 'I think he did not want to trouble you, especially as you do not approve of war and fighting. And I don't suppose he thought I would be so foolish as to take it to him myself.'

'So he said.' He sighed. 'Ah, well, we will say no more of it. Edward Lampeter has been repaid and you have come back married. Are you happy, child?'

'Yes,' she lied.

'Who wouldn't be, married to the heir to an earldom?' Alice put in, pouring tea. 'That can't be bad. I am so thankful I advised your uncle against that match with Edward Lampeter. After all, he is nothing but a sea captain and his father a mere baronet.'

'He is also a very nice man, Stepmama,' Kitty said. Her stepmother did not change; she was still manipulating the truth to suit herself, forgetting that she was the one who had wanted to send Kitty away. Now it pleased her to think she had been instrumental in marrying Kitty off so advantageously.

'Yes, of course. Now, drink your tea and we will go up to the nursery to see Johnny. I wonder if he will remember you. Children forget so easily, do they not?'

Johnny had not forgotten her. He showered her with kisses and exclaimed rapturously over the toy soldiers she had brought him as a present, asking her if she was going to stay.

'No, my love, but I shall visit you again and you may come and visit me soon.'

She took her leave and returned to Beauworth House, thankful to escape Alice's sharp tongue. How her uncle bore it, she did not know. Even if she and Jack never lived together, if the marriage came to an end, she would not live at home again. Too much had happened and she knew Alice would never let her forget her infamous conduct, whatever her uncle said; there would be hints and innuendo and cruel taunts, just as there always had been. Whatever happened, she would keep her hard-won independence.

Her father-in-law had only in the last hour returned from Horse Guards. 'All day I've been there,' he complained to Kitty, as soon as she had taken off her pelisse and hat and joined him in the withdrawing room. 'Everyone seemed intent on passing me on to someone else. They were too polite to tell me to go away, but too cautious to tell me what I wanted to know. I had to go right to the top, the Minister himself.'

'What did he say? Is he going to recall Jack?'

'He said he could not. He said communication was so bad, he could do nothing until Jack himself sent word.'

'But what is he doing in France? He cannot save the whole French nobility single-handed.'

His lordship smiled a little grimly. 'No, but he might try to save one in particular, someone extra special…' He paused.

'The Queen?' she queried. 'The young King?'

'I am sworn to secrecy,' he said enigmatically, but she knew she was right by the look in his eyes.

'It is, though, isn't it? Oh, how could they ask it of him? Surely her Majesty is closely guarded?'

'Undoubtedly she is. We must pray for a successful outcome.' He paused and reached across to take her hand. 'I have been told that the *Lady Lucia* with Captain Lampeter on board is standing by off the coast of Brittany to take them all to safety.'

'If they succeed.'

'Even if they do not, the sloop will wait two days for Jack.'

'When is the attempt to be made?'

'I was not told the exact date. The Minister told me he had already given me more information than he should have done and we must be content with that.'

'Yes, I understand.' But it was so very difficult to accept and her imagination was already running riot with all the things that could go wrong.

He smiled reassuringly. 'We will go home tomorrow and wait and pray for Jack's safe return. And Kitty…' He paused. 'We will say nothing of this to anyone, do you understand?'

'Of course.'

'Not even the Countess. Especially not the Countess. We must shield her from worry, she has had to endure enough already. Her country torn apart by bloodshed and her son so confused and unhappy, he must expunge it by flinging himself into ever more dangerous situations. But now he has you and a chance to settle down. To be honest, I am a little peeved with him for volunteering to go. He had no business to leave you so soon after your wedding.'

'I expect he thought it was his duty.'

'Duty, bah! His duty is to you and his family. He is my only son and heir and I want to see a grandson before I call in my accounts. If I lost him…'

'Oh, pray that you do not,' Kitty said, reaching out to touch his arm.

He took her hand from his sleeve and squeezed it. 'This is no way to go on, is it? We will be patient and cheerful.'

'Yes, my lord.'

'Can you not call me Father? I should like that very much.'

'Yes, Father,' she said, shyly. She was beginning to love this man and the thought of disappointing him as a daughter-in-law weighed heavily on her. She sensed that he needed her, that her presence was a comfort to him in the absence of his beloved son. 'We will go home.'

If only Jack would come back, if only they could somehow learn to get along together.

The forger had been busy again and Jack now had a new identity. His cover as Jacques Faucon was blown. Now he was Pierre Bandol, a gunsmith. Because there had been mass conscription of all young men to fight the war that was sapping the country's life-blood along with that spilled daily in the Place de la Guillotine, he was obliged to pretend to be lame and had practised a strange limping gait, as if one leg were longer than the other. It was tiring, but it did mean he was left alone when recruits were rounded up and marched off to be soldiers.

The Luxembourg and Tuilleries Gardens had been turned into massive forges and the fires were kept going night and day, making weapons. In the buildings nearby women were set to work stitching tents and uniforms, and children were making bandages. Men too old to fight were directed to repair roads and public places and encouraged to preach patriotism, the invincibility of the Republic and the hatred of kings.

The need for more and more weapons made it easy for Jack to find work, to listen to gossip, to find out exactly where in the Conciergerie the Queen was held. It was becoming even more urgent that something was done because there was open talk of putting her on trial for treason. But it seemed no one had any communication with the prisoner. She was kept in solitary confinement and even her guards had guards and were watched.

It was the end of August before any progress could be made. After weeks of careful nurturing the prison administrator, a former lemonade seller called Michonis, was persuaded to let the Queen have a visitor.

The Chevalier de Rougeville, who had led the Queen to safety from the attack on the Tuilleries just before the royal family were taken to the Temple prison, was allowed to have a few words with Antoinette and left her a message hidden in a carnation. 'We have men and money at your service. I will come Friday.'

'Now, we wait,' he said to Jack and the other conspirators when he met them afterwards in the cellars of a wine merchant. 'And pray she found the message. I was watched all the time and could give no indication that she should examine the flower.'

It was one of her guards, a man named Gilbert and a distant cousin of Jack's, who brought her reply, pricked out with a pin on a scrap of paper. 'I am watched. I speak to no one. I trust you. I shall come.'

The scene was set for one of the most daring attempts of rescue Jack had ever been involved in. Shortly before eleven on Friday the second of September, dressed as a guard, he accompanied Michonis and Gilbert to the Queen's cell, deep inside the prison.

The room was only a few feet square, sparsely furnished with three beds, one for the Queen, one for her woman and one for the two guards who never left her. It had no fireplace and no lighting, save for a glimmer of light which came from a lamp in the courtyard. It was bitterly cold and had a sour-sweet smell of medicines and herbal concoctions, having once been the prison pharmacy.

Jack was shocked that the queen of a great country like France should be treated so harshly, but he could say nothing, nor show her any politeness or good manners. He did not speak at all and neither did Gilbert.

'I have orders to conduct the Widow Capet back to the Temple,' Michonis told the guards.

Flanked by Gilbert and Jack, dressed as a gendarme, and preceded by Michonis, the Queen left the cell and began to walk down a long corridor and through several gates, each of which had to be unlocked. So far so good. There was only one more to be unlocked and then they would be at the main exit, where Rougeville waited with a carriage. Nervously Michonis fumbled with the keys, but at last they were through and could see the dim outline of a vehicle in the courtyard.

Suddenly Gilbert stopped. 'What ails you, man?' Jack demanded.

'I saw something,' he whispered, shaking from head to toe with fear. 'A guard with a musket, hiding in the shadows.'

Jack looked. 'There is no one there. Come on, we have no time to lose.'

'I can't. It is not right…'

Jack was all for knocking him down and continuing without him, but Michonis himself seemed to lose his nerve. He placed himself before the Queen, who appeared to be on the verge of fainting. 'Go back.' He glanced towards the main gate as he spoke. The sentries there were watching them intently, their muskets off their shoulders, ready for use. 'Our bluff has been called. Go back, *citoyenne*, back to your room.'

The Queen gave one despairing look at Jack, turned and walked slowly back through the gates they had just left, followed by Michonis and Gilbert. The sentries moved forward, muskets pointing. Jack could not go back into the prison; his only hope of escape lay with Rougeville, who was pacing impatiently beside the carriage, wondering what had delayed them.

He strode towards the sentries, hoping they had not recognised the Queen. 'A slight hitch,' he said, and passed them at a run. They levelled their muskets and called to him to halt. 'Get into the coach!' he yelled at Rougeville, as bullets spattered round him. Rougeville, startled, ran back to the coach and scrambled inside, holding the door open for Jack, while the driver whipped up the horses.

They rattled out of the courtyard followed by musket fire, across the bridge and into the maze of alleys on the north side of the river. Behind them they could hear shouts of command and the sound of horses in pursuit.

'What happened in there?' Rougeville demanded.

'Gilbert got cold feet.' Jack had been hit by a musket ball and his arm was hurting him. 'We were within a hair's-breadth of pulling it off and the spineless fool has to go and be frightened by a shadow. Michonis realised the game was up and quietly took the Queen back where she came from.'

'Damn! We'll never have another chance to save her. They'll be doubly watchful now. Did they recognise you?'

'I don't know, but it is of little consequence. I am not going to go anywhere for a little while.'

Alerted by his tone, his companion turned to look at him. 'You've been wounded?'

'Yes. And please do not suggest taking me to a hospital.'

'You need attention.'

'I've had all the attention I need, I thank you, sir. I'll get out here.' He put his head out to tell the driver to stop. 'You save yourself.'

'Where are you going?'

'Best you don't know.' He opened the door and yelled at the driver. 'I told you to stop, damn you. At least slow down.'

Reluctantly the man pulled the horses up, but long before the wheels had stopped turning Jack had jumped into the road. He stumbled and put his hand against a wall to save himself, jarring his injured arm, forcing a grunt of pain from him. The coach rattled on and he dashed into an alley as their pursuers passed.

Ten minutes later he half-walked, half-fell into Jean Clavier's furniture workshop among the wood shavings and chair legs.

'Jack! What in heaven's name are you doing here?' his friend demanded. 'And wounded too. Well, do not say I did not warn you. Come on, let me get you upstairs. Thérèse will bind you up.' He put Jack's good arm about his shoulder and helped him up the stairs and into his living quarters. 'But do not tell us what happened. We do not want to know.' He gave a cracked laugh, as he guided him through the sitting room into a bedroom beyond it. 'Not that it would help much if a wounded man were seen coming in. There is a new law. Anyone can denounce anyone anonymously. They call it the Law of the Suspect.'

'I know. I do not ask you to hide me. Simply bind me up and let me be on my way.'

Jean let him down onto a bed. 'Where do you go?'

'Home.' The sound of the word conjured up visions of England, of Chiltern Hall, of his parents and Kitty. Most of all, of Kitty. He had been a fool not to tell her he loved her, a bigger fool not to stay at home where it was safe and where they could learn to love each other. She had a great capacity for love, he knew that without being told; all he had to do was make her fix some of it on him.

Edward Lampeter on *Lady Lucia* was standing by off the coast of Brittany, watching for the signal to send a boat ashore to pick up the Queen and her rescuers. They had failed, but he must still make it to the rendezvous and then home. Home and Kitty.

Thérèse was digging around in his wound, trying to find the musket ball, and the pain was making him sick and dizzy. Jean handed him a bottle of cognac and he gulped at it. It dulled the edge of the pain. Kitty hovered in a kind of fog just out of his reach. He lifted an arm feebly beckoning her to come to him. Thérèse put it back under the covers.

'To England?' she demanded. 'How will you get there? You will be lucky if you do not catch a fever from this wound.'

'No, no fever…' He yelped as the ball came out and Jean fetched the poker from the fire to cauterize the wound.

'Be quiet, would you have the whole *armée revolutionaire* down on us? Drink some more brandy.'

'You're a hard woman Thérèse Clavier,' he murmured, half-drunk, half-fainting. 'But an angel.'

'You can stay here tonight, tomorrow you go, understand?'

'Yes.' He rolled his head towards Jean. 'Get me a cart.'

He was far from fit to travel the next day, but it was not because of Thérèse's insistence that he went, but his own determination to reach the coast. They dressed him up as an old woman, an old woman with a fever, so that no one would come near him, then they loaded him on to the back of an empty farm cart and covered him with sacks which had once held potatoes. The stench made him feel sicker than ever.

The owner drove him through the *barrière* at Saint-Denis and took him to the farmhouse on the Calais road, where, having been paid generously in gold coin, he left his passenger to the tender mercy of Lucie and her mother.

The jolting had made his wound bleed again and he was only semi-conscious. It took all their strength to haul him from the downstair room where the farmer had dumped him like a sack of potatoes, up to his own bedroom, by which time he was past caring.

Lucie, who loved him, would not let him die. She would take any risk for him and set off for Paris to buy salve and ointment and laudanum for his pain, hiding her purchases in her petticoats in case she was stopped. She did not go through the barriers, but out over a broken wall and through a cemetery. As soon as she was clear she began to run.

He was worse by the time she arrived. Her mother had been sitting at his side all day, bathing his brow with cool water, giving him sips of water to drink, and praying loudly to every saint she could think of who might help. 'He has been calling Kitty's name in his delirium,' she told her daughter, when she returned. 'And he thrashed about and made his wound bleed. What shall we do if he dies? How shall we get word to his family?'

'He is not going to die, *Maman*. I will not let him. Come let us wash him down and dress that wound again with this new ointment and see if we can get him to swallow a little laudunum.'

It was three days before he came to his senses; by then he knew it was useless to go to the coast. Edward Lampeter had his orders not to wait above two days and he would obey those orders. Now everyone would know the attempt to rescue Antoinette had failed and they would assume he had died. He might do so even now, if news of his whereabouts reached the Revolutionary government.

He must escape, if only for the sake of Lucie and her mother, who would forfeit their lives for giving him succour; it would take only a malicious neighbour to denounce them. All the ports were blocked. Save one. Toulon was in the hands of Admiral Hood. Five hundred miles away. Five hundred miles across enemy terrain, and this time without the woman whose company had delighted him before. Did he have the strength for it?

Chapter Ten

It was September and the leaves were beginning to turn colour in the woods on the estate before the news reached Chiltern Hall that the attempt to rescue Antoinette had failed.

Kitty had gone downstairs to breakfast as she was in the habit of doing, though Lady Beauworth rarely rose before midday. She found his lordship alone, eating toast and reading his mail. Bidding him good morning, she seated herself at the table to be served her own breakfast.

'This is a letter from Captain Lampeter,' he told her. 'He docked at Portsmouth two days ago.'

Her heart began to beat so fast she could hardly breathe. The sloop had been in two days, long enough for Jack to have reached home if he had been on board. Where was he? Had he had taken one risk too many? 'Jack?' she queried. 'Oh, tell me he is all right. Tell me has has only gone to London to report and will be here soon.'

'I only wish that were so.'

'What does Edward say?' She could only pick at her

food; her stomach was too queasy in the mornings to eat heartily.

'Only that the sloop waited a full twenty-four hours longer than the allotted time, but there was no signal from the shore. They had to leave without any of our people.'

'That doesn't mean anything, does it?' she said, clutching at straws. 'There could be any number of reasons why he missed the rendezvous. It is early days yet.'

'Of course,' his lordship agreed, sounding positively cheerful. 'If the Revolutionaries had captured him, they would not have kept silent about it, the French papers would have been full of it. An English peer, trying to free the Queen! My goodness, the whole world would have heard of it by now.'

'What shall we tell her ladyship?'

'Nothing. Not yet. I shall invite Captain Lampeter to visit us. He will perhaps be able to tell us more.'

But when Edward came there was little else he could tell them. He had landed Jack secretly on the coast of Brittany where the remnants of a counter-revolution had not yet been entirely eradicated. 'There were sympathisers there waiting for him,' he said.

'And that was the last you saw of him?' Kitty asked. They were talking in the library where his lordship had received his visitor. It was afternoon and her ladyship had taken the carriage to call on friends. Kitty had declined to go with her, preferring to stroll round the grounds. Seeing Edward arriving, she had hurried back to the house to join the two men, knowing her father-in-law would not exclude her.

'Yes.'

'So you do not know if he even reached Paris?' his lordship asked.

'No, but we know the attempt to free Antoinette was made and one must suppose he had a hand in it. It was his mission, after all.' He paused, knowing something more was expected of him, but unable to give them the reassurance they needed. 'It is a pity it failed. If it had succeeded, it would have been a great coup and every exiled Frenchman would have rallied to her. The other great powers might have renewed their efforts to rid France of the scourge. As it is…' He shrugged.

'Do you think Jack stayed behind to try again?' Kitty asked him.

'It is possible, but very unlikely. The Queen will be more closely guarded than ever and the latest intelligence is that she is to be tried for treason. Our sources say it was talked of at a secret session of the Committee of Public Safety, but as the man most wanting the Queen's execution, besides being a *procureur* of the Paris Commune, is also the editor of *Père Duchesne*, a popular newspaper, it did not remain a secret very long.

'He is reported to have said he promised his readers Antoinette's head and, if there was any further delay in giving it to them, he would go and cut it off himself. The Public Prosecutor has been called in to make a case against her.'

'Have they one?' Kitty asked.

'I don't know. The report is non-committal, but no doubt they will fabricate one.'

'Jack is missing, not dead,' Kitty said stubbornly. 'He has simply gone to ground. He knows where he can be safe.'

With Lucie, perhaps?

The thought of Lucie and Jack together in that shabby

but comfortable farmhouse filled her with jealousy. Lucie loved Jack, she had made no secret of it. How long before Jack, in hiding and cut off from home, came to reciprocate that feeling? He was not made of stone, he had told her so, had demonstrated it in no uncertain way.

Lucie had known Jack longer than she had; Lucie had made no demands on him, she had simply given him her love. And if Jack chose to ignore his clandestine marriage... What had he said? 'How do you know that, in these heathen times, a wife cannot be discarded as easily as a grubby cravat?' Oh, she did not want to think of that. She would not.

They had unfinished business, she and Jack, and he must come home. He must. She had put their quarrel firmly behind her, pretending it was nothing but a tiff, her innocent reaction to the act of love which she had not understood, and she wanted to tell him that. She wanted to tell him that the result of that one night's union, unnerving as it had been, was to be a child. And the waiting was tearing her to shreds.

Her theory that Jack had stayed behind to make a second attempt to free the Queen was blown away a month later when they learned she had been tried and executed.

'A week ago on October the sixteenth,' his lordship said, tapping the newspaper which had been delivered that morning. 'She was accused of conspiring with her brother, King Leopold of Austria, against France and sending him money; organising a counter-revolution; forcing Louis to veto the deportation of priests; having a hand in appointing her husband's ministers favourable to herself and trying to start a civil war.'

'*C'est incroyable,*' Justine said. They were seated at nuncheon and this time the Countess was included in the discussion. ''Ow can anyone believe that nonsense? Why, she is nothing but an empty-headed pleasure seeker. I 'ave met her and anyone less likely to meddle in politics I cannot imagine.'

'They tried at the preliminary examination to trap her into a confession, but she came out of it very well,' her husband went on, referring to the report. 'At the trial itself the prosecution maintained that she had influenced the King into doing whatever she wished, that she made use of his weak character to carry out her evil deeds. They called dozens of witnesses, including her son. His evidence was vile.'

'Poor little Louis loved his mother,' the Countess said. ''E must 'ave been coerced into giving evidence.'

'Was she not allowed to say anything in her own defence?' Kitty asked, remembering her own so-called trial.

'She was allowed to speak at the end, but it did no good. The jury took only an hour to find her guilty and she was sent to the guillotine the very next day. The report says it took nearly an hour for the tumbril to reach the Place de la Guillotine because of the press of the crowd. She had to be helped out of the cart and up the ladder to the scaffold. Four minutes later she was dead and her head held up for all to see. According to this, the crowd cheered themselves hoarse.'

Kitty shuddered. 'Whatever is the world coming to? Where is their Christianity?'

'Denounced, along with everything else.' He sounded weary and dispirited. 'Sunday has been abolished, the churches closed or turned into what they call Temples of Reason.' He laughed suddenly. 'It is bizarre. All the

months now have thirty days divided into ten-day periods. *Décades*, they call them. And they have new
names. October is called *brumaire* now.'

'I cannot imagine anything more likely to cause
chaos,' his wife said. 'Surely the people will rise up
against that? They are most of them Catholic, they will
want to say Mass and go to confession.'

'They will do it secretly,' Kitty said. 'The priest who
conducted the marriage ceremony for us at Haute Saint-
Gilbert did it in secret because he was one of those who
would not take the new oath, but he said it was no less
legal.'

'When Jack gets back we'll make doubly sure,' his
lordship said. 'We will have another ceremony.'

'Oh,' she said, shocked. 'Do you think it wasn't legal?'

He smiled and reached out to pat her hand. 'Of course
it was, my dear. You and Jack believed it was and that
is good enough for me. Think no more of it.'

But now the doubt had been planted in her head,
Kitty could not shake it off. Had Jack known the marriage wasn't legal? Was that why he was able to say
they could have it annulled and why he was so angry
with her on their wedding night? Now, added to the
worries over Jack's absence was added the anguish of
a marriage that was no marriage at all and of bringing
an illegitimate child into the world. How could she be
sanguine about that? She had not told anyone of her
condition, but it would soon become obvious, and then
what? Would they accept the child?

'Now perhaps Jack will come 'ome,' the Countess
said, then smiled when she saw the startled look her
husband and daughter-in-law gave each other. 'Do not

look so surprised. Did you think I did not know 'e 'ad gone back to France?'

Kitty smiled. 'We hoped to save you distress.'

'What about your own distress, Kitty? You must be as worried and afraid as I am.'

'No, Mama, I am not afraid,' she lied. 'Jack will come back soon. I have no doubt he has gone south to Toulon, as we did before.'

'Then perhaps 'e has gone to Haute Saint-Gilbert and will bring us news of Anne-Marie.'

Kitty agreed, not daring to say what was in her mind. With the whole of France undoubtedly searching for the conspirators, Toulon, in British hands, was an obvious place to look for them. And if Jack's identity was known, they would also be watching Haute Saint-Gilbert and Malincourt.

For his lordship's sake and for the Countess's, she had to sound confident, but inside she was crying.

As the autumn days shortened towards winter and still there was no news of Jack, hope began to die inch by inch.

France was slipping into anarchy. According to some reports reaching England, the Law of the Suspect was being used to feed the guillotine, often several at a time, and those who had been at the forefront of the Revolution were themselves being put to death. No aristocrat was safe and even men of letters and science were obliged to watch their tongues and be continually looking over their shoulders. What hope had a foreign agent of staying undiscovered?

The Earl wrote frequently to the War Department, but they had nothing to tell him, except that the situation in France was so confused that there was little information coming through. 'We are forced to the conclusion that Viscount Chiltern has been apprehended and may have met his death,' they wrote. 'Until lines of communication are reopened, we cannot confirm this but must counsel you against false hope.'

Kitty, in her fourth month of pregnancy, was in despair. Had Jack died? Had he given his life for a foreign queen, not knowing she loved him, that he was to be a father? Knowing about the baby helped the Earl and Countess to bear their loss and Kitty herself was a little comforted by the small being growing inside her. She must live for her child, watch him grow healthy and happy and pray that the dreadful deeds being perpetrated against humanity in France would never be repeated.

She corresponded with James and Nanette frequently, and that November they arrived for a short visit. Nanette, too, was expecting a baby, though she was not as far advanced in pregnancy as Kitty, and the two young women were able to talk and even laugh a little over it so that the dreary atmosphere was lightened a little.

James and the Earl talked a great deal about the war with France, expressing the hope that, when it was won, the monarchy could be restored in France and that it would be safe for Nanette to visit her parents, or for them to come on a visit to England. She worried about them constantly.

They were two weeks into their stay when everyone's rest was disturbed at eight one morning by a loud knocking at the front door. Apart from the servants, Kitty was the only one already astir.

She had slept badly and had decided to dress and go down to the kitchen rather than summon a maid to bring her a dish of hot chocolate. She paused on the stairs as Fletcher, slow and ponderous, went to open the door.

The man who stood on the step was tall and gangly, dressed in a plain dark suit of clothes over which he wore a cloak and a black tricorne hat, both of which glistened with damp. It had rained during the night and now a thin mist covered the ground and hung in the air.

'Captain Trent!' Kitty cried, dashing down the rest of the stairs. 'How good it is to see you! Have you news of Jack?'

'My lady.' The one-time roadmender bowed to her, while his cloak dripped on the tiled floor. 'No, I am afraid not, but I have brought someone to see you.'

He turned back to a hired coach which stood on the drive and opened its door to assist a lady to alight. She was of middle years dressed in a rich taffeta gown with a woollen riding cloak, both of which were creased and travel-stained. The long feathers in her high-crowned hat drooped in the damp air. It was a moment or two before Kitty recognised the Marchioness de Saint-Gilbert.

'My lady!'

Anne-Marie smiled feebly. '*Bonjour*, Kitty.'

Although it was only a few months since Kitty had last seen her, she had aged. She seemed smaller, shrunken almost; her eyes were dull and there were deep lines about her mouth.

Kitty ran forward to help her into the house. 'Come in. Come into the morning parlour. I believe there is already a fire in there. Take off your cloak. Fletcher will have it dried for you. You too, Captain Trent.' Then, to Fletcher, 'Please tell the Earl and Countess and Mrs Harston we have visitors.'

She led the Marchioness and the Captain into the parlour and invited them to sit down by the fire. 'I'll have some refreshment brought in. You must be cold and hungry. Lord and Lady Beauworth will be here soon.' She rang a bell and ordered coffee and food to be prepared, then sat down, biting her lip in an effort not to bombard them with questions.

'Nanette is here,' she said in French. 'Did you know?'

'No, I didn't.' Anne-Marie's eyes lit briefly with pleasure. 'I came here first because I did not have her direction. I assumed my sister would have it.'

At that moment the Countess came into the room, clad in a dressing robe over her nightgown, and with a cry of joy ran to her sister and embraced her. 'Oh, my dear, dear Anne-Marie, I am so pleased to see you. But how did you get here? Where is Louis?'

'Louis is dead.' She spoke flatly as if repeating something someone had told her.

'Oh, no! I am so sorry. How did it happen? No, do not tell me now. Here is Annie with some refreshment. Eat and drink first. When John and Nanette come, you must tell us together.'

Kitty, suddenly remembering Thomas, who was sitting silently contemplating the fire, turned to her mother-in-law. 'Mama, may I present Captain Thomas Trent, a friend of Jack's.'

The Countess turned to face him, her face alight. 'Captain Trent,' she said, reverting to English. 'You 'ave news of Jack? You 'ave seen 'im?'

'Yes, I have seen him.'

The Earl came in at that point. He had dressed in breeches and shirt, but no neckcloth, and his feet were encased in soft slippers. Fletcher must have told him their visitor came from France, for he would never normally appear in a state of undress. Like Kitty, his first thought had been of Jack. He was closely followed by Nanette who had hastily flung on a muslin day gown and pulled a brush through her hair.

'*Maman!*' She flung herself on her knees in front of her mother's chair. 'Oh, *Maman!* I could not believe it when the maid told me. It is so good to see you.' She paused and looked round the room. 'But where is Papa?'

Her mother reached out to stroke her daughter's hair. 'My darling, your papa…' She paused to swallow. 'He is dead.'

'Dead?' She looked wildly round the room. 'How? What happened? Was he ill?'

Her mother leaned wearily back in her chair. 'Let Captain Trent tell you. I don't think I can bear to recount it.'

Everyone turned to Thomas, who cleared his throat before beginning the tale. He was aware of Kitty watching him, knowing she was anxious to learn what he had to say about Jack, but holding back for Nanette's sake. In any case, the two stories were really one.

'The Marquis was denounced,' he said. 'I don't know who it was, one of the servants, I suspect. He and his wife were arrested.'

Nanette turned to her mother. 'You too?'

'Yes. They took us to Lyons prison. They said Louis was a friend of the *ci-devant* King and went to Paris last year with the purpose of helping in the escape of the Royal family. When they failed, he had connived in the escape of a wanted criminal and an English spy.'

'I can hardly believe it,' Kitty said. 'Why, he was at great pains always to placate the new regime, you know

that. Thomas, you were there when he informed on
Jack…'

'He informed on Jack!' his lordship repeated. 'You
did not tell me this.'

'No, it would have made no difference and I wanted
to spare the Countess.'

'Continue,' his lordship instructed Thomas.

'They had been in prison less than two days awaiting
trial when Jack turned up unexpectedly…'

'At the château?' Kitty asked.

'No, he had more sense than to do that. He came to
my cottage. He was injured. During the abortive attempt
to free Antoinette, he took a musket ball in the shoulder.' He ignored Kitty's gasp and the little cry from the
Countess, who was sitting bolt upright in her chair, with
the Earl standing behind her, his hand on her shoulder.
'He had friends who took the bullet out and other
friends who nursed him, but he missed the rendezvous—'

'I knew it,' Kitty interrupted. 'Oh, please go on.'

'He decided to try for Toulon, which was why he
came to me. He was very weak, having walked most of
the way, and had not dared to call on his old contacts
for help.' He paused to sip his coffee. No one else
spoke.

'As soon as he heard about the arrest of his uncle
and aunt, he insisted on trying to free them. It was madness. The Marquis…' He bowed his head towards the
Marchioness. 'Begging your pardon, my lady. The Marquis had already betrayed Jack to the authorities; they
knew who he was and would be only too eager to get
their hands on him. I tried to dissuade him, but it was
useless.'

Kitty hardly dared breathe. This story was looking

more and more like the tale of a man determined on death. Thomas's next words seemed to confirm that. 'His plan was nothing short of reckless. I told him it would fail, that he would forfeit his life, but he didn't seem to care. He had a wild sort of look about him. I thought he had a fever from his wound.'

'He went ahead despite that?' Kitty murmured.

'Yes. His idea was to waylay the tumbril on the way to the guillotine.'

'By 'imself?' Justine gasped.

'No, I helped him and two others. There was a big crowd round the guillotine and all along the route, all very noisy and shouting for blood. We planned to ambush the cart when it passed the end of a narrow alley that went under the houses to the road on a lower level. Lyons is like that, you know, full of secret little tunnels and alleyways. One of us would pull the horse up and tackle the driver, two others were detailed to pull the prisoners out of the cart and bundle them away. Jack was to fight off anyone who tried to come after us.'

'They managed to free me because I was on the near side,' Anne-Marie said in French. 'But they could not reach Louis. One of the guards clubbed him over the head with his musket so that he fell unconscious into the bottom of the cart.'

'Jack struggled with the guards,' Thomas said. 'He fired his pistols, but I do not know if he hit anyone. He shouted to us to go, he would follow.' He paused. 'I am sorry. I wanted to stay with him, but I had the Marchioness to look after and she was all but fainting in my arms.'

'You think he died?' the Earl asked.

'I don't know how he can have survived. I am sorry, but the last I saw of him one of the guards had floored him and…' He looked doubtfully from Kitty to the Countess.

'Go on,' her ladyship said. 'I want to know it all.'

'He was sticking his bayonet into him. I went back into the town later, after I had taken the Marchioness to safety. The Marquis had been guillotined, that much I could confirm, but no one would admit to knowing anything about Jack. I dared not tarry.'

'No, of course not,' Kitty reassured him, though it was an effort to speak at all. She could imagine the scene, could imagine her brave, proud husband taking on the guards single-handed. If he had not been suffering from a wound, he might even have succeeded. 'You did your best.'

'We came by sea from Toulon,' he went on. 'It is still in British hands, though how much longer it will stay that way I do not know. The Revolutionary Army with all its conscripts is being surprisingly successful.'

'Thank you for telling us,' the Earl said as his wife began to sob quietly. He sat down beside her and put his arm about her. 'Let us hope his end was mercifully quick.'

'You were very brave,' Kitty said.

'No braver than Jack,' he said. 'He was truly a great man. And I can do no better than follow his example. I have to return, there is still work to be done.'

'You must stay and rest first,' his lordship said. 'Nanette, take your mother up to your room until one can be prepared for her.' He bent to his wife. 'Come, my dear, you need to rest too. I shall have a tisane sent to you.'

He gave orders to the servants, a task his wife would normally have done, but she was clearly incapable of it. And Kitty, who might have deputised for her, was numb, though dry-eyed. She could not believe they had really been talking about Jack's death. She could not mourn him; it seemed too unreal. How could he have died and she not know it? She had been living with hope for so long that it would take time to realise it had been dashed.

Thomas left again and a few days later Nanette and James took Anne-Marie to Richmond where they had acquired a little house not far from the park. It was peaceful there and yet within a day's ride of London, a good place for the Marchioness to recover and for James to continue his chosen career as a writer.

Their departure left Chiltern Hall very quiet. Kitty tried to lead a normal life, keeping her mother-in-law company, sewing, visiting friends and neighbours and writing letters during the day, reading or playing the harpsichord and singing a little in the evenings. But her thoughts constantly returned to France, to the château on the hill at Haute Saint-Gilbert. To Jack. Her husband. The man she loved.

She found herself more and more thinking back over what had happened. She had run from home. Anyone could have taken advantage of her. She could have been robbed or raped; she could have been flung into the gutter and left to die. Instead, a kindly fate had sent Jack Chiltern. It was not so much that first meeting of strangers, but the later one on the packet to France which had sealed her fate.

Something had passed between them when he kissed her, a flash of something akin to lightning. No, she decided on reflection, it was nothing so violent. A thread perhaps, passing from fingers to fingers, lips to lips, or heart to heart, a thread so fine it was invisible, so strong it could never be severed. It had been there all through their long journey from Paris to Lyons, even when they quarrelled, even when he had taken her so forcefully on their wedding night.

It had survived the journey to Toulon, and home. She was quite sure it was still there, linking them when he left again. If he was somewhere, alive and well, wouldn't he be able to feel it too? Had it at last been broken? Would she have felt it go? But how could it, when she carried his child in her womb? That link was unbreakable.

For her child's sake, she must be strong, to accept what had to be accepted, but, oh, how she wished she had told Jack of her love before he disappeared. They would not have parted so coolly. Or would they? He had shown no sign of wanting to end their estrangement. 'It will not happen again,' he had said. And he was a man of his word.

When, the week before Christmas, they learned that a French army officer named Napoleon Bonaparte had recaptured Toulon, that all foreign invaders had been forced to retreat from French soil and all counter-revolution suppressed, even the Countess admitted she had given up hope of seeing her son again. Kitty, seeing the dull misery in her mother-in-law's eyes, felt the last vestige of her own hope shrivel to nothing.

'It will soon be Christmas,' her ladyship said, sitting with Kitty in her boudoir, staring into the fire, as if conjuring up images in its flames. 'Jack loved the festival when he was a child. We would help bring in the Yule log and deck the hall with holly. And after we had been to church, we would eat goose and roast beef and apples and nuts. All the servants would put on their best

' clothes and come to eat with us. Jack was such a favourite. I could not have any more children and…'

'Please, don't,' Kitty said, putting her arm round the older woman's shoulders, weeping herself. 'I can't bear to see you cry.'

'No, I must not. It upsets 'is lordship and I would not for the world upset 'im. 'E is such a strength to me, but underneath 'e is as miserable as we are, more because Jack was his heir.' She sniffed and rubbed at her cheeks with a minuscule lace handkerchief, forcing herself to smile. 'But we shall soon have another heir and we must look to 'im.'

Kate did not have the heart to wonder whether it might be a girl and not a boy. Whichever it was, it would be an only child. 'We can still enjoy Christmas,' she said. 'I am sure Jack will be with us in spirit. He will always be with us, don't you think?'

'Of course. You are right. Life must go on and it is expected of us. We cannot let our people down, can we?' She got up from her chair. 'I must go and give the orders. We must cook festive pies and cakes and kill the goose.'

'And tomorrow, we will bring in the holly and the Yule log,' Kitty said. 'It will be a pleasant diversion decorating the house.'

Her ladyship, her hand on the door knob, turned back to Kitty. 'You are so good for me, Kitty. Every day I thank God Jack brought you to me. It is almost as if 'e knew.'

'Knew what?'

'That I should need comfort and solace and that you were the one to provide it. I think 'e must have loved you very much.'

And that was more than enough to make Kitty cry.

She managed to hold back her tears until Justine had left the room, and then she sank to her knees on the hearthrug and allowed them to fall unheeded. She did not deserve their good opinion of her. If she had had a little more sense, been a little more mature about it, she and Jack would not have quarrelled and he would not have made that last trip to France. They could have had a good marriage. Now it was too late.

No one knew of her tears, she told no one of her feeling of guilt, she simply scolded herself and joined in the preparations for Christmas as if her sanity depended on it.

The next day, dressed in a voluminous cloak which disguised her condition, she set out for the nearby woods with half a dozen servants to take part in the traditional task of dragging home the Yule log. The day was crisp and frosty and the sun shone, gleaming on the crystals which hung from the branches.

They selected a huge branch which would fill the hearth of the hall and everyone had a hand on it, dragging it through the fallen leaves, laughing as they went, their breath hanging in the frosty air. Kitty gave only token assistance, but she was happy to be involved and walked alongside the workers, carrying an armful of berry-laden holly wrapped in canvas to protect her from its prickles.

When they came out of the wood and could see across the park, they stopped to rest a moment and it was then Kitty looked up and saw a hired carriage bowling along the road towards the gates of Chiltern Hall. She stood a moment, watching it, shielding her eyes with her hand, the better to see it in the strong sunlight.

Strange carriages were a rarity at Beauworth, where everyone instantly recognised a neighbour's equipage.

It turned into the gates and made its way up the drive. It stopped at the front door and a man alighted. 'Jack!' she cried aloud, dropping the holly and gathering up her skirts in order to run.

It was not her husband, she decided, as she came a little nearer; this was an older man. He walked slowly and stiffly, his shoulders hunched. She paused, panting for breath. But supposing he had news? Good news or bad? From a distance he did not look joyful. She watched as the door was opened and Fletcher came out and hurried down the steps to help the caller inside. The carriage was driven away. He was obviously known to the footman. She began to run again and, reaching the front door, raced in in time to see the newcomer disappearing into the library. He turned when he heard her.

She stood and stared for several moments before she found the voice to speak. '*Jack!* It is you!'

He was as thin as a beanpole, his normally tanned face ashen, his eyes sunk deep in their sockets, his clothes hanging on him in loose folds. One arm was tucked uselessly inside his coat. He could hardly stand and was still being supported by Fletcher. She curbed her inclination to throw herself at him; she would bowl him over. A feather would fell him.

She stopped. 'Jack! Oh, how good it is to see you!'

'Good?' he queried with a twisted smile. 'A wreck of a man appears on the step and you call it good.'

'At least you are alive. Fletcher, does the Countess know he is here?'

'I was about to inform her, my lady, as soon as his lordship was seated.'

'I'll go and tell her. Jack, can you climb the stairs? You should go straight to bed.'

'Later,' he said, pushing the footman away and walking unaided towards the library. 'I need a drink first.' Kitty ran to support him. He waved her away. 'I can manage, I am not ill.'

She stood back and watched him, afraid he would fall. 'Fetch the Countess,' she said to Fletcher. 'Then see that his lordship's room is made ready.'

Fletcher disappeared at a run as Jack sank into an armchair before the hearth. Kitty went and knelt beside him, taking his hand in both her own. 'Oh, Jack, we have been so worried, especially when Thomas arrived with the Marchioness…'

He gave a twisted smile. 'They made it, did they?'

'Yes. Nanette and James were here when she arrived. She went back to live with them.'

'Not an entirely wasted trip, then.'

'No. Thomas said you were very courageous. In fact, he said you were reckless considering you had been wounded in the attempt to free Antoinette.'

'That very nearly succeeded,' he said. 'It would have if certain people had had a little more backbone.'

'Not everyone can be as brave as you are, Jack. But do not talk about it now. It will tire you and you need to rest.'

'Rest,' he murmured. 'Yes, I think I may rest now.'

'Jack! Jack!' Lady Beauworth ran into the room, her skirts bunched in her hand. 'Fletcher tells me…' She stopped at the sight of her son. 'Oh, my dearest, what 'as happened to you?'

He tried to rise, to make his obeisance, but sank back into the chair. 'A slight wound, Mother, nothing serious…'

'Not serious! You look at death's door.' She came forward to kneel at his feet and take the hand Kitty had relinquished. 'You must go to bed at once and Dr Seward sent for.'

'Don't fuss, Mother. All I need is rest.' But it was evident there was more than fatigue wrong with him. He was in a state of collapse.

The Countess called Fletcher back to carry Jack to his bedchamber, sent his valet to him, sent a groom on horseback to fetch the doctor, another to find the Earl who was out riding somewhere on the estate, and ordered the cook to prepare nourishing broth.

Kitty waited until the valet came out of Jack's room and then went to sit with him. He was delirious and did not know her; he hardly seemed to know where he was. She sat watching him, wringing out a cloth and mopping his brow every so often, trying to stop him thrashing about.

The doctor arrived half an hour later. Kitty left the room while he made his examination and paced up and down the corridor outside. Justine came to her, her soft skirts rustling. 'How is he?'

'I cannot tell, he is not fully conscious. Dr Seward is with him now.'

''Ow did he manage to come home like that? Fletcher said 'e came alone, there was no one else in the carriage that brought 'im.'

'He is in no condition for explanations. We must wait until he has recovered.'

'Yes, of course. Let us give thanks that 'e is back with us.'

'No! I will not have it!' The sound of Jack's voice

came clearly through the closed door. 'Clean it up, then leave me.'

They looked at each other, wondering whether to go in, but before either could do so, Dr Seward came out of the bedchamber looking grave. 'He has sustained a wound, perhaps more than one, which was not properly attended to. I cannot be sure, but it looks as if a musket ball is lodged in his upper arm and has been there some time. The area round the wound has putrified. I have told him he must lose the arm.'

'And he has refused?' Kitty queried. 'Is there no alternative?'

'I think it will be unwise to wait. I tried to explain to him, but I fear he is not fully aware of his condition.'

'Go to 'im, Kitty,' her ladyship said. 'Talk to 'im.

Kitty crept into the room. Jack was lying on his back, his face a pale mask. 'You still here?' he queried weakly. 'I had thought you would be long gone.'

'Why should I go? I am your wife. This is our home.'

'So it is.' His tone was full of wry irony.

'You wish me gone?'

She waited, with her heart in her mouth for his reply. He smiled lop-sidedly. 'That fool wants to take off my arm.'

'Yes, I know.'

'I won't have it. It will heal, given time.'

'Jack, please, do not take any more risks. You are home now and I would rather have a husband with one arm than no husband at all.'

'I am not your husband, I never have been.'

She rose and ran from the room. He knew. He had known all along. He had arranged that ceremony simply to make her conform, to obey him. She passed the Countess, still pacing up and down the corridor, and fled to her room, where she laid herself on her bed. To have him home when they thought him lost, to see him so obviously in pain and be able to do nothing to help, to have continued to hope when all hope should have faded—surely she deserved a reward for that?

While he had been away, she had been able to convince herself that, as soon as he came home, all would be well and he would love her and their child. She had been deluding herself. Now what could she do? Where could she go? How could she explain to the Earl and the Countess, who had both been so good to her, that her marriage was a sham?

Jack lay back exhausted. What had made him say such a terrible thing to her? Why didn't she understand that he loved her, that he had been to hell and back and all he wanted was the peace and quiet of Chiltern Hall, his parents and a wife who loved him and wanted him? She didn't want him, she had not even tried to touch him when he arrived.

He could not blame her for that; he must be a ghastly sight, but if she cared for him at all, she would have ignored that. It had been his disappointment that made him lash out. It had been the thought of being reunited with Kitty which had driven him on, helped him to ignore the pain, the hunger, the sore feet from walking miles every day, the danger of being spotted. Kitty, always Kitty. Now he was home and too weak to say and do the things he had planned.

His mother came into the room and sat beside the bed, not speaking, just watching him tenderly. He smiled lop-sidedly. 'I do not make a good patient.'

'Are you going to let the doctor amputate your arm?'

'No.'

'He says the ball is still in there and is poisoning your system.'

'He is wrong. It was taken out. The wound never healed properly because I could not rest. And in Lyons a gendarme stuck his bayonet into it. Filthy it was, so I don't wonder the wound has gone bad. But, now I am home, it will mend.' He paused to gather his strength. 'See, already I am growing stronger.'

She sighed. 'Why did you send Kitty away?'

'I didn't. She went. Mother, keep her away. She only stays from duty…'

'I never heard such nonsense! You are delirious. Why, she loves you. She 'as been beside herself worrying about you, worrying about the child…'

'Child?'

'Did you not notice? Oh, Jack, I can only think your fever has affected your eyes.'

'She is expecting a child? But how could she? We…' This was something he had never envisaged. It put a completely different light on the matter. 'Where is she? Fetch her back.'

'Later.' She stood up as the doctor came back into the room. 'Here is Dr Seward come back.'

'With his chopper and his saw, no doubt.' He lifted his head. 'Take them away. You may clean the wound, no more.'

'But, Jack…' his mother protested.

'You risk your life by refusing,' the doctor said.

Jack's smile was more a grimace of pain as the doctor removed the bandage which had been strapping his arm to his body and peeled off the dressing. 'I have risked my life many times in the last three years, sir. I am… used to it…' His voice faded away as he fainted.

'Good,' the doctor said. 'Now we can get on.'

'No.' The Countess's voice was quite firm. 'I will not let you do it against 'is wishes. Clean the wound and bind 'im again. We shall see how 'e does.'

Dr Seward sighed. He had seen brave men brought down when it came to amputation and many had at first refused, but when the pain and putrefaction became too much to bear they had been willing enough. The trouble was that delay usually meant the infection spread and the final cut was all the more severe; because the patient had been weakened by his obstinacy, he frequently did not survive the operation.

'I will take the responsibility,' she added, when he hesitated. 'Tell me what we must do to nurse 'im and we will do it.'

Reluctantly he gave in.

For three days Justine and Kitty nursed him in turns, never leaving him alone for a second. He grew more and more feverish and restless, tossing this way and that, crying out and mumbling in delirium. Sometimes Kitty thought he called her name.

'He cannot go on much longer like this,' Kitty said to her mother-in-law. 'Are you sure we are doing the right thing?'

'No, I am not, but Jack would not forgive me if 'e came to 'is senses and found we 'ad agreed to let the doctor take 'is arm off.'

'It is better than letting him die.'

''E did not die in France when there was no one to nurse 'im. 'Ere, where 'e 'as every attention, 'e will survive.'

'You are as stubborn as he is,' Kitty said. 'I think he would rather die than stay married to me.'

'What? What nonsense is this? You must not say

such dreadful things. 'E came 'ome to you. It is for you 'e wants to get better…'

'Then why is he getting worse?'

'Is 'e?' Justine stood looking down at the form in the bed. For once Jack had stopped thrashing about, as if his soul had already accepted death and welcomed it. He was no longer fighting.

'Yes. Please, send for the doctor again,' Kitty whispered. 'Tell him to do as he thinks fit. I would rather die myself than be the cause of his death…'

'Kitty, go to bed,' the Countess commanded. 'You are so exhausted, you talk as much nonsense as Jack. It is not good for the child.'

'Send for the doctor, please.'

'Very well. But go to bed, child. I'll send Rose to you with a tisane. I will call you if there is any change.'

Slowly Kitty dragged herself to her own room. Jack was dying and, whichever way you looked at it, it was her fault. His innate sense of chivalry had made him offer to escort her in the first place, to try and take her to freedom, to marry her. And having done so, he had brought her to safety, left her in possession of his home and gone off again, risking his life to save a doomed queen.

It was all her fault. He thought so too. She could not forget his words: 'I am not your husband, I never have been.'

Rose came into her room with a glass in her hand and persuaded her to drink the bitter draught it contained. She needed oblivion. She would not be able to think clearly until she had slept. She stripped off her gown and lay down in her petticoat. Her last conscious thought was of her child.

How much were unborn children affected by their

mother's upsets? Did the little one know the anguish she suffered? Was he equally disturbed? She felt him kick, quite violently. 'Oh, you do know,' she murmured. 'You are determined to punish me too.'

Forced into sleep by the drug, she did not wake until the next day. The sun was shining through the fabric of the curtains and she could hear the church bells ringing. For a moment she was confused, wondering what day it was. Then she remembered it was Christmas Day. She rose and went to the window, pulling back the curtains to peer out.

It had snowed a little in the night. The path was glittering with it and it hung on the branches of the bare trees and piled itself against the hedgerows, white and pure. Today was a day of purity; the birthday of the Saviour. 'A child is born,' she murmured, turning back towards the room as Rose came in.

'I thought I heard you about, my lady. I've brought you hot chocolate and water to wash. Shall I help you dress?'

'Yes, please. Lord Chiltern?'

'The Earl sat with him during the night while her ladyship rested, my lady. I believe she went back to him after she had breakfasted.'

'Has the doctor been?'

'Expected any minute.'

'Then let us make haste.'

Fifteen minutes later, Kitty crept into the sick room. It was uncannily silent. The Countess sat beside the bed, watching her son, with tears raining down her cheeks. He lay very still, a hump in the bedclothes, no more. The single candle left burning all night guttered and went out.

Kitty gasped and moved forward to fall on her knees beside the bed, her heart screaming against the outrage, but no sound came from her throat. What she felt was beyond speech.

Justine put a hand on her shoulder and gripped it. 'He sleeps,' she said.

At first Kitty did not comprehend; she thought of eternal sleep, not the sleep from which one awoke refreshed. 'Yes,' she said softly.

'Thank God. Now he will not lose his arm. We can send the doctor away again.' She looked down at Kitty. 'Oh, this is so wonderful. Happy Christmas, daughter.'

A small sound from the bed made Kitty turn startled eyes towards it. Jack was looking straight at her, his dark eyes clear and bright.

'You still here,' he murmured, just as if there had not been four full days since the first time he had uttered the phrase.

It was a second chance. She had a second chance to frame her reply. It was worth fighting for, she told herself. If fate had been kind enough to give you what you most desired, then you would be a fool to throw it away for want of a little honesty. 'It is the only place I want to be, the only place I shall ever want to be.' She smiled and bent to kiss his forehead. 'I am afraid, my darling, you are stuck with me.'

He grinned. 'You mean that? I cannot drive you away, however boorish I become?'

'No. I love you.'

'I do not know what you are talking about,' the Countess said brightly. 'Why should you drive Kitty away? And you are never boorish. Why, you are the most even-tempered of men.' She paused and gave a light laugh. 'Most of the time, anyway. I own you were dreadfully ill-tempered when you arrived, but that was because you were so ill. I am sure Kitty has forgiven you, for I 'ave.'

'Have you?' he queried, looking at his wife.

'Yes.'

He raised his eyebrow at her. 'For everything?'

She knew what he meant. 'For everything.'

He grinned lop-sidedly. 'Love is the strongest force of all, isn't that what you once said to me?'

'Yes, though you said it was a tyrant.'

'I was wrong. And you were right. I love you, Lady Chiltern. I have loved you since the moment you berated me at the Paris *barrière*, a veritable fishwife.'

'But you were not at all pleased with me for that.'

'Oh, indeed I was. I thought you were wonderful.' He reached out and put his good hand up round her neck, drawing her face down towards him so that he could kiss her. 'My little tyrant.'

The Countess crept from the room. They hardly noticed her go.

Epilogue

The sun was shining and the daffodils were nodding on the day Justin James Chiltern was christened. Wearing the christening robe Jack himself had worn, he was taken to the church by his proud parents in the family coach, where the ceremony was witnessed by his doting grandparents, his Uncle James, who had provided one of his names, and his Aunt Nanette, determined to be present though the birth of her own child was imminent.

Great-aunt Anne-Marie was also present, and Great-uncle William and Kitty's stepmother, who, unusually for her, was overawed by the grandeur of the occasion and had little to say, apart from cooing over the baby. Captain Trent and Edward Lampeter also arrived, both resplendent in uniform. And all along the way almost the whole population of Beauforth stood to cheer the new heir.

It was a day on which to be happy and Kitty was happy. She could hardly believe there had been that appalling quarrel on her wedding night. Her first wedding night, for there had been a second that was very different.

* * *

When Jack had been sufficiently well to speak of what was on his mind and had been on his mind ever since it happened, he had once again begged Kitty's pardon. It was the first time he had dressed and come downstairs and, though he was still pale and a little weak, he was making rapid strides towards a full recovery. She had wrapped a rug about his knees and put a cushion behind his injured shoulder, before sitting in a chair beside him.

'I was so sure you wanted an annulment and that was the last thing I wanted,' he went on. 'It made me feel so frustrated and confused, I wanted to lash out against it, against the circumstances that had brought us to such a pass, at myself for being such a fool as to think I could win your love after we were married when I had not succeeded before. It was a feeling that was new to me and I suppose I needed to prove I was my own master. Instead, I lost control.'

'Why did you not say so? It was a strange way to ensure the marriage endured. And so unnecessary. I would have given myself to you willingly.'

'I did not know that. I thought you had agreed to the marriage simply to help us get out of France and keep your reputation intact.'

'Jack, that was how you put it to me when you suggested it. It was not what was in my mind. I wanted a true marriage. And when you…when you…' She could not bring herself to put into words the horror of that night.

'I must have been out of my mind, there is no other explanation. And I knew, as soon as it was over, that I had forfeited your love for ever. Nothing I did afterwards could redress the wrong.'

'So, instead of trying to work things out, you brought

me home and disappeared again. Jack, we were so worried about you and, when the War Department as good as said you must be dead, we almost lost hope.'

He smiled wryly. 'Only almost?'

'I could not bring myself to accept it. I had this strange feeling that we were joined in some way, and that if the thread that bound us had been severed by death, I should know it when it happened. I know that sounds fanciful, but I was right, wasn't I?'

'Yes, thank God. When I found you still here...'

'Where else would I be? I am your wife. This is our home. It will be the home of our child.' She paused. They had to be open and honest with each other, or any doubts they had would never be quite erased. 'But the question is, do you want to be bound to me?'

'Do you need to ask? My bonds are easy to live with. I loved you in France, I love you now, I will love you in a hundred years if we should live so long.'

'Oh, Jack, how I have longed to hear you say that!'

'In spite of what I did to you?'

'I cannot believe the marriage bed is always like that.'

'Oh, believe me, it is not. If only you would forgive me, then I could show you a very different husband, one who cares deeply for you. I would hope, in time, to expunge the memory of that dreadful wedding night.'

She looked at him shyly. 'Jack, it was a proper wedding, wasn't it? Legal, I mean?'

'Yes.' He looked at her sharply. 'You surely do not think I contrived it to—'

'Now, don't fly into the boughs, all I meant was that we could make doubly sure. It was your papa put the idea into my head. He said we could have a second ceremony, here, in Beauworth church, and then there could never be any doubt about it.'

'And you would like that?'

'I should like it very much.'

'Then, this time, I must do the job properly.' He flung the rug from him and slipped from his seat to kneel in front of her, taking both her hands in his. 'My darling Kitty, I adore you, I cannot live without you. Will you make me very happy and consent to become my wife?'

'La, sir,' she said, entering into the spirit of the occasion. 'I shall have to think about it and give you an answer later.'

'How much later?'

'Oh, I think thirty seconds will suffice.'

He waited the prescribed time, his eyes dancing with happiness, while she smiled down at him. 'And your answer?'

'Yes, of course, silly. And do get up, you will soil your beautiful clothes.'

He stood up, drawing her to her feet to kiss her very gently, very tenderly, afraid of being too forceful. 'When, my love? Tell me when.'

'As soon as maybe.' She laughed. 'After all, our child must be born in wedlock.'

The ceremony, witnessed by Lord and Lady Beauworth, took place a week later, a year almost to the day since they had first met. And that night, in spite of her ungainly bulk, he had taken her in his arms in their bed and kissed her tenderly, beginning with her face and working his way down to her throat and breasts, putting his hand to her swollen stomach and laughing delightedly when he felt the baby kick. 'I am half afraid to touch you,' he murmured.

She lifted his head in both her hands and smiled at

him. 'He is tougher than you might think. He will not mind.'

'You are sure it will be a boy?'

'No, but it does not matter in the least, there will be others. We are going to be one big happy family, God willing.'

'Amen to that.'

He kissed her rounded stomach and stroked her breasts and thighs, gently and tenderly, taking infinite pains not to alarm her. But their love was not to be denied; she was as passionate as he was and she had waited too long already. Instinct told her what to do and instinct served her well. It was all about loving and being loved and when they came together in one glorious frenzied peak of fulfilment, they both knew that this wedding night was one not to be forgotten.

*   *   *   *   *

MILLS & BOON®

Makes any time special

Enjoy a romantic novel from
Mills & Boon®

Presents...™ *Enchanted*™ TEMPTATION.

Historical Romance™ ⋀ **MEDICAL ROMANCE**™

MILLS & BOON®

Historical Romance™

THE MASTER OF MOOR HOUSE
by Anne Ashley

The dawn of a new century…

For Megan Drew, the arrival of 1800 brought back
Christian Blackmore into her life. Both of them had
changed immeasurably, but if Megan were truthful, *one*
thing had never changed—her feelings for the man she
loved beyond words.

THE QUIET MAN
by Paula Marshall

The dawn of a new century…

For Allen Marriott, 1899 was proving to be a tumultuous
time. Not wishing to reveal his connection to his employer,
Gerard Schuyler, he was forced to involve Trish Courtney
in his secret, heightening the thrill of their illicit meetings…

On sale from 3rd December 1999

Available at most branches of WH Smith, Tesco,
Martins, Borders, Easons, Volume One/James Thin
and most good paperback bookshops

FREE!
2 Books
and a surprise gift!

We would like to take this opportunity to thank you for reading this Mills & Boon® book by offering you the chance to take TWO more specially selected titles from the Historical Romance™ series absolutely FREE! We're also making this offer to introduce you to the benefits of the Reader Service™—

- ★ FREE home delivery
- ★ FREE gifts and competitions
- ★ FREE monthly Newsletter
- ★ Books available before they're in the shops
- ★ Exclusive Reader Service discounts

Accepting these FREE books and gift places you under no obligation to buy; you may cancel at any time, even after receiving your free shipment. Simply complete your details below and return the entire page to the address below. **You don't even need a stamp!**

YES! Please send me 2 free Historical Romance books and a surprise gift. I understand that unless you hear from me, I will receive 4 superb new titles every month for just £2.99 each, postage and packing free. I am under no obligation to purchase any books and may cancel my subscription at any time. The free books and gift will be mine to keep in any case.

H9EB

Ms/Mrs/Miss/Mr ....Initials...
BLOCK CAPITALS PLEASE

Surname...

Address...

....

....Postcode ....

Send this whole page to:
UK: The Reader Service, FREEPOST CN81, Croydon, CR9 3WZ
EIRE: The Reader Service, PO Box 4546, Kilcock, County Kildare (stamp required)

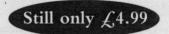